Rachel SINCLAIR
THE ALIBI

By Rachel Sinclair

Kansas City Legal Thrillers

Bad Faith
Justice Denied
Hidden Defendant
Injustice for All
L.A. Defense
The Associate
The Alibi
Reasonable Doubt
The Accused
The Hate Crime
Secrets and Lies
Until Proven Guilty

Vinci Books

vinci-books.com

Published by Vinci Books Ltd in 2026

1

Copyright © Rachel Sinclair 2017

The author has asserted their moral right to be identified as the author of this work in accordance with the Copyright, Designs and Patents Act 1988. This work is a work of fiction. Names, characters, places and incidents are the product of the author's imagination or are used fictitiously. Any resemblance to actual persons, living or dead, places and incidents is entirely coincidental.
All rights reserved. No part of this publication may be copied, reproduced, distributed, stored in any retrieval system, or transmitted in any form or by any means, including photocopying, recording, or other electronic or mechanical methods, nor used as a source for any form of machine learning including AI datasets, without the prior written permission of the publisher.
The publisher and the author have made every effort to obtain permissions for any third party material used in this book and to comply with copyright law. Any queries in this respect should be brought to the attention of the publisher and any omissions will be corrected in future editions.
A CIP catalogue record for this book is available from the British Library.
Paperback ISBN: 9781036703219

The EU GPSR authorised representative is Logos Europe, 9 rue Nicolas Poussion, 17000 La Rochelle, France
contact@logoseurope.eu

Chapter One

I HAD TO ADMIT, Gina Degrazio, my current client, entertained me to no end. She had no filter to her mouth, zero, so that was refreshing, in and of itself. I was used to people trying to bullshit me. That was what my clients usually did. They told me the story that put them in their best light and it was up to me to figure out the truth. Criminal defense required you to be a great study of human nature. It was human nature to not admit to faults and highlight virtues, and criminals were no different. That was why I chose not get too angry with my clients for hiding the truth – they were humans, so they would naturally be hesitant to admit to what they did wrong.

But with Gina, it was different. I felt I could trust what she said because she came across as refreshingly honest. She seemed to not understand that sleeping with her husband's identical twin brother was wrong, and she also didn't seem to understand that admitting, out loud she fantasized about burning her husband alive in a car would be something that most people wouldn't want to admit to on a first meeting.

Still, I knew I couldn't get too taken in by the brash New Yorker. She was a mob wife, after all. A low-level mob wife, as Vittorio Degrazio was more of a street-level thug than anything else, but a mob wife nonetheless. In the hierarchy of the mafia, Vittorio was considered a soldier. If there was someone to be beat up, he was the one to do it. If there was a cop to be shaken down, or a store owner to be threatened, Vittorio was your man. He was 45 years old and hadn't risen through the ranks, which told me he probably wasn't terribly bright. Or, maybe he was bright, but he was just violent, and wanted a job that expressed that violence.

Gina had explained to me she had an air-tight alibi – she was with Enzo Degrazio, Vittorio's identical twin brother.

"Yeah," she said, "me and Vittorio hadn't hit the sack in years and years." She shrugged. "So I started having sex with Enzo instead. I figured, he looks just like Vittorio, so it was really just like shtupping my own husband, you know?"

I nodded my head as I wrote. "I guess. So, you were arrested for his murder and you're now out on bail." I looked at my notes. "The bond was set at $3 million." I looked at her and raised one of my eyebrows. "Suffice to say you know somebody who has access to that kind of cash. Who would that be?"

She shifted uncomfortably in her seat. "I know people," she said. "Pay no mind to that. I wanna keep talking about my case. I didn't kill that bastard. It's so stupid I'm even here. Vitty was a mob enforcer for the love of Christ. Those goddamn pigs who arrested me told me they have evidence I did it. Evidence. Like what? That's what I asked. Like what? They tell me they got evidence the gun used in the hit on Vitty matched the caliber and barrel of a gun registered to me." She shook her head. "I'm thinking they're full of

The Alibi

shit. If I would off my own bastard husband, I wouldn't have been dumb enough to use a gun I registered. Jesus Christ, can those assholes please use just a bit of plain logic?" She shook her head. "But I didn't say that to those pigs. I didn't tell them nothin'. But I sure was thinking it in my head, let me tell you."

I didn't like her evasive answer on who paid her bond. Somebody had access to that kind of money. She couldn't just post 10% of the bond, and, even if she used a bondsman, she had to come up with at least 10% to give to the bondsman. And most bondsmen wouldn't touch a bond that high without some kind of collateral. Gina didn't look the type who would have access to that kind of cash. She looked cheap, with her blue eye shadow, teased black hair, bright red lipstick, red dress that was at least two sizes too tight, and faux fur coat. She was probably in her early forties, although she looked much older – her skin was crepey, slightly grey and there already were deep lines playing around her mouth. She kept hacking the deep cough of a heavy smoker and I smelled the faint scent of old cigarettes on her clothes.

She looked like the wife of a two-bit gangster, which was what she was. Yet, somehow, she managed to make a $3 million bond. How?

"We'll get back to the details of the case," I said. "I want to circle back around to my original question. You posted a $3 million bond. How did you manage that? Who gave you the money?" I looked again at the documents in my file and didn't see the name of anybody but Gina. That told me somebody just gave her the cash to post her bond. I just couldn't imagine who would do that.

She nervously brought her index finger and thumb to her mouth and rubbed the sides of her lips. One bony hand with long red nails flew up to her stiff hair and patted the side of the tangled mane while she furtively looked me in the eye and then looked away. Then she sat up straighter in her chair, seemingly determined she wouldn't let me intimidate her.

"Enzo got me the money," she said, almost defiantly. Her body language told me she was nervous as hell but she managed to get it together long enough to proudly pronounce just who was bankrolling her. "Anything else you need to know?"

"And where did he get the money?" Enzo, according to my notes, was apparently not in the mafia business. He owned an Italian restaurant downtown. Of course, I would have to look into the finances of said business. Chances were that restaurant was just a front, a laundromat, so to speak. Dirty money usually poured through legitimate businesses and came out "clean." Whether or not Enzo's restaurant, which was simply called "Enzo's," was one of those legitimate businesses that cleaned dirty money was something that remained to be seen. I was determined to figure that one out.

"From his bank," she said. "You can check that out if you want."

"Then why didn't you want to tell me that in the first place? Why all the smoke and mirrors, all the nervous tics? You're hiding something from me, Mrs. Degrazio, and, believe me, I'm the last person you want to lie to."

Gina looked out the window and then rapidly looked back at me. "I knew you would think there's a rat in my story," she said. "Enzo is my alibi and he got me the money to get out. I thought maybe you would think Enzo was behind this murder all along and set me up. That's what I

The Alibi

thought you would think so I didn't want to tell you Enzo got me out."

I dropped my pen and just stared at Gina for a few minutes. Then I shook my head. "Mrs. Degrazio," I began.

"Gina," she said. "I don't answer to no 'Mrs. Degrazio.' Not no more, I don't."

"Gina," I began. "I don't understand why I would think Enzo killed his brother just because he supplied the money to get you out. It's interesting your mind went there. It's also interesting you offered this explanation to me unprompted." I put the words *Enzo a possibility?* on my sheet of paper and then looked back at Gina. Gina was definitely the type who spoke before thinking. It was odd those particular words came spilling out of her mouth.

She shrugged. "You're gonna think that about me. That maybe me and Enzo were in on it and maybe we agreed I was gonna take the fall and that's why Enzo would get me out of jail." She nodded. "But that's not how it went down."

"Then how did it go down?"

"I told you, I don't know how it went down. I didn't even know that the rat bastard died until I got the pigs showing up at my door to arrest me. Showed up at Enzo's door to arrest me, that is." She shook her head. "I got no idea how they knew to look for me there but somebody narced on me that's for goddamn sure."

I looked down at my notes. "Okay," I said. "Now, let's see. Vittorio was found at his home, shot in the chest. It looked like he had been dead for several days at the time he was found. It looks like he was reported missing by one Vincenzo Delagarza. Do you know who that is?"

She shrugged. "Never heard that name in my life. Who is he to Vitty?"

"Looks like he's a friend. I guess Vittorio was supposed

to show up to a weekly poker game he never misses. When he didn't show, it looks like Vincenzo went to Vittorio's home and found him in the living room. As I said before, he had been dead since Wednesday of that week and he was found on a Saturday." I looked at Gina. "So, I can assume you and Vittorio weren't living under the same roof at the time he was murdered."

"No. I told you, I've been shacking up with Enzo."

"And that's where you were at…" I looked at the police report and my notes. "February 18 at around 10 PM?" I squinted, seeing the time of death was estimated to be between 9:30 and 10 PM that night. "You were with Enzo Degrazio, right?"

"Right." She nodded. "That's where I was when that rat bastard was being shot down like the dog he was."

"Please," I said, putting my hand up. "I hate expressions like that. I happen to love dogs."

"It's just a saying," she said. "Somebody came into Vitty's home and shot him dead."

"Right. And there was no forced entry," I said. "At least it doesn't appear there was a forced entry." I clacked my pen on the desk. "No forced entry, so it was probably somebody Vittorio knew. Can you give me a list of people who would be seeing Vittorio on a regular basis? That would be the place to start to try to figure out who might have done this."

"Sure," she said. "I'll give you that. It's a long list, I'll tell you that. Vitty was into all kinds of nonsense."

"Was he seeing anybody? Any woman? Or anybody else who might have been intimate with him? Maybe staying with him? That would be extremely helpful to know."

She shrugged. "I don't know who he was shtupping. I don't think there was anybody special sleeping with him. I'll try to find that out for you though."

The Alibi

"Please do." I went further down the police report and then scanned the interrogation transcript included in the file. "Okay, it looks like you did the right thing. You asked for a lawyer right away, and they didn't really get a chance to ask you any questions."

"Yeah. Look, I don't know why I was arrested for this. Aside from the fact that my gun was apparently used in the killing, but, come on. I'm really going to register a gun and then use it to kill my husband? Seriously? How stupid do they think I am?"

"Then who would have access to that gun registered to you?"

"I guess anybody who can get into that house. It was right there, that gun, right there. Underneath the bed. I didn't keep it locked up or nothing like that. It was fully loaded, too."

"So you moved out of Vittorio's home and were staying with his identical twin brother and you didn't take the gun with you? Can I ask why?"

She sighed. "Because I moved out with nothin' but the clothes on my back, that's why. Vittorio beat on me, and got out the belt, and I ran out of there. That's what happened. I didn't go back, either, ever."

"And you never went back into that house for anything? Not to get clothes, belongings, or your gun. Just moved out and never went back."

"Yeah, that's right. Just moved out and didn't go back ever. I should have sent Enzo over there to get my things, but Vitty and Enzo, they don't talk. They hate each other. Hated each other for years, even though they lived only a couple of blocks apart. So, yeah, I couldn't exactly send him over there with a bundt cake to get my shit back."

"And there wasn't anybody else who might have been

able to do that for you? At least go back and get your gun out of there?"

She rolled her eyes. "What's somebody supposed to do? Go over there, all kinda casual-like, and say 'excuse me while I go into your bedroom and look under your bed?' I'm sure that was gonna work. No, nobody went over there to get my gun out of that house. I didn't think it was gonna be a problem until it was."

"Okay. Well, then, we can feel safe in assuming that whoever got that gun out of there must have known right where it was. Unless Vittorio moved it after you left the house. That's a possibility. But you raise a good point – if there was a casual friend visiting him, or any other acquaintance, they had to have known the gun was underneath the bed. And then they would have somehow snuck into the bedroom to get it. I suppose that wouldn't be difficult to do if they would have waited until Vittorio was in the bathroom or something like that and then sneaked into the bedroom to get the gun while Vittorio was on the pot. So, let's see, I should probably ask you about Vittorio's house. Specifically, where is the bedroom and does he lock the bedroom door?"

"The bedroom is on the second floor," she said. "Our home is one of the old homes with the three levels. We got bathrooms on every floor. I guess that somebody could have run up to the bedroom while Vittorio was using the bathroom and got the gun beneath the bed. And ran back down and shot him in the living room. And then left. Yeah, that's possible."

I sighed. "Is it possible? No, scratch that. Of course it's possible, but is it probable? I mean, who knew the gun was underneath the bed? Who would know that piece of information? You're asking me to buy that it was a friend or an acquaintance in the house, but you're not really telling me how that friend or acquaintance would know exactly where to find your gun."

Gina narrowed her eyes. "You don't believe me. You think I did it, don't you?" She crossed her arms in front of her and gave me the stink-eye. "Listen, you're my lawyer. You can figure out why somebody got in that house without breaking in, found my gun and shot Vitty with it. That's for you to figure out. The cops aren't doing nothing about finding the real killer. They think they got the real killer and that's me. The cops aren't doing nothing, so you gotta do the work for them. You gotta figure out who did it."

"Motive, means and opportunity," I said. "I have to show the jury who had the motive, means and opportunity to kill him. So far, you're cover all those bases. That's what I'm trying to say. You knew where that gun was, so that covers means and opportunity. He was beating on you, so you say, and it's pretty evident you hated him. From everything you've told me here today, it's more than obvious you had motive to kill him. Now, I'll admit that, because Vittorio was a gangster, there were plenty of others who probably had motive to kill him. And I'll try to track down everyone with motive. But we have to figure out who on the list of suspects not only had motive but also would know how to get their hands on your gun. That's where I'm stuck."

"Figure it out," she said. "That's your job."

"Yes," I said. "That's my job. And I'll get my investigator on it as soon as I can. But you're right about one thing. As your lawyer, I won't lie to you. I think you did it. For now, it looks like it was you. You told me you have an alibi, but you've also said a few things about Enzo that make you look suspect."

"What did I say about Enzo that made me suspect?"

"You told me you thought I would somehow think you and Enzo planned this murder together. You volunteered that information. Now, you haven't yet told me how Enzo managed to get his hands on $3 million, because it looks like you paid cash for your bond. No bail bondsman was even listed in this file. You haven't told me why Enzo would put all that on the line for you. I'm sorry, Gina, but it doesn't sound like you and Enzo have a great love. Why would he sacrifice that kind of money for you? Things in your story are just not adding up, Gina, so, yes, I think you did it."

"I was with Enzo at the time of the murder," she said. "I told you that."

"Yes, you did," I said. "You told me that. But I somehow think that Enzo won't exactly be an airtight alibi for you, no matter what you and he have cooked up as a story. If he tries to say you were with him at the time of the murder, be prepared for the prosecutor to rip his story to shreds. Be ready for that, and, I hate to be the one to tell you this, but I have the feeling the prosecutor will be able to shred that story about you being with him that night. Unless you were out with him somewhere, where people know the two of you, at the time of the murder. Then maybe that would be a different story. But to just tell me you were at Enzo's home with him isn't going to cut it."

Gina stood up. "You don't believe me. Well, then, maybe you don't need to be my lawyer. Maybe I'll find somebody else to represent me."

I leaned back in my chair. "Be my guest," I said. I didn't need the money, that was for sure. After settling that wrongful death case last year, and getting $5 million in the process, a million of which went to Harper, I didn't have to take any case I didn't want to. That was liberating. I worried, when I left the Public Defender's Office and my wife Sarah decided to divorce me, I couldn't make ends meet. That $5 million windfall from that case eased my concerns immensely. I wouldn't take cases that were dead-ends unless I truly believed in them. And, right at that moment, I wasn't believing in Gina. Not at all.

She sat back down. "I want you," she said. "I want you to represent me."

I raised an eyebrow. "Why do you want me so much? Plenty of other attorneys are out there to take your money. You and I are off to a bad start. Maybe your instinct is right – maybe you and I aren't meant to be lawyer and client. No skin off my nose. Probably not yours, either."

"I got a recommendation," she said. "From somebody who knows a friend of yours in Cameron. Nick Savante. I know a guy who knows Nick, and Nick says you're the best in the business."

I closed my eyes. Nick recommended me. "Who's the guy who knows Nick?" I asked her. "What's the name of the guy who gave you the recommendation?" I would have to pay Nick a visit to ask about this whole situation. I hadn't seen him in awhile, and it was time for me to visit him anyhow. Might as well ask about Gina while I was there. It gave me a good excuse to make the drive to Cameron.

"The guy who told me about you, the guy that knows Nick, his name is Joey Caruso. He's a lifer in the prison, but he's one of Enzo's best friends. He gave me your name. I trust Joey. He knows who's on the up and up. And that's what he says about you – you're on the up and up. He says you won't try to pad your billing with bullshit. He also says you know your shit and you'll fight for every client. Even people like me, you'll fight to make sure I don't serve a day in prison. So, yeah, I want you. Only you."

"Well, I don't necessarily know if I want you," I said. "As a client. Let me talk to Nick about this, let me do some preliminary investigation into what you're saying, and I'll get back with you. In the meantime, if you want to find different counsel, I'll understand."

Gina screwed up her face and then looked out the window again. Her bright red lips were pursed. "You look into it," she said. "You'll find out I'm telling the truth. But see for yourself. Talk to Nick if you need to talk to him. He'll tell you all about Joey Caruso, and you can even talk to Joey yourself. Then you can take me officially on as your client."

I nodded my head. "I'll get back with you in a week or so and let you know my final decision about this. In the meantime, as I said, look for other counsel. I can't guarantee I want this case."

At that, she stood up again and walked out of the office without another word.

Gina left, and Harper came into the office. "How did it go?" she asked. "Sorry, I know I was supposed to be around for intake, but I got caught up in traffic court, of all things." She shook her head. "Always a line at traffic court."

"Not a biggie," I said. "I think Gina's lying about where she was and whether or not she did it. The only thing that's making me think I should take this case is the fact that she apparently got my name from a good friend of mine. I need see him and talk to him about Gina and this Joey Caruso guy. I've never heard of him, Joey Caruso, so I need to see if Nick knows anything about him."

Harper sat across from me and opened her mouth and shut it again. I could tell something was on her mind.

I waited for her to ask me about what was on her mind, but she shook her head.

The Alibi

"What?" I asked her gently. "You look like you want to ask me something."

"No, nothing," she said. "It's none of my business."

"You want to know why I apparently have a friend who knows somebody who would know someone like Gina." I nodded as I saw her expression, which told me I had hit a nerve. I still hadn't told Harper about the guys. I didn't quite know why I never told her about them. It was a sore subject for me, of course, but she and I were in business together. We were even talking about becoming partners. Her other partner, Tammy, was on board with my coming in as a partner and Harper, Tammy and I were having talks about doing just that. Yet, I was still hiding my past from all of them.

"No," she said, shaking her head, but I could read her better than that. "I wasn't wondering about that."

I stared at her for a few seconds and then shook my head. "Okay," I said, taking a deep breath. "I'll come clean with you. You might want to fire me after I do, and, if that's the case, I understand. But…"

I felt nervous telling Harper about my stint in prison. I was totally innocent, but not really. I was innocent as far as not taking part in that armed robbery where the poor off-duty guard was shot, but I certainly took part in many other crimes in my youth. I guess I didn't really want Harper to know the kinds of people I knew. The kind of crowd I ran with. That was the embarrassing part, more than anything.

At the same time, I felt ashamed for being embarrassed about the guys. Why should I apologize for knowing them? They were a part of me. They still were. That hadn't changed. I was still just as tight with them, in my heart, as I ever had been. So why should I hem and haw and beat around the bush about the fact I was good friends with four guys currently serving life sentences in prison? They were up for parole this year, too, at least Nick, Tommy and Jack were. Connor wasn't because he actually killed the off-duty guard.

So, hopefully, Harper would meet the guys sometime soon. I might as well tell their stories. And, in the process, tell my own.

She was still looking at me, searching my face, trying to ascertain what I was thinking. I finally bowed my head, took a deep breath, and decided to just come out with it.

"I had a bit of a rough life growing up," I said. "I never knew my dad. The reason I never knew him was because my mother had no idea who he was. Or who he could be. She was a drug addict and a prostitute. All of which would have been okay, I guess, even though she brought her johns home while I was in the next room, playing with my toy soldiers. But she eventually did marry, briefly, and that was how I got my name – Harrington. That guy, whose name was Steven Harrington, beat my mom and me, and put me in the hospital twice. I was only 10 years old at the time and I ran away after the second time he put me in the hospital. I lived on the streets for a year, hiding out from my mother, but she tracked me down and put me into a reform school. Ozanam. You've probably heard about it."

Harper nodded her head. "Yes. I have."

"Okay. Well, I met some guys when I was at the reform school. Nick Savante, Tommy Arcola, Jack O'Brien and his baby brother Connor. We became really tight and committed a lot of crimes in our younger years. Nothing massive – some burglaries, some shoplifting, we stole a car or two. Mainly we stole the cars for joy-riding, although we stole one of the cars because we wanted to use it in a burglary. We were dumb kids, all of us from violent and

The Alibi

broken homes. Just blowing off some steam, really. We needed the money, so we pawned the stuff we stole from homes and stores, but the main reason we committed crimes was because we were pissed-off at the world."

I could tell Harper knew where this was going. She didn't say a word, though. She just stared at me, unblinking, her green eyes focused on my face. She put one of her hands on mine and squeezed it.

"So," I said. "The guys, the other guys, decided to hold up a liquor store. I wasn't involved in it. They didn't even tell me they were doing it. I guess that the reason why I didn't partake in the festivities was because I was against actually robbing people. I thought that was too risky. There were too many chances something could go horribly wrong. Which it did. There just happened to be an off-duty security guard at the store, and the guy was packing. When the guys were cleaning out the cash register, the guard got his gun out and pointed it at Connor. Connor panicked and got his own gun and shot the guard in the leg. Just shot him in the leg. It shouldn't have been fatal, really. However, the guy ended up dying from a MRSA infection he got in the hospital. That meant everybody's charges were upgraded to felony murder."

"Anyhow, I wasn't involved. However, it was known to the police that I ran with the guys, so they put me into a lineup. I looked pretty similar to Tommy Arcola. We both had long curly hair and olive skin. Both of us skinny, both of us about the same height. An eyewitness identified me as the guy who drove the getaway car. That was actually Tommy. The funny thing was, Tommy was also identified as taking part in the robbery, by the same eyewitness. Tommy actually was in the robbery, but that eyewitness didn't identify him as the getaway driver. The upshot was, all five of us went on trial for that robbery and felony murder, and we all five of us were convicted in separate trials. All of us got life in prison with the chance of parole except Connor. He got life in prison without the possibility of parole."

Harper's eyes were big now, and she was staring at me with tears in her eyes. "Go on," she said. "Oh, Damien, I can't believe that happened to you." She shook her head and looked down. "How did you-"

"Get out? Well, I broke out, actually and I'm living on the lam." I put my finger to my lips. "Shhhh. You don't know this, but my real name is actually Donny Moore, and…" I smiled when I saw Harper was actually believing that. "No, really, I got out of prison through the Innocence Project. See, I became a jail-house lawyer and was winning new trials for guys. Winning appeals for them. So, the *Kansas City Star* came to interview me, and I told the reporter at that time I was completely innocent. I had nothing to do with the robbery."

"That newspaper article drew the attention of the Innocence Project lawyers. They came to see me in prison and I told them my story. I was assigned a lawyer by the name of Chuck Riegel, and Chuck worked his ass off to get me a new trial. They found the car used in the robbery, tested it for DNA, and found my DNA wasn't in the car. My DNA wasn't in that liquor store, either. That was enough evidence to get me a new trial. Then I got this kick-ass, take-no-prisoners Public Defender to try my case. That was Colleen Sutton. That's how I first came to know her. She tried my case, got a not-guilty verdict, and, well, I got out of prison, rocked my SATs, went to college, hard-rocked my LSATs, got into UChicago law school and here I am."

"And what about the others? They won't be eligible for parole for quite a few years, right? They have to serve 85%

The Alibi

of a life sentence, which is calculated to be 30 years. That means they'll be eligible in about 8 years."

"Well, right. But their sentences were commuted to 20 years, all except for Connor. The reason why their sentences were commuted to 20 years was because my lawyer, my Innocence Project lawyer, went to the press about our case. It looked bad the guys were sentenced to life in prison when the only reason why the victim died was because he got an infection in the hospital. And Chuck was able to show this robbery was never meant to involve a weapon - the guys didn't bring a weapon onto the premises, only Connor did, and he came in after the robbery was already in progress. So, it really would have been a Second-Degree Robbery if not for that. Plus, they were all so young when it happened and were absolutely model prisoners behind bars. Absolutely stellar. I guess the governor was tired of hearing about our case, so he commuted the sentences down."

"Really? I'm surprised the governor would do something like that."

I smiled. "Well, I might have had a hand in that. I actually had pretty good grounds for a lawsuit against the prosecutor's office after what happened to me. They were so aggressive, too aggressive, and they ignored some inconsistencies in the statement of the eyewitness who fingered me. I also suspected they suppressed evidence that would have exonerated me. I was ready to go to the media, ready to splash my story far and wide."

"The head of the prosecutor's office wanted to cover up what had happened, and he was in tight with the governor at that time. I told the prosecutor's office I would keep quiet if the governor agreed to commute the sentences of at least Nick, Tommy and Jack. I tried for a commutation for Connor as well, but the governor wouldn't go that far. I took what I could get and that was the real reason the governor commuted their sentences. But don't tell anybody that. That arrangement was strictly confidential"

"I won't say a word, of course," Harper said.

She looked stunned. She was still gripping my hand and still had tears in her eyes. "Wow. I never imagined something like that happened to you. I mean…" She shook her head. "I mean, I guess it's guys like you that make this job worthwhile, huh? To be given the chance to give an innocent man another lease on life – that's why we do what we do. That's why criminal defense is a calling. Yeah, we get the scumbag clients, like Erik Gregorian, and we do our best to make sure they're unleashed back onto the streets. But, every once in a while, you get a case that makes you realize why you chose this profession. For Colleen, I'm sure that case was yours."

"For me, it was Darnell Williams," she continued. "He's an African-American boy accused of murder, a murder that had been committed by his arresting officer. There have been others. I would like to think that cases like Darnell and cases like yours make this job completely worthwhile. That they cancel out the bad guys we end up releasing back onto the streets. That's what I would like to think in my head."

I nodded my head. "Well, now you know where I'm coming from. Now you know why I have committed to this job with a passion. Because you're right – that old axiom about it being better to release 100 guilty men than to see one innocent man go to prison is right. When you are the one innocent person serving a life sentence, well, you couldn't imagine anything worse than that."

"And I guess Nick is in Cameron. Is that right?"

"Yeah. Cameron. All the guys are in Cameron. I still go up there to visit them, at least once a month. Nick, Tommy and Jack are all up for parole this year. Connor isn't and won't be. He's serving a life sentence without the possibility of parole."

"Hmmm," Harper said. "How old was Connor when he was convicted?"

"Only 16," I said. "And, I know, I've done the research. There have been some promising Supreme Court cases that have come out in the last few years about sentencing juveniles to LWOP. One case, *Miller v. Alabama*, ruled that mandatory LWOP sentences were unconstitutional when applied to juveniles. Another, *Montgomery v. Louisiana* said the *Miller* case applied retroactively. But those cases don't apply to Connor, unfortunately. He wasn't mandatorily sentenced – the jury had discretion, and they decided he deserved LWOP. It's not right that he's in there for the rest of his life. He's now 32 years old and hasn't caused a lick of trouble inside. He hasn't so much as participated in a fist-fight in prison. He was just a scared kid when he was sentenced. Just a scared kid who wanted to show his big brother he could be useful. He was only supposed to be the lookout, but he decided he wanted to actively participate. That was why he ended up in that liquor store with that gun at that time. One stupid, brash decision by a 16-year-old who knew nothing but violence his whole life, and, just like that, he finds himself locked up until he dies."

"There are studies about juveniles," Harper said. "There are also cases coming out all the time. Let's keep an eye out on any Supreme Court cases that might apply to juveniles who weren't mandatorily sentenced to LWOP. Or, better yet, why don't we find a good attorney who specializes in this type of case to see if there is anything that can be done to have Connor's sentence commuted to life in prison with the possibility of parole."

I nodded my head. "I've been on that for awhile now. I'm always doing research on it. I can't imagine Connor having to remain in prison once the guys get out. It's bad enough that he's in there now, but it's not as bad because his brother and two of his best friends are serving time with him. But once those guys get out and he's still in there…" I shook my head. "I just can't imagine how he's going to react to that. Believe me, I've been working every angle to try to get him out of there with the other guys. That *Miller* case is fairly recent – 2012. The *Montgomery* case was decided in 2016. I've been on the lookout for cases that might be winding their way through the courts that would apply to guys like Connor. I keep hoping something might turn up."

Harper put her hand on my shoulder. "They might. They might. Don't give up hope."

"Yeah." I sighed. "At any rate, I need to see Nick in prison. I need to ask him about this Joey Caruso guy. See what he knows about him. That might tell me something, in turn, about Gina. I have the feeling she's not being truthful about Enzo Degrazio. I don't know. Something seems off about her story."

"What feels off?"

"Just some details. She didn't want to tell me, at first, that Enzo supplied the money for her bail. When I asked her why she wasn't more forthcoming, she told me she was afraid I might have suspected she and Enzo were in on Vittorio's murder together. What was odd was that she, at first, said she was afraid I would think Enzo set her up to take the fall. So, her story changed in the blink of an eye right there. And I personally think it's odd that Enzo would give her the money for bail in the first place. As I told her, it didn't sound like she and Enzo had a great love story. So why would he stick his neck out and give her $3 million for her bail? And how did he get that kind of money, anyhow? He owns an Italian restaurant downtown, that's true, but I really wasn't aware that owning a restaurant made you wealthy enough to just toss around $3 million like it's water." I shook my head. "I don't know. A few holes in her story are bothering me."

"What else is bothering you about the story?"

"The fact that her gun was used in the murder. It was registered to her. She said she kept that gun underneath the bed when she lived with Vittorio. Which would mean that, if somebody else decided to use that gun to murder Vittorio, they had to know where to find it and then stolen it while Vittorio wasn't looking somehow. And there wasn't a sign of a forced entry. It's all adding up to Gina having done the murder. I just think she's lying when she said she had nothing to do with killing her husband."

Harper nodded her head. "So, you're going to the prison to see Nick. Could you do me a big favor?"

"What's that?"

"I have an assistant I've been training. Her name is Heather Morrison. She was a client of mine a few years back. She's very bright and very good at research. She can find just about any case you want her to find. Anyhow, she would love to see what goes on during a prison visit. She's been to the Jackson County jail quite a few times to do intake. But she's never been inside a prison. Could you take her with you when you visit Nick?"

"Sure, why not? I'm always willing to help somebody learn. I'd be happy to bring her along."

"She's transgendered," Harper said. "She was born with the name Heath."

"And?"

Harper shrugged. "And nothing, I guess. I didn't know if you'd have a problem with that."

"Why would I have a problem with it?"

"Well, a lot of people do."

"A lot of narrow-minded people do. Anyhow, no, I don't have an issue with her being transgendered."

"Good. She's coming in an hour. Maybe you could meet with her then."

"Sure."

HEATHER APPEARED in the office about an hour later. She looked enough like a female that I never would've known she was biologically male if I didn't see her prominent Adam's Apple on her throat. She was dressed in a slim black skirt, a tight red long-sleeved t-shirt, tights and high-heeled ankle boots. She looked me up and down and smiled. "You must be Damien. Hello, Damien." Her eyes got big and she smiled broadly. "Harper, you didn't tell me he was so cute."

Harper laughed. "I didn't, did I? Well, he is. As you can see."

"Sorry for being unprofessional, Dami. Do you like being called Dami? Like that old bat on *The Exorcist* calling her son Dami?"

"Believe it or not, I did get some teasing about my name growing up. Mainly because the demon child in *The Omen* was named Damien, but sometimes because of the priest in *The Exorcist*."

"Oh, that's right! I forgot about *The Omen*. How weird that two devil-related shows had main characters named Damien in them. One good, one bad."

"You can call me Dami," I said with a smile. I had the

The Alibi

feeling I would get along with Heather. "I've been called worse."

Heather rubbed her hands together. "Well, I'm totally excited about going to Cameron with you. Harper told me all about it. Guess you have a client there you need to see?"

I looked at Harper who looked at me and shrugged. I guess she didn't tell Heather about who Nick was. "Actually, I'm seeing a friend of mine. His name is Nick Savante. He's a lifer, although he's up for parole this year."

"Oh, you got a friend in prison?" She smiled and nodded. "I get it, I guess."

"Yeah. Long story. I'll tell you about it on the way to the prison. I'm going there on Saturday. I'll pick you up at 8?"

"Sure. I live in Mid-Town. I just got an apartment there. Thanks to Harper, I can get an apartment in Mid-Town. If it weren't for Harper, I'd be in prison right now."

I smiled as I realized both of us had a story to tell each other. "You tell me your story and I'll tell you mine," I said. "On the way to the prison. In the meantime, I'm glad to have met you. Harper speaks very highly of you. She tells me you're one helluva researcher."

"I *am* one helluva researcher. Harper also tells me you guys got an investigator. Tom Garrett. I was hoping I could learn some tricks from him, too. I'd love to be an all-around legal eagle – doing investigations, doing legal research, learning the ropes. Learning everything I need to know about practicing law. Not that I ever want to go to law school and become a lawyer or anything like that. But I really enjoy doing the grunt work."

"Actually, investigation and research isn't grunt work. It's the backbone of what we do. Without research and investigation, we're nothing."

Just then, Pearl poked her head into my office. Harper,

Heather and I were sitting there when she came in and whispered into Harper's ear.

Harper looked at me. "Excuse me. I need to see about something."

At that, she got up and left. Then she came back in a few minutes. "I think that we have a new case. Possibly another wrongful death case."

"Oh? Tell me about it."

"It's Darnell Williams. His aunt Arnetta has died. He told me she's been sick for awhile, and, after she was taken to the hospital this last time, it was found her house is full of toxic black mold. I think it's time to do some investigating on this issue. The landlord, the guy who owned the apartment complex that Arnetta lived in, owns apartment complexes all over the city. We should find out how many of those apartments have the same problem as Arnetta's apartment, and if anybody else has gotten really sick or has died from the mold. This could be just the thing for poor Darnell and his family. He's at MIT right now, doing great, but he's only a Freshman in college and his family is still very poor. He worries about them all the time. I hate that his aunt died, but if we could get some money for his family, that would help out a lot."

I remembered Harper telling me Darnell's story. He was a young African-American guy working at a Church's Chicken when he came across the body of a policeman. He found it as he was taking out the trash. He was trying to call 911 when another policeman came along, told him to spread up against the wall, and then found drugs on him. He was arrested for drug possession and murder. It turned out the policeman who arrested Darnell was the actual killer who planted those drugs on Darnell. It was a shameful case, made even more shameful by the fact that Darnell apparently was a really, really good kid. A bright one, too. He got into MIT, where he was apparently thriving.

And now his aunt was dead, apparently because the landlord, the person who owned the house she rented, was a slumlord who didn't care about the conditions of the apartments he rented out. At least, that was apparently what was preliminarily shown by the facts.

"Let's do the preliminary investigation," I said. "And we'll have to figure out if it's worth it to file some cases. We should do an investigation on all of his properties and see if it's worth it to file a class action lawsuit against him."

"I'll get Darnell in here and see if there's anything he can tell me about his aunt. I do know one thing – she didn't have any children. That would mean her two sisters – Violetta and Anita, Darnell's mother, will get the compensation for this case. As I said, I hate that Darnell is experiencing even more tragedy in his young life, but I can't help but think that any money from a lawsuit would do wonders for his family."

I was skeptical about the lawsuit, for much the same reason I was skeptical about my other wrongful death lawsuit involving the negligent doctor – I wondered how much this Arnetta's life was "worth." Damages in a negligence lawsuit depended upon the earnings potential of the victim, extrapolated over the years of life the person was expected to live. If Arnetta truly died because of the toxic mold, then it implied she must have had underlying medical issues. Generally, toxic mold isn't fatal unless the person was weakened to begin with, unless the person was very old or very young. At any rate, I had personally never heard of a case where toxic mold killed an otherwise healthy person.

Assuming Arnetta was already sick, the case became complicated in two different ways. First, there was the issue of causation. If Arnetta was sick, who is to say what truly killed her? Sure, toxic mold might have contributed to her death, but who was to say that her underlying illness, whatever that illness happened to be, didn't cause her death? The other issue was that of life span. If Arnetta was really sick, then her life span wasn't expected to be very long, even if the toxic mold didn't get her. That would mean our compensation would be very limited.

Nonetheless, it was worth it to at least meet with Darnell. And it also was worth it to investigate if the owner of the property had other properties with the same issue. Filing a class action against that individual might be the best way to get some money for everyone, while also bringing money into the firm. Then again, we were also limited by the fact that the individual, whoever that happened to be, might not have millions to pay out for damages.

"Pearl," Harper said. "Call Darnell. See if he can't meet with us sometime soon. I know he's in Massachusetts right now, but we can pay for his flight if he wants to meet us Saturday afternoon. He'll probably go for that, because I'm sure he wants to see his mother and siblings."

At that, Pearl got on the phone and called Darnell. Five minutes later, she said that it was a go. Darnell would be in our office at 2 PM Saturday.

"That means my visit to Nick will be on a tight schedule," I said. "Which is fine, because I don't generally spend more than a half hour there anyhow." Cameron prison was about 45 minutes away from where I lived, so the round trip would be about an hour and a half. Assuming Heather and I started around 9 in the morning, I would be back to the office with plenty of time to spare.

I had my work cut out for me, but that was okay. I really wanted to see if I could get some kind of justice for the

The Alibi

people who were harmed by the toxic mold. If there was one thing that burned me, it was a slumlord. That was because my mom and I grew up in rancid apartments that were freezing in the winter and insufferably warm in the summer. Rats were always around, as were cockroaches. We had to have pans all over the house because the roof would always leak whenever it rained. It smelled like mold and mildew. Worst of all, nobody ever bothered to do anything about the issues. My mom would call and complain, but she never got anybody to even come out and look at our place.

I suppose that, if I really wanted to analyze the issues, I would discover I wanted to nail the slumlord bastard to the wall because I wanted justice for my own shitty upbringing.

Then again, analysis was never my thing.

Chapter Two

THAT EVENING, when I got home, I found a most unpleasant surprise. Sarah, my estranged wife, was sitting in the living room. Just sitting there, watching a movie on Netflix. She smiled when I walked through the door.

"Damien," she said pleasantly. "I'm so glad you're finally here. I sent Gretchen away with the kids."

Gretchen was my new baby-sitter. Nate, my nine-year old and Amelia, my seven-year-old, loved Gretchen because they thought she was fun. And I guess that, to a kid, she probably *was* fun. She played video games with them and let them watch as much television and streaming as they wanted. I didn't mind that Gretchen was permissive – I tried to always get home by 6, so I could have dinner with the kids and make them do their homework.

Amelia was doing fantastic, health-wise. She seemed to be beating her non-Hodgkins Lymphoma. Even though it seemed, last year, that Amelia would probably die, she didn't. Just the opposite – she was getting stronger every day.

The Alibi

I supposed that was why Sarah was in my house. Now that Amelia was out of the woods, for now, she wanted to come back. I wasn't prepared to let her back, however. Not after what she did. Not after she abandoned Amelia and me when we needed her the most. Not after she began an affair with John Gibson long before she officially told me she wanted out of the marriage.

No, I wouldn't just roll over and play dead.

"What are you doing here?" I asked Sarah as I stared at her big blue eyes filled with tears. Those eyes of hers used to slay me. Not anymore. "You don't belong here anymore. I changed the locks when you moved out. I changed them for a reason."

"I know," she said softly. "I heard you're dating Ally Hughes," she said, forcing a smile. "I must say, I was surprised. I thought you only liked blondes."

Ally was a brown-eyed brunette with olive skin. In other words, she was just about the opposite, looks-wise, from Sarah. Sarah was a blue-eyed blonde with alabaster skin. They were both beautiful women in their own right, but only Ally was beautiful to me because Sarah had shown her ugly, ugly side.

"Who I am dating is none of your concern."

"Have the kids met her yet?"

"No. Where are the kids right now, incidentally?"

"They're at the Oak Park Mall with Gretchen. I sent them there with her this afternoon. I called Gretchen and asked her totake the kids before I got there."

I took a deep breath. "You did. Why?"

"Because I wanted to talk to you. You won't return my phone calls."

"That's because my divorce lawyer has told me not to speak with you directly. My lawyer has been calling your lawyer, however. Which is how it's supposed to be. Perhaps you don't know that."

She crossed her arms in front of her, but then slowly dropped them back down to her sides. "I do know that. But we aren't forbidden to speak to one another, are we?"

"No. But it's not a good idea. So, I think you should leave."

She sighed. "Damien, I-"

"Leave."

"I won't. I need to talk to you." She lowered her head and then looked back up at me. "I miss you. I miss our life together. Our family."

I nodded. "Translation. John Gibson kicked me out and Amelia seems to be getting better, so I want to come home. Well, you're not welcome at this house. I haven't gotten a restraining order against you, but I swear to God, Sarah, if you don't leave right this minute, I'll be at the courthouse getting a restraining order so fast your head will spin."

Her eyes were pleading with me. She put one of her hands on my face and rubbed it.

"You don't mean that," she said softly. "You know you don't mean that."

"Like hell I don't. Now get out."

She put her other hand on my other cheek and then rubbed my hair. That always got me. Her rubbing my hair used to be one of her loving gestures. Whenever I was feeling down or stressed, she would always make me a whiskey sour and give me a neck massage and rub my hair. It used to work with me – whenever I was angry with her for some shit she pulled, she would just stroke my cheeks and rub my hair, and I would inevitably calm down.

Was it going to work this time? As I looked at her, my emotions were roiling. On the one hand, I absolutely hated her. Hated her. She jacked me around, she cheated on me, and she abandoned Amelia. On the other hand, there was still a lot of residual love I had for her. I really had never stopped loving her, even if I didn't like her. Even when I hated her, I was in love with her.

And the divorce hadn't been finalized. In fact, nothing had even been filed. My divorce attorney, Olivia Wilder, had the petition prepared and ready to go. She even had a tentative property settlement drawn up and a parenting plan. Sarah told me she wouldn't fight me on any of it. All I had to do was get my lawyer and Sarah's lawyer, Arnold Hamilton, to call a settlement conference and then everything would be ready for the uncontested divorce docket. The uncontested divorce docket was easy-peasy – the parties simply had to go in front of the judge and testify the documents represented our agreement, and then the judge would sign off and we would be done.

Yet, I hadn't been pressuring Olivia to call for the settlement conference, and she hadn't even heard from Arnold Hamilton. He hadn't returned her calls. This wasn't all that unusual for attorneys – they get busy, or, sometimes, they become negligent, so they don't always keep in touch with one another.

The truth of the matter was, I didn't want the settlement conference. Deep down, I didn't want to end the marriage. That wasn't fair to Ally, of course. We were casually dating, and I did really like her. But I hadn't told her I didn't really want a divorce from Sarah. I never told anybody I secretly hoped there was a flicker there. That maybe marriage counseling and individual counseling for Sarah might bring us back together. I thought I owed that much to Nate and Amelia to try to keep the family together.

I owed it to myself, too. I never wanted to go through life wondering what if?

"Sarah," I said, realizing my anger had faded away. "I still love you. But the trust is gone. Completely gone. I can't forgive you for abandoning Amelia. I can forgive you for abandoning me, because I know you were going through an emotional crisis. I know Amelia being sick brought up a lot of awful memories for you about your brother Noah. I understand that, believe it or not." I took a deep breath. "However, you owed it to Amelia to keep trying. To stand strong. I know you didn't agree with my decision to ask the doctors to keep treating her. I know you felt it was fruitless and we were just torturing our daughter. I understand that. I've been to family therapy with the kids, and the therapist has told me you were most likely experiencing some sort of PTSD about the whole thing."

Her blue eyes were becoming warmer, yet sadder, with every word I said. She swallowed hard and then hung her head. "You know why I ran away? You understand it?"

"Yes. I do. I know you couldn't handle Amelia being sick because it reminded you of Noah. But Sarah, it was up to you to find the strength to be there for her. Even if you couldn't be with me, you needed to be there for her. That's what I can't forgive."

"Right now? You can't forgive me about that right now?" Her voice was hopeful. "Or is there a chance we could find our way back and you might forgive me in the future? Is there that chance?"

I sighed. "I don't know. See, if it was just you taking time away somewhere, maybe going to stay with your mother in New York, I would be much more ready to let you come back. I would be angry, but I could get over it. But you didn't just go and stay with your mother. You went into the arms of another man. That's what gets me. You betrayed our vows. Remember how we promised to forsake all others? You threw that in the trash." I was feeling the anger boiling up inside me again. "Why would you do that?"

She shook her head. "I don't know, Damien. I don't know. John and I aren't together anymore. I broke up with him because I wanted you back. I wanted my family back. My life back. I was confused, Damien. I didn't know where to turn. I couldn't talk to you about Amelia. Your mind was made up and all we did was fight about her. That's all we did. I could talk to John about my feelings about our daughter. He listened to me and didn't judge. I felt safe talking to him about how awful I felt about wanting my own daughter to die. What kind of a mother was I to want that?" She bowed her head. "I was suicidal," she said, in a very quiet voice. "And I couldn't talk to you about that, either. I couldn't put that on you, not when you were so focused on Amelia getting better."

Was she manipulating me with this talk about her being suicidal? She had never been suicidal to my knowledge.

"I don't believe you were suicidal."

She got up and went over to an accordion file she had positioned on the floor. She reached into the file and silently brought out a document. She handed it to me, and I looked at it.

It was a discharge document from Shawnee Mission Medical Center. She had apparently stayed there in the psychiatric ward for five days. I looked at the paper, and it indicated that Sarah had appeared at the hospital one day, afraid she would take her own life. She told the intake doctors she had a plan for killing herself and was afraid she would carry it out.

"I wanted to end it," she said. "I wanted to hang myself. I fantasized about doing it. I bought a rope. I tested it on a tree branch – I made a noose and ordered a doll that weighed over 100 lbs. I hanged that doll from a branch in the woods of Swope Park. I was ready to do it. That's when I knew I needed help. I went to Shawnee Mission and they held me inpatient for five days. I couldn't tell you about that. That was right after I moved out of our house. John didn't even know about it – I told him I was staying with my mother during that time. I just needed to get mentally straight completely on my own. That stay in the hospital cured me of wanting to commit suicide, but I've still been struggling with severe depression. I need to be back with you and Amelia and Nate. I know I really screwed up and you're right, I need to be stronger. I'm in therapy, though, working through my issues."

She was in therapy. I felt she was telling the truth about that. I could see it in her eyes.

I closed my eyes and wrapped my arms around her. She clung to me and, in a matter of seconds, she was crying. "I'm so sorry, I'm so sorry, I'm so sorry," she said, over and over and over again. "I love you. I love our children. I can't live without you and I can't live without Nate and Amelia."

"I know," I said. "Listen, here's what I'll do. I got a very nice settlement for a wrongful death case last year. I know you know about it, because I told Olivia, my divorce lawyer, about it. It was marital property, so I had to disclose it. Anyhow, I would like to set you up in an apartment on The Plaza. And we can see each other a few times a week and see how it goes. I'm not ready for you to move back in. I'm not yet ready to trust you like that. But we can go to marital counseling and try to pick up the pieces. I'll break things off with Ally and you have to promise me you won't see other men. I won't make any promises, but, if we can rebuild, if it's possible to rebuild, I would like to try."

She looked at me, her eyes grateful. "Yes. Yes, I would like that. I don't want to live apart from you guys, though I understand why you need that. I'll do anything to make you realize I won't go off the deep end like that again. I won't ever make the mistake of cheating or abandoning or anything like that. Just give me one more chance and I'll show you."

"Okay. Well, next week, let's look for an apartment for you. Someplace close to here. And we'll see how it goes. No promises."

She nodded her head eagerly. "You can't imagine how much this means to me. I can't tell you how much it means to me."

"No promises," I repeated.

I looked out the window and saw Gretchen was coming up the driveway with Nate and Amelia in tow. They each had shopping bags in their hands and were laughing. They walked in the door and saw the two of us together and they all stopped dead. Gretchen's mouth was hanging open and Nate and Amelia both looked stunned.

Sarah plastered a smile on her face. "I was just leaving," she said, in a sing-song voice. "But I'll see you guys later." She looked back at me and I nodded.

Amelia looked at me when her mom left. "What was that? Why was Sarah here?"

I took a deep breath.

"A long story."

Chapter Three

THAT SATURDAY, I picked up Heather at her apartment. It was in the Hyde Park area in a four-plex built in the 1920s. It was a brick building with stone balconies and the cornerstone in front of the apartment building read "1922." The Hyde Park area was actually one of my favorite areas of town. It was a blend of turn-of-the-century mansions and small houses, all of which were built between the turn of the century and the 1930s. Her street was tree-lined and quiet.

I went in the front door of the building and headed up to the second floor. I knocked on her door, and she opened it. "Dami," she said. "Come on in."

I walked in and saw Heather had a style all her own. Her couch was bright blue, her curtains were bright red, blue and yellow and she had a throw-rug made of white fake fur. The place was small, with hardwood floors and low ceilings.

As for Heather, she was dressed in tight jeans and a long sweater layered over a black t-shirt. A colorful scarf was around her neck. I assumed she wanted to wear scarves because she had to hide her Adam's Apple. Harper told me she always wore high heels, and today was no different, as she was in boots with three-inch heels. Her long black hair was up in a bun.

"I'm almost ready," she said. "I just gotta clean out Frisky Bun Bun's litter box."

It was then I noticed the black cat sitting on the window ledge, looking out. Her tail was twitching and she was looking at me suspiciously, as cats often do.

Heather went over to the corner and sifted out some lumps out of the litter box and tossed them into the trash. "Now I'm ready." She went over to her couch and picked up a leather bag and slung it over her shoulder. "Let's go."

We walked down to my car and got in. "Okay," she said. "Now, tell me who we're seeing again and why?"

"His name is Nick Savante," I said. "And he's one of my oldest and closest friends."

"And he's a lifer?" Heather looked at me with a mixture of approval, admiration and subtle curiosity. "I don't need to tell you that you look like the last guy who would have a good friend serving LWOP."

"He's not LWOP. He's up for parole this year."

"Umkay," she said skeptically.

I took a deep breath and told her my story.

"Okay," Heather said. "So, you were in prison and you grew up with these guys serving life sentences. Got it."

"Yeah. What do you think about that?"

She shrugged. "I can't believe you got to where you are, considering what happened to you when you were young. You're kind of a bad-ass."

I smiled. "And you are too," I said. "Harper told me your story."

"I guess. I mean, I killed my psycho adoptive mother with a butcher knife because she would kill me first. But that doesn't mean I'm a bad-ass. I was just unlucky."

"Oh, but you are," I said. "You're getting your shit together. You went through a lot, too, and you're putting it all behind you. That speaks volumes."

"Thanks for saying that." She looked out the window. "Anyhow, I'm really excited about visiting this prison."

I had to smile at her youthful effervescence. When I was her age, I was in prison, wasting away. In a way, it made me angry I couldn't experience the hopeful optimism that Heather was displaying. I never got the chance to capitalize on what it meant to be young and feeling the world was at my feet. I would have to live vicariously through Heather.

After about 45 minutes, we came up on the prison grounds. Cameron Prison is a medium security prison less than an hour outside Kansas City. We went in the prison, filled out a questionnaire, were searched and then led into a room where inmates meet their visitors. All around me were tables with inmates talking to people. Guards stood around and made sure nobody got out of line and nobody was slipping something to somebody.

About twenty minutes later, Nick appeared. He saw me and smiled. I stood up and we hugged. "Buddy," he said. "Man, I thought you were never coming around."

"Aw, come on, man. You know I would never ditch you. Womb to tomb, right?"

"Right, right," he said, still smiling broadly. "I told the guys you were coming. You gotta see them, too, you know. They're all wondering about you."

"I will, I will. Anyhow, I wanted to see how you were. I also need to ask you about a guy in here. His name is Joey Caruso. Name ring a bell?"

Nick looked up at the ceiling and put his hand on his chin. "Sure, I know Joey."

He just then looked over at Heather, who smiled at him. "Who's this?" he asked.

"Heather Morrison," I said. "She works for our firm as an investigator and researcher. She's wanting to learn the ropes. I agreed to bring her along. I hope that's okay."

"Sure, why not?" Nick shrugged. "Now, about Joey. Who is he to you?"

"Nobody. I just got a client, Gina Degrazio, and she hired me to represent her. She told me you gave Joey my name as somebody who should represent her. What can you tell me about him?"

"He's a good guy. He was a transfer from a maximum security prison, got here because of good behavior. He's a lifer, in for Murder One. Killed his wife when he caught her in bed with another man. Can't say I blame him for killing her, but he probably should've killed him, too."

At that, he smiled at Heather. "Oh, sorry, I shouldn't say things like that around a young lady."

"Trust me, Heather has heard it all at this point," I said. "Right, Heather?"

"Oh, God yes," Heather said. "I've been working for Harper for about a year now, meeting with people, doing research and all sorts of stuff. You don't have to police your language around me."

Nick nodded his head. "Thanks, then. So, yeah, Joey is a good dude with a bad rap. You know, he's not really a violent guy. He didn't beat on his wife or anything like that. He just lost his shit when he caught his wife in bed with another dude. That's all. Now, why were you asking about Joey again?"

"I have this new client-"

"Yeah, yeah, Gina Degrazio. Right. Joey talks about Gina all the time."

"Now, tell me about Joey and Gina. Why does Joey talk about her all the time?"

"Gina's his girl," he said. "She's been his girl for quite a few years, according to Joey."

"Really? Joey doesn't mind that she's married and sleeping with her husband's identical twin?"

"I don't know about all that. Joey did tell me that Gina was married, but he said Gina and her husband are name only, you know? I don't know about her sleeping with her husband's identical twin, though. I never heard about that one."

"Okay. What else do you know about Joey Caruso? After all, you told him I would be a good lawyer for Gina. You wouldn't just tell anybody that, so you must know something about him and something about Gina. By the way, I'm thinking Gina will be one of my pain in the ass clients. You know, I'm always telling you about how 20% of my clients produce 80% of my work. I have a feeling Gina will end up part of that 20%. A sneaking suspicion."

"Well, let's see...Joey tells me that he's one of those guys who's low-level on the crime scene. One of those guys who runs robbery and burglary rings but who never gets caught for shit like that. At least, that's what he tells us guys inside. He swears this is his first time down and that if he hadn't been yanked for killing his wife, he would still be on the outside, making his living by knocking off liquor stores and running underground gambling rings. But, between you and me, I think he's full of shit."

"What do you mean?"

"What I mean is, I think Joey is more connected than what he lets on. There's some other guys in here more connected in the Italian mafia world and Joey runs with them inside. He seems to know them all pretty goddamned well. They're not the hit men and the soldiers, more like capos, the guys who have men under them. The ones who order the hits, not the ones who carry them out. They're not the guys who get their hands dirty. The only reason why they're inside is because they're taking the fall for guys even higher up than they are. I'd expect that if Joey was as two-bit as he lets on, these guys literally wouldn't even know him in here. So, yeah, I think Joey has some connections."

"That's interesting. So, you think Joey has connections in the mob, more than he lets on."

"Yeah. I mean, he doesn't even let on that he's connected with the mob at all. He lets on that he's unaffiliated. Says he leads his own low-level crime ring, and doesn't mess around with the big boys. I don't know about that, though."

"Maybe it's just that he's Italian and the mob guys are Italian, and they all have things in common?"

"No, it's not that. Joey's from New York, he's not from the old country. He speaks perfect Italian, though. He said his parents were from the old country and spoke not a word of English so that's why he's bilingual. When he's with those guys, those mob guys, they all speak Italian to each other even though they all know English. Drives the guards crazy. The guards keep telling them to speak English to each other, but they won't do it. Because of that, one of them is always in the hole at any one time, but they don't care. They say it's a free country and have a right to speak a foreign language if they want to."

"And you can understand what they're saying to each other when they speak Italian, right?"

"Yeah. My Italian is kinda rusty, but I remember it well enough to keep up."

"What do they talk about when they speak Italian?"

Nick rubbed the back of his neck and smiled. "They're planning their escape." Then he smiled again. "Nah, really, I don't think they talk about anything important. They talk about what they got when their ladies come in to see them and two of the guys are with each other. They're not gay or nothing like that, but they're lonely, you know. But they're like two old married people, bickering constantly, back and forth. Like cats in a bag."

"But there's not really anything they talk about that's important?"

"Depends on what you think is important."

"Well, anything you can tell me about what Joey says about Gina would definitely be important."

Nick looked up at the ceiling. "Well, he talks about how Gina and her husband, they've been married for twenty years, but the husband isn't interested in her and never has been."

"He ever talk about Vittorio beating on Gina?"

"Nah. I never heard nothing about that." Then Nick narrowed his eyes. "But then again, now that you mention it…" He cocked his head and then pointed at me. "Hold on now, I kinda remember some things that some of the guys are saying around here about Joey and Vittorio. Word gets around here, you know, about what guys have done on the outside. And there was a rumor going around about Vittorio and how he's associated with Joey."

"What is that?"

"Joey was Vittorio's fixer. You know, if Vittorio got into trouble, Joey would fix it for him.

"What kind of problems would Joey fix for Vittorio?"

The Alibi

"Well, you know, Vittorio himself, from what I hear from Joey, was involved in the mafia. He wasn't a hit man but an enforcer. He roughed people up, gave them warnings, that type of thing. He found girls for the prostitution end and collected money from the johns. He also collected money from the people the organization was shaking down. The shopkeepers, the pimps, the dealers, the people who were using the organization's turf. Everybody had to pay the piper, you know, and Vittorio would collect from everyone. That was his main job, from what I understand. He was the shake-down artist."

"Okay. What would Joey have to fix for him?"

At that, Nick got a little closer to me. "Well, the word is, Vittorio was into drugging ladies. You know, put those roofies into their drinks, they pass out and he has his way with them. That's what Joey told me about Vittorio."

I sat up straighter in my chair. "Really? You got any names of these ladies?"

"Nah. Listen, it's all talk, anyhow. Joey said he fixed all those things for Vittorio. He fixed them with the cops and all that. Joey's got connections, Joey knows all the cops, they're all in his pocket, and the ones that aren't, Joey gets information on them he can use to blackmail them into doing what he wants. You know, nobody is an angel on the police force, everybody's got a skeleton in their closet. Joey finds out what that skeleton is and holds it over their heads. So, yeah, Joey had everyone on the force dancing to his tune. Nobody found out anything about those women, though, except one decided to squeal. Most of the other women were shut up by Joey – he either threatened or bribed them. The same way he deals with the cops, he deals with the ladies – threatening and bribing."

"What kind of skeletons do these cops have?"

Nick shrugged. "You know. Some are on the take some are on the make. Some got problems with kids others got issues with drugs. That's not all of them, of course. Lots of cops are clean and bright. But even those ones got family members into all kinds of issues and Joey gets to the family members and ends up blackmailing or threatening them. Listen, everyone's got black sheep laying around, black sheep that can end up being very useful. At any rate, Joey has a special talent for using every trick in the book to make sure he never gets arrested for nothing he does. And he did the same for Vittorio."

I turned to Heather. "You getting all this?"

She nodded. I saw she was writing down a lot of notes, and I smiled.

"Yet, he ended up in prison," I said. "How did that happen?"

"Well, you gotta understand something. Joey had the cops on his side when he was doing two-bit stuff. But they couldn't look the other way when he got caught for murder."

"But he could fix things for Vittorio when he was raping women?"

"Yeah. Joey fixed things for Vittorio by paying off the women he was raping. And, if that didn't work, he would threaten them. Most of those women had kids at home, and all Joey had to do was make a threat against their kids and these women shut their mouths real quick. So, the upshot was, the women were either too scared to bring charges against Vittorio or they got paid off. Either way, they didn't go to the cops."

I would have to get Garrett involved in this story. I would have to send him out and find me some names of

The Alibi

women who knew Vittorio, hopefully some names of women who Vittorio raped. That would give me an avenue to explore so I could figure out who really killed Vittorio. Assuming, of course, Gina was as pure as the driven snow on this matter. Which I had a feeling she wasn't.

I nodded my head. "So, how did Gina get my name? Did she get my name from you, directly, or from Joey? In other words, did you get a chance to meet Gina herself?"

"I never met Gina. I only know of her 'cause Joey talks about her every time she visits. You know, they even got a conjugal visit the other day. I mean, not the other day, it was awhile ago, but you know what I mean."

"Sure, sure. So, you didn't actually meet Gina."

"No. Never met her."

I got the information I needed. I could always come back and see Nick again if I wanted to know other things, after I got Garrett investigating on the case. But, for now, I had some avenues I could explore. From what Nick told me, there were possibly scores of women who would have wanted Vittorio dead. I would imagine they were unbelievably enraged by what happened. They would be thirsty for justice, and yet, Joey came around and threatened them with even more violence if they spoke a word to the authorities. That would make them even more enraged.

One of them would certainly be angry enough to have killed Vittorio. The question was – who would have been that angry? Who would have been most likely to have taken matters into their own hands? Garrett would have to give me names and I would investigate these victims and try to narrow it down.

I could also look at the victims of Vittorio's other crimes. He was a low-level criminal in addition to apparently being a serial rapist. He stole from people, he burglarized, he shook people down, he beat people up. They were also on my possible list of alternative suspects. They had to be.

The problem with a guy like Vittorio, though, was that there were probably so many people who wanted him dead. I didn't quite know how to narrow it down. I also would have to figure out how to get Vittorio's crimes into evidence. I would have to show the jury that Vittorio made enemies around the city, enemies who would have been angry enough to kill, and that would mean I would have to introduce the evidence of his crimes to the court if I would have any chance for acquittal for Gina.

I knew one thing, though – I could figure out how I would narrow the list of suspects down by figuring out which of the suspects would have access to Gina's gun. Who, among the women enraged by Vittorio's actions, would know about Gina's gun? It stood to reason that if I would be successful in finding out who the alternative suspect was, I would have to look for the nexus between Gina and Vittorio. It would have to have been somebody angry with them both – because the person killed Vittorio and deliberately framed Gina by using Gina's registered gun.

That's if Gina was being framed. It didn't look good for her. I still thought she did it.

"Okay," I finally said. "Thanks for the info. Now, let's talk about you. Your parole hearing is coming up in a couple of months. I don't think I need to tell you that I'll represent you, Jack and Tommy in all of your hearings. I'll do whatever you need me to do."

"I got ya," Nick said. "You're my brother. Jack, Tommy

The Alibi

and Connor are too." He looked sad. "But Connor, man, he's just going to die if we all get sprung. We're all tight back here and the other guys in prison still don't mess with us because we're friends with you. I have to tell you, Damien, I'm more than a little worried about what will happen to Connor if the three of us get out."

"Me too." I sighed. "Listen, it's not hopeless. There's been two different Supreme Court cases that have come down saying minors have no business being sentenced to LWOP. These cases don't exactly fit the particulars of Connor's case, but I'm keeping an eye on anything that might. And I'll get in touch with my attorney from the Innocence Project and see if he can do something to reopen Connor's case." I put my hand on Nick's shoulder. "So, yeah, my ultimate goal is to make sure all three of you guys get out of prison soon. I'll give all of you guys a job, too. I got that huge settlement from my wrongful death case last year and I know I can find jobs for all of you. You're right about all of us being brothers. We're all in this together. Don't you forget that."

Nick bowed his head and the guard came over to him. "Well, I guess I gotta get out of here." We bumped our fists and he smiled. "'Til next time, bro." Then he got up from the table and walked away.

I looked over at Heather. "Okay. Now, Heather, you heard the same information I did from Nick. What do you think? What kind of strategy should be taken from here on out?"

"Well, it sounds like Vittorio probably made a lot of enemies. I'd talk to the women involved in his perverted crimes and see if any of them got reason to see Gina in prison. Then I would figure out who in that bunch would be the most likely to have had access to Gina's gun. That's how I would narrow it down."

I smiled. "Smart girl. Harper did well when she hired you."

Heather beamed but didn't address the compliment. "You want me to work with Garrett to run those women down? I would definitely start with the women threatened to keep quiet, as opposed to the ones who accepted the bribes. I think that's the best way to go about it."

"I think so too. Okay, here's how we're gonna do this. Garrett can probably find the names of the victims at least some of them. It'll be tricky, but we can figure out, by looking at Vittorio's bank account, who was getting hush money. It's going to be even more tricky to find out the ones threatened into silence, but I have a feeling most of these victims have some kind of commonality. Maybe they all frequented a certain bar, which is where Vittorio met them, or perhaps they live in the same neighborhood. If Vittorio was somebody who was a creature of habit, he probably met his victims in much the same way."

"Perhaps he ran in a certain circle, and people in that circle would know both him and the women he met," I continued. "I don't know, but I'm sure Garrett can figure out how to run down at least some of the women involved with Vittorio. Then, you're right, we can triage them to figure out who might have been the most likely suspect."

Heather and I left the prison, and I was thinking I might – might – have a good lead on who to look at for this murder. The cops weren't going to do much more investigation – they knew Gina had motive and the gun was registered to her, and they had so many other cases on their plates. They would take the path of least resistance. So, it was up to me, Heather, Garrett and Harper to do the legwork for them.

If there was somebody out there who had it in for Vittorio, I would find her. Or him. That was the only way I could pull a rabbit out of the hat and see Gina acquitted.

I had my work cut out for me. That much was for sure.

Chapter Four

WHEN I GOT into the office after my prison visit, I saw Harper was there with a tall, slim African-American kid. The kid was dressed in jeans and a t-shirt with high-topped tennis shoes. He stood up when I walked in the room, and shyly extended his right hand.

"Hello," he said with a smile. "My name is Darnell Williams."

I smiled back and shook his hand. "Damien Harrington," I said. "I'm Harper's new associate."

"Let's go back to the conference room," Harper said. "I've been chatting with Darnell for a bit. He was early for his appointment, and I was just here in the office, so we've had a chance to catch up."

"I understand you're a freshman at MIT," I said to Darnell as the three of us walked back to the conference room. "How do you like it up there?"

"It's a lot of work," he said. "But I love it. Everybody knows what happened to me with that cop, Officer Cooper.

The Alibi

They all have been very supportive, though. It hasn't been a black mark against me at all."

"Nor should it," I said. "Believe it or not, I can relate to the feeling of being wrongfully imprisoned. There's no bigger frustration in this world. Harper told me about what happened to you about how that cop deliberately framed you for murdering that other cop, and I have to say, I wouldn't be as calm about it as you've been. You're to be commended, buddy."

"You were wrongfully imprisoned?" Darnell asked.

"Yeah. But mine was because of an honest mistake. I couldn't imagine how pissed I would have been if I knew I was in prison because somebody else was trying to cover his ass." I shook my head. "Harper also told me Officer Cooper is serving a life sentence for the murders he committed. I would imagine he's probably being harassed and beaten on every single day. Dirty cops don't have an easy time in prison, trust me when I tell you that. They have to face the people they railroaded into prison and they also have to face the people they legitimately put into prison. They usually have a target on their backs. From what Harper told me about Officer Cooper, if he's getting beaten up in prison, it couldn't have happened to a better person."

We all went into the conference room. Harper got a pitcher of water out of the fridge and poured all of us a glass. "Okay," she said, getting out a legal pad and handing one to me. "Let's get started. Now, Darnell, tell me again about your Aunt Arnetta. You said she was suffering from diabetes. Is that right?"

"Yes," he said. "That's right. But it was under control. She was controlling it with diet, medication and exercise. Lifestyle changes. My mama, she's kinda big, but Arnetta really kept up on her health. She didn't let herself go the way my mama has."

"And when did you start to notice Arnetta was getting sick?"

"Well, as I told you, she suffers from Type 2 Diabetes, so I used to notice, when I was a kid, she was tired a lot and would get really winded from just a little bit of exercise. She would complain about pain in her joints and was thirsty all the time. We didn't know what was wrong with her because she wouldn't see a doctor. She finally did when she went into a diabetic coma. We almost lost her. But you know, the doctors did all kinds of tests on her and they diagnosed her with diabetes. They also found out what kind of allergies she had, and it turns out she had a severe allergy to mold spores of any kind. She was really sensitive to mold."

I was writing this down on my sheet of paper and I wondered how Arnetta survived in that house as long as she did. She had the pre-existing condition of diabetes. It sounded like she had it under control, but that definitely weakened her. And having a severe allergy to mold would exacerbate the issue as well.

"So, she was living in an apartment on the East Side," Harper said. "It looks like this was an older apartment, built around the turn of the century. And she started getting sick when-"

"This is all second-hand knowledge, because I didn't know she was getting sick when she actually was sick. But this is what my mama told me the other day about how it went with Arnetta. Mama told me Arnetta moved into that apartment about a year ago and started getting sick right away. She started getting really tired and had migraine headaches. She has never been a migraine sufferer before. She started coughing all the time and getting stiffness in her joints. She had all kinds of other issues, too. Memory issues, difficulty in concentrating, diarrhea and bloating and would get lightheaded all the time. She didn't know what was going on. She went to the doctor, who said she was suffering from chronic fatigue. He put her on medication for that. But she kept getting sicker and sicker. She was always suffering from the flu, it seemed like. She started to have problems breathing. She told my mama she would wake up at night and find she couldn't catch her breath. She got rashes and she bruised all the time. She even started to lose her hair."

"And she saw a doctor about all of this?" I asked Darnell.

"Yeah. But, you know, she only could afford the free clinic most of the time. She didn't have insurance. They didn't really want to deal with her. She went to Truman a few times, went to the ER, but they seemed to think she was drug-seeking so they didn't want to help much. They didn't know what was wrong with her. They did tests for pneumonia and even tested her for Lyme Disease, but they couldn't figure it out."

"Did they ask her about her mold allergy?" Harper asked. "Did any of these doctors bother to check her records and find out she had a mold allergy?"

"No. Apparently, none of them did. And Arnetta, she didn't even think about the mold allergy thing herself. Nobody knew what was going on. All we knew was she was getting weaker and weaker and her symptoms were getting worse and worse. And then, one day, my mama tried to call her and she didn't answer. That wasn't that odd, though, because Arnetta didn't always answer the phone. But mama tried for several days and got really worried, so she went over to Arnetta's apartment. She found her in the living room. She had been dead for several days."

"Okay," Harper said. "And was there an autopsy done?"

"Yes. My mama requested it. The doctor found there was mold everywhere in Arnetta's organs. In her throat, on her liver, in her lungs, in her brain, everywhere. So, the mold investigators went to her apartment and did tests and found mold everywhere in that apartment."

I looked at the results of the environmental evaluation of the home and found the apartment tested positive for some of the most deadly strains of toxic mold – *Stachybotry, Aspergillus/Penicillium, Cladosporium* and *Chaetomium*. I knew something about toxic mold, and I knew these were some of the deadliest mold strains, especially *Stachybotry* and *Aspergillus*.

"Now," Harper said. "We've established that mold either killed your aunt or contributed to her death. We established her apartment was filled with toxic mold. The only other thing we have to know is whether the owner of the apartment complex knew about the mold and did nothing about it, and for how long that owner knew what was going on. That's going to be the kicker. Did your Aunt Arnetta call her landlord and complain about the mold? And, assuming she knew about the mold, and she could remember she was allergic, why didn't she move out of the place?"

"She was in a lease," Darnell said. "And, yes, she called the landlord about the mold. But Arnetta never put two and two together about the mold. I guess she forgot she was highly allergic and I think she just didn't realize there was a connection between the mold she could see on her walls and her getting so sick. Arnetta didn't really use the Internet all that much – she's kinda old-school like that – and my mama never considered it, either. Neither did Aunt Violetta. I wish my mama would have told me what was going on

The Alibi

with Arnetta, but I was so busy with my criminal case, and then, when we beat down the criminal case, I was focused on getting ready for college. I wasn't paying attention to her and what was going on. If I was, I would have went right over to her apartment, saw the mold, and then told her to get out of there as soon as she could. I know about toxic mold and what it can do. I've known about that for years. We've studied it in Biology Class. But Arnetta and mama, they're not as up on things as me. They haven't had a lot of education or anything like that. So, Arnetta never even thought the mold in her apartment was killing her."

I saw Harper rummaging through the file, and she found what she was looking for – a log the landlord kept about Arnetta's complaints. It showed she complained to the superintendent about a leaky faucet, a toilet that constantly overflowed, a garbage disposal always on the fritz, and mold on her walls. It showed the superintendent fixed the toilet, the garbage disposal and the faucet, but there was not a work order that showed that the superintendent, or the landlord, did anything about the mold problem.

Furthermore, Harper and I went through a history of Arnetta's apartment and it was discovered the mold issue was pre-existing. Apparently, three different tenants, dating back six years, had complained about the mold issue. In other words, that apartment had a mold problem for six years and nobody did anything about it.

And now a woman was dead because of it.

Harper nodded at Darnell. "I forgot to tell you how sorry I am for your loss. I know you don't have a lot of family members, except for your siblings, your mother and your aunts. I also know your mother is still struggling financially. I know this is cold comfort, but it looks like negligence. The landlord had a duty to make sure the premises he rented out were safe. That would include eradicating any mold issue and apparently he didn't do anything about it for six years. The other families who lived in that apartment, prior to Arnetta, complained about the same issue, mold, and still nothing was done. So, that's a clear breach of their duty to provide safe premises to his tenants. Causation is pretty clear – thank goodness there was an autopsy done, so we could establish with certainty what caused Arnetta's death. Granted, her diabetes was a pre-existing condition, and that's what the other side will argue, but with this many mold strains found throughout Arnetta's body, the other side will be hard-pressed to argue the toxic mold didn't cause Arnetta's death. Especially since her diabetes was controlled. So, the only other thing we have to think about is damages. Essentially, what is the life of Arnetta worth? A part of damages is also pain and suffering, but the main part will be calculating what she was worth."

Harper put her hand on Darnell's. The poor kid looked shaken and devastated, and we had to somehow put Arnetta's life into dollars and cents. This was always the hardest part – trying to reduce somebody's life to a dollar amount. But it had to be done.

"How do you determine how much you can get for her life?" Darnell asked.

"Well, we have actuaries that can do that for us. Basically, the actuaries figure out how much Arnetta was making at her position and extrapolate that forward. It also matters how much education she has, how many skills, that type of thing."

Darnell swallowed hard. "Arnetta was working in a nursing home," he said. "Making $13 per hour. 40 hours a week. She didn't have much education. She dropped out of high school. She had three babies, but they're all gone – her youngest was hit by a car when she was six, her boys ended up getting killed on the streets by gang-bangers. Arnetta had a hard life."

"And she was 45 years old. Is that right?"

"Right."

"And she didn't have any health issues except the diabetes, and that was controlled. Right?" Harper asked.

"Right."

"Well, we can probably assume she would have worked until the age of 65, which is retirement age. Actuaries can do a good job of calculating her lifetime earnings. You have to understand, she's making $13 an hour now, but that amount was bound to increase year by year, even if she didn't change positions. Even assuming she only made $13 an hour, at 40 hours per week, that's a half million in lost earnings. Not to mention money for pain and suffering," Harper said.

"But," I cautioned. "You also have to realize your mother and your Aunt Violetta aren't situated as a dependent might have been. In other words, the damages that Harper is talking about, the loss of income, might be reduced because Violetta and your mother, Anita, weren't dependent upon Arnetta's income. We'll have to show the jury that Anita and Violetta were entitled to Arnetta's income in some way. That's not to say you guys won't get any kind of damages, but they will be reduced. That said, you can still claim for pain and suffering and possibly punitive damages. It all depends on what a jury might do with these facts. They're pretty egregious on their face – the fact that there was mold in that apartment for years and nothing was done might be egregious enough facts that a jury will award punitive damages."

"And," Harper chimed in. "I have a feeling Arnetta

wasn't the only one harmed by this particular landlord. I'll have to do some digging, but if this landlord was somebody who owned decaying apartments and homes around the city, and there were other people who got sick because of mold in his or her properties, then we can start a class-action. That would bring the other side to the table pretty damned quick. I have a feeling we can force a settlement from them within a matter of months. I won't promise anything, though. I don't know if a class-action lawsuit is even a possibility right now, and I won't know until I can figure out exactly who owned the apartment that Arnetta lived in and whether or not that person owns other properties. I'll also have to inquire with the former tenants of Arnetta's apartment and find out if they got sick, too. Most of them are outside the two-year Statute of Limitations, but the people who lived in the apartment right before Arnetta might be qualified to sue as well."

Darnell nodded his head. "I hope you can do something for mama and Violetta. They're struggling. I mean, I hope to be making good money when I get out of school, but I plan on pursuing my Masters's Degree, at the very least, so I can't support either of them for many years. My mama needs a break from all her money problems. I hate to be greedy, and I really hate to profit on Arnetta's death, but if something good can come of her illness and her dying so young, that would be the best thing."

"Okay, then," Harper said. "We'll begin our investigation on who was at fault in this entire scenario. I won't rule out suing her doctors for malpractice, because somebody should have investigated her background and saw Arnetta had a severe allergy to mold. Plus, her symptoms were classic for toxic mold exposure. Somebody dropped the ball when they didn't even think to go there. But malpractice is always a tricky thing, so I won't promise anything on that front."

Harper then explained medical malpractice, and how it was different than regular personal injury cases. She explained how she had to find a doctor willing to sign off on the lawsuit, basically, and she had to show the doctors somehow breached the medical standard of care to their patients. The standard was one of reasonableness, and you had to show the doctor did not perform reasonably before you could collect. That was an ambiguous term, but it was defined by how other medical professionals with similar backgrounds and in the same medical community would have behaved under the same circumstance. Mold exposure was one of those things that not every doctor would consider, even when somebody presents with persistent symptoms such as Arnetta, so it would be hard to prove that a reasonable doctor would have tested for mold exposure in Arnetta's case.

After about an hour of talking back and forth with Darnell, we all stood up and I shook Darnell's hand.

"It was a pleasure to meet you," I said. "We'll be in touch."

Darnell smiled, nodded and headed out the door of the suite.

"Poor kid," Harper said. "That kid has gone through so much heartache. I really hope we can come through for him on this."

"I think that we can. We just have to do some digging. Obviously, we can sue the landlord and the superintendent, but, let's face it, they probably don't have a pot to piss in, as my mother would say. We have to figure out who owned this apartment, and find out if that person or group owned other properties around the city. I'll get Garrett on that as soon as possible."

"Thanks for that," Harper said. "How did things go with your friend? Did you find out anything important from him?"

"Yeah, I did. I found out Vittorio was apparently a sex offender. A repeat sex offender. He drugged women and raped them."

"Really?" Harper looked confused. "Did Gina say anything about that to you? Did she tell you she thought Vittorio was doing things like that? That's not generally something that can be hid by a spouse."

"No, she didn't say anything about that to me. But that doesn't concern me. From what she told me, she and Vittorio weren't that close, to say the least. And, don't forget, she was sleeping with Enzo. I'll have to ask her if she ever suspected Vittorio was a repeat and habitual sex offender. I have a feeling she didn't know about it, though. I mean, if she did know about it, why wouldn't she bring that to my attention? That's her get out of jail free card, if you think about it. Vittorio was threatening the women he raped. That would certainly widen the list of suspects in his murder."

"Well, talk to her about it. Find out what she knows. You're going to need her cooperation on this, anyhow, to find out who Vittorio might have been involved with. She might have some kind of knowledge about where he used to hang out. That's probably where he met his victims, I would imagine – at bars. That's usually the way it goes with the date rape drug thing. What, was he using GhB or something like that? Doing a Bill Cosby thing?"

"That's what Nick told me. I'm going to get Garrett on it, see if he can round up any names of victims, but you're right – Gina also might know people who Vittorio attacked and Gina probably would also know the places Vittorio went. So might his poker buddies, the ones who figured out he was missing. They might also be good people to talk to about this."

"Good. Let's start with talking to Gina and get Garrett on the case. In the meantime, I have to get home. I told my girls I would take them to the movies tonight with some friends of theirs. Don't ask me why I'm agreeing to chaperone a bunch of middle-schoolers. They're gonna give me a headache to beat the band, I'll tell you that." She gathered up her things from the center of the table. "What are your big plans this weekend?"

I took a deep breath. "I'm seeing Sarah," I said. "We're having dinner tonight with our kids."

Harper furrowed her brows. "Sarah? Are you talking about-"

"Yes. The mother of my children. My estranged wife. Yes. That's who I'm talking about."

"Didn't she-"

"Abandon me and Amelia when we needed her the most? Have an affair with a guy who she later moved in with? Yeah. She's guilty as charged for all of that."

Harper sat back down. "And you're having dinner with her because?"

"It's a long story. We aren't getting back together. Not yet, anyhow. But we're cautiously moving forward."

"And Ally knows about this?"

I sighed. "No. I haven't told her. I don't yet know what I want to do with Sarah. I love her. I never stopped. I mean, there was a long period where I didn't like her and an even longer period where I hated her. But, even while I hated her, I still loved her. I know, I know. It doesn't make any goddamned sense to you. It doesn't make sense to me, either. I wish I could make sense of it. But I'm not going to stop seeing Ally just because I'm going to maybe see how things go with Sarah. Is that shitty of me?"

Harper smiled. "Of course that's shitty of you. You don't have to even ask that question. It's *prima facie* shitty of you. But it's your life. Just don't be surprised if you have to recuse yourself from every case that Ally's on the other side of, because she'll have it out for you if you string her along and then dump her." She shook her head. "That's why I never shit where I sleep. But, as I said, it's your life."

I was stung by Harper's words, even as I privately acknowledged she was right. I was hedging my bets, which was why I didn't break it off with Ally. I was figuring that Sarah would go off the rails again, sooner rather than later, and I would have Ally to fall back on. That wasn't fair to her, of course, but I did really like her. I didn't want to hurt her.

Yet I knew I would if Sarah and I officially got back together.

I was caught between a rock and a hard place, and I didn't know what direction to turn.

Chapter Five

ON MONDAY, I met Gina in my office. I would have to pick her brain about what I had found out about Vittorio. I was mainly trying to see how much she knew about Vittorio's "predilections," and why she didn't come clean with me about them.

I knew that, when she came into the office and sat across from me, and I asked her about Vittorio's sex crimes, my initial hunch was right. She had no idea Vittorio was involved in these things.

"No," she said, shaking her head. "I didn't know Vittorio was drugging women." That was all she said, though, and I decided to press her a bit more.

"Okay. Let's go through this step by step. I'm just going to treat this like a cross-examination, if you don't mind."

Her back straightened and she looked me clearly in the eye. "Go ahead. I got nothin' to hide."

I thought her saying she had nothing to hide was odd, but I pressed on. "Now, you and Vittorio were living together until a few months ago, right?"

"Right."

"When, exactly, did you move out and start to live with Enzo?"

She took a deep breath. "I don't got no calendar," she said. "I don't know."

"Give me an estimate. Did you sign any contracts with Enzo? He owns the house you're living in, right? Did he give you anything to sign to make sure you pay him rent or anything like that?"

"No. I don't pay him rent. I just live there and I service him. That's my rent." She stared at me briefly. "Listen, it's no different than those ads on Craigslist where those guys are looking for sex instead of rent. With me and Enzo, it's the same."

"Today is April 1," I said. "And you first talked to me the early part of March. The murder occurred February 18. You said you weren't living with Vittorio on the day he was murdered. So, it's safe to say you moved out sometime before February 18, right?"

"Well, yeah, that's a given."

"Let's take some landmarks here. Was it before or after Valentine's Day?"

"Like I give a crap about Valentine's Day." She shook her head. "I got no idea. That day is just like any other day to me."

"How about New Year's Day? Before or after New Year's Day?"

"I don't know. Listen, what is all this about? Why you asking me all these questions?"

"I need to know when you lived with Vittorio. I'm going to find these women who Vittorio is accused of raping. I'm trying to get approximate dates on when it happened, and from there, I can tell if you're lying to me about how you didn't know what was going on. That's why I'm asking you these questions."

"I'm not lying. I didn't know Vittorio was a pervert. And if I were you, I'd leave this whole thing alone."

"I'm not going to leave it alone. This angle is the best way to get you acquitted. There are an untold number of victims out there who have a damned good reason to want Vittorio dead. I'm going to track these people down. But I swear to God, if I find out you either knew what Vittorio was doing or, God forbid, you somehow approved of it or helped out with it, I'll be off your case faster than lightning."

"Just leave it alone," Gina said.

I sighed. "When did you move out of Vittorio's house, Gina? When? Did you live there with him, he disappeared for hours and you didn't question it? Did he come home and tell you what he was doing and you looked the other way? Did he threaten you to keep you quiet about it? Or did you get off on it? Did you get some kind of perverse pleasure about it?"

"What the hell do you think about me? Getting some kind of perverse pleasure on something like that? Who does that?"

"Oh, you would be surprised. Believe me, I've dealt with cases like this before, and you'd be surprised how many of the wives were actually involved with all the dirty deeds. Now, I'm going to ask you again. When did you move out of Vittorio's house?"

"I don't remember."

"You don't remember? At all? You can't remember if you moved out of the house sometime last year, or early this year, or two years ago, or whenever?" I stood up. "Or maybe you never moved out of that house at all. Maybe you made up that whole story about living with Enzo. You know I'm going to talk to Enzo and ask him. Hopefully the two of you got your stories straight about what you're supposed to tell me, but, from where I sit, I have a feeling you're lying. You never did move out of Vittorio's house, did you? You weren't really with Enzo on the night of the murder, were you?"

"Why are you asking me all these questions?" She crossed her arms in front of her, a sure sign she was getting defensive. I was a student of body language, and her language told me she was ready to blow. "I'm not on the witness stand."

"No, but you will be. You will be, unless I think you're lying, and then I probably won't put you on. But, for now, I'm trying to make sure you get your story straight before the prosecutor cross-examines you and makes you look like an idiot."

"I'm not an idiot. I resent you calling me an idiot. I graduated high school. I'm not dumb."

"No. But you're lying. And you don't even have a good answer for me. Me, your attorney. You don't have a good answer for the questions I'm asking you, so you sure as hell won't have good answers for the prosecutor."

I realized I wouldn't get anywhere with Gina with my bullying tactics. So, I decided to try something else. I would try to get on her good side and see if she told me the truth that way.

"Listen," I said softly. "You say Vittorio beat on you. Maybe he has frightened you. Maybe he has men out there who will take care of you if you tell the truth about what happened the night Vittorio was murdered. Maybe you really know what happened. If that's the case, then just tell me. Just tell me, and I can get you into a good witness protection program. You'll change your name, change your identity, the government will pay for you to live anywhere you choose. Paris, Rome, wherever you want to go. If you have information that will bring down a big fish, somebody the government really wants, they'll make sure you are protected."

"No." She shook her head. "Vittorio didn't know no big fish. He was a soldier, a low-level guy. He didn't even carry out hits. He just shook people down. Did the occasional burglary, sometimes found working girls for the family, that kind of thing. He didn't know no big fish. He didn't know nothing about none of that. He had no information the government would want, and neither do I."

"Well, okay then." I took a deep breath. "But maybe you have your own reasons for lying. Maybe you do. At any rate, I'm your attorney, and you need to be straight with me. You need to tell me everything, down to the letter. If you don't, I'll have to withdraw from your case."

"You're not going to withdraw from my case. I'm paying you big money to represent me. Joey told me that-"

"And that's another thing. You lied to me about Joey. About who he was. You were sleeping with him. You go and see him in the prison on a regular basis. You have conjugal visits with him. Why would you lie to me about that? You knew I would find out. All I had to do was see my friend in prison, Nick, and he would tell me everything he knew about Joey. And about how Joey knows you. So why lie?"

"I didn't want you to know. I thought if you knew about that, you wouldn't believe me about my story about Enzo."

"I *don't* believe you about Enzo. Worse, I don't believe a word that's coming out of your mouth. You're playing a game, and I don't like it."

When I worked for the Public Defender's Office, my

clients played games with me all the time. They would lie and hide things. Omit things. Make me try to guess what their game was. I always figured it out, but, sometimes, I would figure it out too late. I would be blind-sided in trial, made a fool of in front of the judge and jury. I got smarter as I went along, however, and I got better at figuring out the puzzles my clients presented.

But when I was in the Public Defender's Office, I didn't have a choice with my clients. I was just assigned defendants and I had to go with them to the end. I couldn't just withdraw from their case. But I had the choice to withdraw from Gina's case. I could do it in a heartbeat.

"That's it," I said, standing up. "I can't work with you. Not when you can't tell me the truth."

"I'm telling you the truth," she said. "You can't withdraw from my case. I won't let you."

"I *am* going to withdraw from your case," I said. "I can't have a client who lies to me."

"Well, maybe if you withdraw from my case, maybe something's going to happen to your friend in prison. Nick. Maybe something happens to him if you withdraw."

At that, I lunged at her. I wouldn't have her threatening Nick or anybody else. "What the hell is that supposed to mean?"

She shrugged her shoulders. "Maybe you're gonna find out. I wouldn't want to find out if I were you."

I turned around and looked out the window. I counted to ten, very slowly, and did some deep breathing. I would have to face this woman calmly. I couldn't speak to her in anger. I had to find out what she was talking about.

I took a few quiet minutes as I closed my eyes and slowly went to my happy place.

Then I turned around. Gina was still there, sitting in the

The Alibi

chair, her arms crossed. She was giving me the stink-eye to end all stink-eyes. I sat down and stared down at my yellow pad of paper.

"What did you mean," I asked, as calmly as I could, "when you said that something will happen to Nick if I withdraw from your case?"

"I told you you gotta withdraw to find out. I'm not gonna say anything more to you than that."

I sighed. "Listen, Gina, no matter what you say, no matter how many lies you tell, no matter how many empty threats you give me, I'm gonna find out the truth. That's what I do. I have a crack investigator who will find these things out for me. So, you might as well tell me."

She shook her head. "I got my Ace up my sleeve, and like hell I'm gonna let you know what it is. Now, you gotta represent me to the end."

I finally just sat down. "Just get out of here, please. Just leave. I'm obviously going to have to find out the facts of this case without your help."

She pointed at me. "Okay. But I gotta give you a warning here. You don't worry about what Vittorio was up to with those women. You got that? You don't worry about that."

"What do you mean, I don't worry about that? You do know that Vittorio's double life is your best chance at acquittal, don't you?"

"No. You try to think of something else. You try to come up with another story that's going to get me off. Not that one."

At that, she turned her back and walked rapidly out of the office.

———

"WHAT DO YOU MEAN, Gina doesn't want you to go there with the drugging women?" Harper asked me after Gina left the office.

"Just what I say. She told me not to go there. She's a sneaky one, I'll give her that. But it's backfiring on her. I now want to go to that defense all the more."

"Well, it's pretty simple, right? You have to defer to your client, whatever defense she wants to go with, but if you don't feel comfortable with what she wants, you have to withdraw. It's early enough to do that, you know. She hasn't even been Grand Juried, let alone formally arraigned. Do a quick motion to withdraw and let her be somebody else's headache."

I bit my lower lip. "I would do that, but I don't know. I think she's bluffing, but goddamn if she's not."

"About what?"

"She said something cryptic about something happening to my best friend, Nick Savante, if I withdraw from her case. See, she's seeing this guy inside, his name is Joey Caruso. Caruso knows Nick. I have no idea what Gina is talking about, though. She just told me I would find out if I withdrew from her case."

"Ah ha. Now, see – you're in the same situation I was with Erik Gregorian. I thought Sargis was bluffing me when he said he would kill me and kidnap my girls if I didn't defend his son and get an acquittal. But I wouldn't find out for sure. It's the same thing with you – she's probably bluffing. She probably can't do anything to your friend, even if you withdrew from her case. But what if she can? Then what?"

"I don't know. I don't know what she's even threatening. I guess I should stay on her case and try to figure out the best way to defend her. But one thing is for sure – she's told me not to worry about the drugging women thing. I'm gonna worry about it. I'm going to do my due diligence on it. I at least want that card up my sleeve just in case nothing else presents itself."

"Something will present itself," Harper said. "The guy was a gangster. He had enemies. You don't necessarily have to show his perverted side to the jury to get an acquittal for Gina. Maybe you should focus on what enemies he might have had with the mob. Try to figure that out."

I steepled my fingers and swiveled around in my chair. "I know what you're saying, but my gut is screaming at me about two things. One, the drugging women had everything to do with why Vittorio was murdered."

"And the second thing your gut is telling you?"

"That Gina is hiding something. She's hiding something big. And I need to find out exactly what it is."

Chapter Six

IN THE MEANTIME, I decided to put Gina's case on the back burner. It was still early in the process. The Grand Jury hadn't yet convened on her case, which meant she hadn't been formally arraigned, which meant, in turn, she hadn't been assigned a trial docket just yet. In other words, there was plenty of time to prepare for her case.

I sent Tom Garrett to do some digging on Vittorio's victims to see if he could scare up some of them. Once he did, I would speak with them and see what I could find out about Vittorio and what he did to them.

Other than that, however, I decided to not do any more work for her. I was at a standstill, and I still wrestled with whether or not I wanted to withdraw. On the one hand, I knew in my heart I should withdraw. She didn't listen to me, she wasn't being truthful with me, and she was against my strategy. Everything was telling me the relationship between Gina and me was toxic and was only bound to get worse.

Instead of actively working Gina's case, I decided to throw myself into Darnell's case. Or, should I say, Arnetta's

The Alibi

case. Harper was busy with a few other murder cases she was trying to plead, along with a ton of other cases, and I was less busy, so I decided that working Arnetta's case would be what I would focus on.

I needed a win with Arnetta's case. I wanted to bring down those slumlord bastards, and I wanted to bring them down hard.

So, the first thing I did was meet with Garrett to find out what he knew about who owned Arnetta's building, whether that person owned other property, and whether or not other people were getting sick because of this person's neglect.

We met at a bar downtown, one of the seedier bars around. It was the kind of bar, with the basic cement floors, exposed overhead pipes and dimly-lit pool tables in the back, that people could be incognito. Not that I cared if people saw Garrett and me together. Of course I didn't. But this was the kind of bar that Garrett liked. He always told me he wasn't comfortable in the "yuppie bars," as he called them – the kinds of bars with wine lists and craft cocktails were not for him. He wanted to go to someplace where he would see somebody puke in the corner.

I walked in, saw him sitting in the back, and joined him. The waitress came around and I saw they had PBR on the menu. I hadn't had PBR since I used to run with the guys, so I felt nostalgic enough to order one. I wasn't so high on myself that I couldn't enjoy some really cheap brew once in awhile.

"Hey, buddy," Garrett said when I walked in. "Sit down. You're gonna love some of the stuff I'm coming up with."

My order taken, I sat down and leaned forward. "Hit me," I said. "I hope you got something juicy to tell me."

"I do. Listen, I managed to track down two different women who knew Vittorio, both of whom are ready to speak with you whenever you want to talk to them. They both told me how relieved they are that Vittorio is dead. I think you can start with them and they might lead you to other women. At any rate, I'll keep digging to find out if I can scare up anybody else for you to talk to about that."

"I knew you could do it," I said. "But boy, that was fast. How did you figure it out so quickly?"

"I got connections. I know guys who knew Vittorio, knew where he frequented, and it was just a matter of going to those places and asking around. It wasn't hard to find people who knew Vittorio at these bars – he was there all the time. It also wasn't hard to find people who saw Vittorio go off with women. From there, it was just a matter of me tracking down the women and asking them a few questions. I don't know if these are the women that Vittorio raped or nothing like that, but I figured it's a good bet we're on the right track."

I nodded my head. "Good, good. Just give me a list and I'll go and talk to them. That is, if I even want to still be on this case. Don't worry, you'll get paid no matter what, but I'm starting to think I need Gina to not be my client anymore."

"Why? She giving you the business?"

"Oh, yeah. I mean, they all do, to a certain extent. But this one…" I shook my head. "I don't think I can believe a word that comes out of her mouth. She's one of those women who you know they're lying because their lips are moving. Anyhow, thanks for that. Now, what you got for me on the Arnetta Williams case?"

"I did a title search and found out that a Robert Davis owns that building Arnetta died in. And, just like you thought, he owns property around the city. I visited some of the other apartment buildings he owns. All I can say is,

The Alibi

where are the condemnation people when you really need them? These places aren't fit for bums to live in. Homeless people on the street wouldn't even want to squat in these buildings. But there are people living in all these places. And, get this – the bastard is loaded. Loaded. You know, sometimes you might find somebody who maintains property and they really shouldn't because they don't really have the money to do repairs. Sometimes real estate doesn't have the best profit margins, especially when you can't charge much rent. In those cases, I feel the person needs to sell to somebody who could make repairs when the repairs are needed. But in this case..." He shook his head. "It's some fat cat who obviously could give shit less about the conditions his people live in. That's what pisses me off the most."

"Tell me about this Robert Davis," I said. "What does he do, aside from being a slumlord?"

"Well, he's one of those goddamn trust-fund babies from what I can see. He comes from old money. His old man is a billionaire and he himself is living off a trust fund of $10 million. So, yeah, he has the money to make sure the people in his apartment buildings are living in safe conditions but he just doesn't care. He's a sociopath if you ask me."

I shook my head. "Bastard. What else did you find? Did you talk to anybody you saw around those apartments?"

"Nah. I just got the addresses. But I did some digging – I know people down at Truman Med. I know record-keepers down there. They give me information when I need it. They aren't supposed to because of the HIPAA laws and all that, so they could lose their jobs if anybody ever found out what they're doing. Anyhow, I was able to cross-check with my people down at Truman to find out how many people have been admitted to the hospital from those apartment buildings. There are three other apartment buildings, by the way, that this prick owns. Anyhow, I found five other cases for you to investigate. All of them sound like your lady, Arnetta. Coming in with all kinds of weird symptoms. A couple of them actually were diagnosed with pneumonia, but they came back in a few months, still coughing, still with body aches, headaches and diarrhea. I haven't found nobody else who has died in these apartments who are complaining of the same types of things, but it sounds like you have some sick people on your hands."

"Seriously? You got names and all that?"

"I sure do. Names, phone numbers, addresses, all that. Listen, you'll have to come up with some kind of story when you approach them. You can't just go on down there and say I told you about them coming to the hospital. You do that and the jig will be up. My people over at Truman won't talk to me no more."

"Goes without saying. Guess I need to have some type of ruse to speak with them."

"It's pretty easy. They're all still living in the same apartment complex. Guess they can't afford to go anyplace else, the poor bastards. Go on over there, tell them you're there to fix their apartments, and then talk to them about what's going on. Listen, these people need help with their problems. They don't know it, though. They probably have limited education, maybe some of them don't even speak English. They might be immigrants, maybe not even legal immigrants. At any rate, they don't know they need a lawyer. They probably don't even know their apartments are killing them. You need to get in there and let them know what their rights are. They won't come to you.".

"I know that. I don't feel comfortable speaking with them under false pretenses, but I don't know what else to

The Alibi

do. God, I never wanted to be one of those ambulance chasers. You know the guys – the ones who hang out at hospitals, hoping to pick up a case. The ones who go to funerals and hand the widows their business cards. But I think you're right – these people won't come to me. I need to round them up. I could send them a letter in the mail, but who knows if they'll get it? They need to know what's going on with them. They probably need somebody to pay their medical bills, at the very least. I would love to figure out some other way to reach them, but I think you're right – I need to get in and speak with them, and I probably have to do it under false pretenses."

"If you want, I'll do it. I'll get in there, look around, see the mold, ask if anybody is sick in the house, and when they say 'yes,' I'll tell them they're entitled to money. I'll ask them to call you. My guess is that if these people are poor, which they are, since they're living in squalor, they'll jump at the chance to speak with an attorney. I'll set it up for you to speak with them."

I nodded. "You might be right about something, though. They might be immigrants. Do you speak Spanish by any chance?"

"I do." He nodded. "I learned it growing up in my neighborhood. I grew up around the Boulevard. You know everybody speaks Spanish around there. What about you?" *The Boulevard* referred to Southwest Boulevard, which was known as "Little Mexico."

"I learned it in prison," I said. I smiled as I realized how much my rough background, and Garrett's, helped us both. "So, if they're immigrants from a Spanish-speaking country, we're golden. But if the people are from other countries, I got nothing."

"Well, none of them had names that sounded Vietnamese, if that's what you're thinking. A couple of them had names that sounded Hispanic though."

"Go ahead, go over there and knock on their doors and see if they'll let you in. Tell them you're there to fix their apartments. They'll let you in. And, hopefully, you can convince them to let me pay them a visit. I'll go to them, of course. Most of them will have problems coming to see me at my office, and that's okay. Just set it up."

"Will do."

I realized, as I spoke with Garrett some more, I was not only hopeful about these mold cases, but I felt energized. Gina, with all her lies and games, was sapping my energy, day by day. She was making me depressed about my job. But this – the possibility of actually helping somebody – this was why I got into law in the first place. It was like when I was in prison and was helping guys who were not only helpless, but hopeless. When I actually helped guys get a new trial or get their convictions overturned, there was no feeling like it.

If these cases turned out how I hoped that they would, with the people not only getting money, but justice and, most importantly, they hopefully could move out of their filthy apartments, then I would feel I actually did something good.

Criminal defense, more often than not, was a thankless job. Not just a thankless job, but one that came with huge risks that I would end up letting a murderer back on the street. I did it with Erik Gregorian – I got him off, but all I did was put him back on the streets, where he was resuming his criminal activity. It was a hollow victory, to say the very least.

But with these mold cases – I had a real chance to get people justice. I had a real chance of actually helping somebody. These people were poor, they were the dregs of society, and they probably never had anything positive in their lives.

I had the chance to maybe give them that, and that's what made it all worthwhile.

Chapter Seven

THE FIRST APARTMENT I went to was that of Enrique Martinez and his wife, Aurelia. Garrett had gone over there on the pretense of fixing the apartment, and then was able to explain to them, in Spanish, what he was really there for. It turned out that not only was Aurelia sick, and had been for quite some time, but they had a newborn child that died of SIDS. I did my research and found out there were quite a few cases, nationwide, of newborns who allegedly died of SIDS but actually died of mold exposure. I also found out that newborns, and the elderly, were the most likely to die of mold exposure. Sometimes young adults died of mold exposure, but usually they, like Arnetta, had some kind of underlying issue that weakened them and made them more susceptible.

Aurelia let me in the door. She nodded and tried to speak in broken English, but I just shook my head and explained to her, in Spanish, that I knew her language fluently. She looked relieved.

The Alibi

"Ah, si," she said, "gracias." Then she told me, in Spanish, what was happening with her.

"A man came the other day," she said in Spanish, "he told me his name was Tom Garrett. He told me he would fix our mold problem. I was hopeful, but then he told me he was actually working for a lawyer. That lawyer is you." She smiled and nodded. "I told him about how I've been feeling. I've never been sick before. Now, I'm sick all the time. Rashes, headaches, trouble breathing. And my son, he was only 6 months old, he died in his crib. I had taken him to the doctor several times because he seemed to have problems breathing. Then he died." She shook her head and started to cry. "He died, just like that. Tom Garrett told me the mold in my apartment might be why I'm so sick and my baby died. He said maybe you could help."

I put my hand on her shoulder and spoke to her in Spanish. "I'm very sorry for your loss," I said. "And I am here to help you. You need to move out of this apartment and do it as soon as possible."

"I'm in a lease," she said. "I can't move out for another three months."

"You must move out," I said. "You find another place to live, and I'll make sure you get out of your lease." I wanted to tell her about the "Doctrine of Habitability," which means that if you showed the landlord the premises were not liveable and the landlord doesn't do anything about these issues, you can withhold rent or repair and deduct. But, in this case, I wanted to threaten the landlord and the owner. I wanted to file suit against them and tell them that if they try to collect from Aurelia and Enrique, I would go public with what they were doing. I had a feeling that they would, at the very least, not sue Aurelia and Enrique for "breaking" their lease.

There was also the concept of "constructive eviction," where a tenant may vacate their property and break their lease if the landlord interferes with the tenant's enjoyment. All I had to do was show that the owner's conduct was wrongful, which it certainly was, and this was another ground for Aurelia and Enrique to move out. Garrett's research showed me that Aurelia and Enrique both had complained about the mold many times and, thus far, nothing was done about it – that showed wrongful conduct right there.

She shook her head. "No. I'm afraid they'll sue us."

"When I file my suit, I'll make sure I can get an injunction against the landlord and the owner. I'll get an injunction against any legal action against you and Enrique. What that means is that they can't sue you. Trust me, you need to move out. Your life might depend on it."

"What do you mean by that?"

"This mold," I said, pointing at the ceiling and the walls, both of which were covered in large black, green and brown spots, "is deadly mold. That's why I want to take your case. I want the owner of the property to pay for this. I want the owner of the property to pay for the death of your newborn baby and I want the owner to pay for your suffering. You're entitled to money, Aurelia, both for your sickness and your baby dying. I want to help you get that money."

She took a deep breath. "Enrique, my husband, he's not here. He needs to make the decision on whether we want to file a lawsuit. He's not sick."

"He works outside the home, right?"

"Yes. He works 40 hours a week at Wal-Mart."

"And you stay home?"

"Yes. I stayed home with Manuel, my son, and I wanted

to go to work after he died, but I couldn't, because I started getting so sick. So, yes, I don't leave the house very often."

"That's why Enrique isn't sick and you are. He gets out of the house, so he gets fresh air 8 hours a day. Plus, I have a feeling you might be allergic to mold and Enrique isn't. That also makes a difference. As for Manuel passing away, he was a newborn, and toxic mold is especially dangerous for newborn babies."

"Where are we going to live? We cannot afford much rent. Enrique's parents are living in Mexico and he sends money to them. He must send money to them, because if he doesn't, they don't eat. It doesn't leave much money for us to live on, though."

It was then that I made a snap decision. I had all this money just sitting in the bank. I made some investments and bought a new house, but I still had $2 million left from the $4 million I got from my wrongful death settlement last year. Why didn't I take a few thousand out of the bank and make sure all my new mold clients had a decent place to live? What good was money if you didn't use it to make a difference?

"I'll make sure you get a good apartment," I said. "Leave that to me. In the meantime, talk to Enrique, tell them I stopped by, and try to convince him to let me take you on as a client. You and Manuel."

"We don't have money to pay you."

"That's okay. I take these cases on a contingency fee basis. That means I take a percentage out of your settlement, whatever that happens to be."

Aurelia took a deep breath and nodded her head. "I'll talk to Enrique and I'll call you."

"Thank you."

OVER THE NEXT FEW WEEKS, I signed up six more clients for my pending class action lawsuit against the rich slumlord bastard Robert Davis.

There was Juanita Davis, a young African-American woman living in a two-bedroom apartment with two boys, age 6 and 4. Both boys had been in and out of the emergency room at Truman Hospital with respiratory illnesses. The youngest had developed a severe case of asthma. Both boys were continually sick with different flus and colds, and they had both developed rashes on different parts of their bodies and they both persistently complained of headaches. Juanita herself wasn't sick, but she explained to me that she worked two jobs and wasn't home that much. She had a baby-sitter come in and watch the boys, and I went and interviewed the baby-sitter, but she said she wasn't sick. I figured that was probably because her exposure to the mold was somewhat limited because she wasn't in the apartment all the time and the boys were.

Juanita, as the guardian for her two boys, Marcus and Jamal, was my second client. The third client was Mariana Alba, an immigrant from Ukraine who, thankfully, spoke perfect English, albeit with a thick accent. It took me some time to adapt to translating what she was telling me, but, after a few hours of speaking with her, I got the gist of what she was saying.

Mariana told me she had moved into her apartment within the past year, and that, prior to her moving into her place, she had never been sick before. After she had been in her apartment for a week, she started to develop a persistent, deep cough. The headaches and the rashes followed. She ended up in the ER at Truman Med several times

The Alibi

because of her symptoms – once because she had a headache that had lasted a week despite her best efforts to cure it with over the counter medicines. Another time was for a severe respiratory illness – she was sick for a week, and then, one day, she woke up in the middle of the night and found she couldn't catch her breath. She was in the ER two more times because of recurring bladder and kidney infections. She also said she was feeling a general sense of malaise – like she didn't want to get out of bed in the morning.

I also signed up Mariana's boyfriend, whose name was Josh Dylan. He had been staying with Mariana, pretty much full-time, even though he technically had an apartment of his own. He, too, complained of respiratory illness, persistent infections, persistent migraine headaches and rashes. He also said he had gone into the ER several times with chest pains – he thought he might be having a heart attack.

Candace Kaine, aka "Candy Kaine," was my fifth client. She was a part-time stripper at a low-class joint who had been bedridden for several months at the time I saw her. She explained to me she had wanted to move out of her apartment and find something better and hoped her stripping job would help her do that. But she had been unable to dance since she had been so sick and was constantly afraid her landlord would throw her out. She had ignored several eviction notices and was more than relieved when I told her what I had told everybody else – I would pay for her to get a new apartment. Candace had the same symptoms as everyone else – debilitating headaches, rashes, respiratory illnesses, constant fatigue, etc. She also had chest pains, like Josh Dylan, and said she felt light-headed most of the day.

Candace cried happy tears after I told her I would pay for her to get a new place. She put her blonde head on my chest and just let loose with a torrent of tears.

"You don't know how much this means to me," she sobbed. "I thought I would die. I thought I would end up on the streets. I've got nobody to help me. I'm too sick to work. I applied for disability, but I was told that it would take months to approve me. I didn't know where to turn. You don't look like an angel, but, to me, you are. You are the answer to my prayers."

The sixth person who became my client was a gay man named Mercury James. He was a pale, skinny guy with blonde hair that was almost white and pale blue eyes. When I explained to him the mold in his apartment was killing him, he, like Candace, broke down and cried.

"I thought I was in full-blown AIDS," he told me. "I was too afraid to get tested. My boyfriend left me because he thought I had AIDS. He's negative right now and didn't want to press his luck. He still loves me. If you think my symptoms are because of this goddamn mold all over this shitty-ass place, then I think me and him will get back together. I hope you're right."

Mercury told me the reason he thought he had AIDS was because most of the symptoms he was having were the same as those patients suffering from full-blown AIDS.

"Man, coughing all the time, rashes all over my body, can't get out of bed most days. Body aching all the time, head to toe. Headaches that split my skull in two. Been in the ER several times, but I've never consented to them testing me for AIDS. I don't want to know if I got that disease."

With each of the people I signed up, I offered them the same deal – they each got a new apartment to live in and I sent each of them to a doctor for testing and treatment. I lined up specialists for them, including ear, nose and throat doctors and doctors who specialize in treating severe headaches. In addition to that, I even found a doctor who specialized in mold-related illnesses. That wasn't his entire practice, but he had a particular expertise in the growing field.

After I signed up Mercury and made sure everyone was out of their apartments, and everyone had seen the doctor, I sat in my office reviewing all their files and thinking about how alive I felt at that very moment. I couldn't possibly alleviate all the suffering of everyone in the world, but I made a huge difference to these seven people – the five adults plus the two children – and I felt energized by it. I approached these cases with a focus I hadn't experienced in years. In my mind, Gina and her issues didn't even exist.

Until Pearl came in the office and informed me that Gina's case had gone through the Grand Jury, which meant I had to be in court for her formal arraignment. That wasn't that big of a deal – formal arraignments were always more of a formality than anything – but, at the same time, I realized her case was moving along and I had to make a decision on what to do with her. If I was going to withdraw from her case, I would have to do it soon. I couldn't just go along and prepare for trial and then withdraw. That wouldn't be fair to her and probably would result in a Bar Complaint. Plus, it would be a lot of time wasted on my part.

No, I would have to figure out what direction I wanted to go with her.

So, I called Garrett.

"Garrett," I said, when he picked up the phone. "You find any more of Vittorio's victims? I need to speak with some of them. I need to make a decision on whether or not I still want on Gina's case."

"Yeah," he said. "I'll e-mail you a list. I got some of the bios from them so you can also determine which one might be at the top, as far as suspects go. I know you were saying you wanted to know which victim might also want to get Gina and I think I found a couple who might fit that bill."

My ears perked up when he said that. "Really? You found some of Vittorio's victims who might also have it in for Gina?" That was what I was looking for, really. The nexus between Vittorio and Gina – somebody who hated both of them. "Go on, tell me who you found who knew and hated both Vittorio and Gina."

"Well, there's this lady. Her name is Bianca Cassavettes. I tried to speak with all the victims I found and asked them some questions about Vittorio and Gina. Most of them didn't know Gina, but Bianca did. So did one other lady whose name is Coretta Taylor. Other than that, the people I talked to had no clue who Gina was. They all spoke freely to me, though. They felt they could be open about Vittorio and what he did, now that he's dead. I tell you, he was a piece of work, that one."

"Tell me about Bianca and Coretta," I said. "How did they know Gina and what did they tell you about her?"

"Bianca said she knew Gina because Gina confronted her in a bar. I guess the two of them got into a cat fight because Bianca was messing with Vittorio."

"Give me Bianca's phone number. I'll give her a call and set up a meeting. I need to hear what she has to say to me."

I decided I to speak with the women and Enzo before I made a decision on whether or not to continue with Gina's case. I felt I could get a good sense on what the truth was if I spoke to those witnesses. From there, I could probably get

The Alibi

a good sense on whether my own client was lying to me or being straight.

I got the phone number and the address for Bianca, I gave her a call and set up an appointment, and then looked at the clock. I was late for traffic court, so I would have to get a move on.

But I never quite made it to traffic court.

Enzo Degrazio was in the suite, talking to Pearl.

I sighed when I saw him, and called Harper.

"Can you cover for me in muni?" I asked her. "It seems I have a surprise visitor."

"Sure," she said. "Give me the name and the charge, and I'll take care of it for you."

"Susan Davis," I said. "Just a speeding ticket."

"Got it," she said.

"Thanks." I looked up and motioned to Pearl to let Enzo come in.

I was actually happy to see him, because I wanted to know what he knew.

Hopefully, he would help me make my decision on Gina.

Chapter Eight

"HEY," Enzo said, when he came into my office. He was around 5'6", black hair greased back, large nose and even larger brown eyes. His ears stuck out of his head. His body was tightly coiled, like a snake. He was dressed in a brown leather jacket, black t-shirt, pale khakis and black sandals. On his head was a black fedora. When he sat down in the leather chair opposite my desk, his stance was casual – he was leaning back, one arm on the right armrest, his foot crossed over his knee. He regarded me with suspicion in his eyes. "Gina told me I should see you. She told me you're on her case and hasn't talked to you in awhile. She's got court in a week and hasn't talked to you. What's up with that?"

"Mr. Degrazio," I began.

"Enzo, man. Nobody calls me Mr. Degrazio." He looked disgusted. "You guys are going to trial next week and you haven't even called her in the last month?"

"Enzo," I said, "we aren't going to trial next week."

"Then what's happening next week? She told me she's

got trial and doesn't know what's happening. I told her I would find out. So, what's going on?"

"It's an arraignment. That's all. Gina will be read her formal charges and will be assigned a trial judge. That's how it's done here in the 16th Circuit – the defendant isn't arraigned until the Grand Jury has met and decides the defendant should be bound over for trial."

"So what was all that business I went to that one day? There was a judge and he told her she was being charged with murder and she got another court date for a Preliminary Hearing. Only I guess she didn't get that Preliminary Hearing. What happened there?"

"She didn't get the Preliminary Hearing because her case went through the Grand Jury instead. That's how it's done in this circuit for murder cases."

"What is a Preliminary Hearing anyway?"

"It's basically an evidentiary hearing," I said. "It's like a mini-trial. The prosecutor puts on their evidence, and I have a chance to cross-examine their witnesses. I wouldn't have the right to call witnesses of my own, however."

"And what happens if the prosecutor doesn't make their case? What happens if they don't have enough evidence for the judge?"

"Then the case gets dismissed. That's a very rare occurrence, however."

"And the Grand Jury? What is that?"

"It's a secret proceeding where evidence is produced and a jury decides whether or not the evidence is strong enough for the case to go to trial. The defendant and the defendant's attorney don't even know when it happens."

"And if there's not enough evidence?"

"Then the case is dismissed. If the Grand Jury finds enough evidence, then Gina is indicted. Which she was."

Enzo nodded. "So, she's not going to trial yet?"

"No. Her trial date will be set at the arraignment next week. I don't even know yet who her judge will be."

He shook his head. "Now, why would she be telling me she's going to trial next week? I swear that ditz would lose her head if it weren't screwed on."

"I don't know where she got that idea. But I'm glad you're here. I wanted to talk to you anyhow."

"Yeah? What about?"

"Well, obviously you're a key witness in the case," I said.

"How so?"

"You're her alibi," I said.

"I am?" He shook his head. "I'm not no alibi. I wasn't within 10 miles of Gina when my brother was killed. I don't know what she told you, but if she told you she was with me, she's telling you bullshit, man."

I sighed. I didn't necessarily automatically think Gina was lying, however. It could be Enzo was lying. I didn't quite know why he would be lying, but I wouldn't jump to conclusions.

"So, why would she tell me she was with you when your brother was killed?"

"I don't know. Listen, I wanted to tell you I think Gina did it. I know you're her attorney and all that, but I just want to lay it on the line. My brother was beating on her, and-"

"And what? Listen, you made bail for her," I said. "$3 million in cash. Now, here you are, in my office, trying to tell me Gina is guilty. That makes no sense to me, none whatsoever."

"Why? Listen, I got the money, I do well in my business, it's no skin off my nose to give her that money. I'm gonna get it back, anyhow, as long as she shows up for trial. Which

The Alibi

she will. If she doesn't, I won't even wait for the bounty hunter to come looking for her. I'll have my own bounty hunters on her and they won't treat her nice. She knows that. So what do I care if I get her out of jail?"

"But why do it? Why not just let her stay in jail and wait for trial? You obviously don't care about her. If you did, you wouldn't be in my office trying to rat on her. What's your game, Enzo?"

"I ain't got no game. I'm just trying to tell you she did it."

"And you're sure of this because-"

"I told you. My brother was beating on her and she hated him. It was her gun, she knew where it was, nobody else did, and she wasn't anywhere near me when he was killed."

"Where was she when Vittorio was killed?"

"Hell if I know. Gina and me, we ain't that close."

"Yet you're close enough to give her $3 million," I said. "Your story isn't ringing true."

"I told you-"

"Spare me the BS about how you wanted to give her the money out of the goodness of your heart. Or you wanted to give her the money because you happened to have it lying around in your couch cushions. $3 million is a lot of money for anybody to part with. I don't know many people who would give that kind of cash to someone they barely know." I crossed my arms in front of me. "So, you mind telling me the truth on why you gave her that money?"

"I told you the truth. Listen, she was in jail and she called me. I didn't want her caged like an animal-"

"Yet you're willing to see her caged like an animal for life. In fact, you seem to want that. Why would that be?"

"I don't know why you're cross-examining me. I'm not the one on trial here."

"I'm cross-examining you because your story doesn't make sense. Yeah, yeah, I know. Your Italian restaurant downtown does excellent business so you're flush with cash. I get that, although I'm surprised you would be that liquid. I would imagine your overhead is pretty high in that choice spot you got downtown. Right in the Power and Light District, the hottest neighborhood in town for restaurants and bars. And what kind of background do you have in the restaurant business? What kind of investors did you attract? Where did you get the cash to open a place in such a hot spot and how did you jump the line in front of your competitors?"

The Power and Light District was the place in Kansas City to see and be seen. The bars and restaurants in that area generally were either chains – national or local – or restaurants opened by highly regarded chefs. Enzo was neither of those. And the spots in the Power and Light District were coveted. The restauranteurs granted a license there had to jump through hoops and wait in line.

As far as I knew, Enzo was just an Italian guy with no particular background in food or the restaurant business. Tom Garrett told me that, prior to Enzo opening his restaurant five years ago, he didn't have a record of any kind of employment or business. That told me Enzo probably was off the books all those years, working for cash for somebody.

He obviously had been greasing somebody's palms, but who? And was that even significant? So what if Enzo had been bribing people to get his restaurant license and his prime-time spot? How did that impact this case?

"That's none of your business," Enzo said. "None of your business on how I got my spot and my license. I got it,

The Alibi

I do great business, and I got money to give Gina to get her out of jail. That's all you need to know."

"So, you won't be straight with me," I said. "Okay, then. Have it your way. I'll send my investigator out to uncover just what happened behind the scenes when you got your lease in the Power and Light District. I have a feeling some serious money changed hands. Either that or you got the goods on somebody in City Hall. Whatever happened, I'm pretty sure it was less than legal. Now, if you don't want my investigator snooping around in your records, I suggest you come clean with me."

He cocked his head and stood up. "I got nothing to hide," he said, spreading his arms out. "Go ahead. Sic the dogs on me. They ain't gonna be finding nothing."

"I will," I said. "I'll do my investigation. In the meantime, you need to think long and hard about what you're doing. Gina said she was with you when your brother was killed. You're here throwing her under the bus. Obviously, one of you is lying. One of you is playing a game. I'm gonna find out who's straight and who isn't. I'm Gina's lawyer. That's my job. Fair warning."

He shrugged and walked out of my office.

The second he walked out, Harper walked in. "I fixed your ticket for you," she said. "But he was going 155 MPH on a bike. The judge said he had to serve mandatory jail time – 48 hours. He'll go to jail every evening after he gets off work for eight hours at a time. You probably should have warned me your ticket was a mandatory jail time ticket."

"Yeah, I'm sorry about that. Anyhow, I think I need to get out of here. I need to meet with Garrett. He'll have to look into some things for me."

"What type of things?"

"Oh, nothing major. It's just that my case is falling apart before my eyes. Gina's whole defense was she didn't do it. The way she proves she didn't do it was through the testimony of Enzo Degrazio, Vittorio Degrazio's identical twin brother. Well, guess what?"

"Enzo came in and told you he doesn't know what she's talking about," Harper said. "How close am I?"

"Pretty goddamned on the nose. Yes, Enzo just told me she wasn't with him at the time of the murder, and, get this, he also told me he thinks Gina did it. Yet, he posted Gina's bond. That was a pretty penny, too - $3 million. He told me he posted the money for her out of the goodness of his heart, and because it wasn't that much money for him, but come on. He's trying to throw her under the bus for his brother's murder, yet he gave her all that money to get her out of jail? Something's rotten in the State of Denmark, I'll tell you what."

"So what are you going to ask Tom?"

"He's going to look into Enzo's restaurant business. There's something rotten there, too. I still think Enzo's restaurant is a money-laundromat for the mob. The only problem is, so what? So what Enzo got mob money for his restaurant? What does that have to do with this whole puzzle?"

"Well, here's why it might matter. Maybe he got the money to give to Gina from the mob."

"Okay. And?"

Harper shrugged. "Maybe he wants her to plead out because that means he'll get her bail money back faster that way. Maybe somebody has called in the loan and he needs the money. Or maybe he just needs the money ASAP for some other reason. Who knows? Maybe he got into some trouble and needs the money he gave Gina. You have to admit, if Gina's alibi falls apart, she'll be much more likely to take a deal. That means her case might be over within a couple of weeks. You guys go to trial and it'll take several months. Maybe Enzo doesn't have that long to wait to be paid back."

"Well, then, that makes me even more suspicious there's something going on. I mean, what you're saying is that Enzo might not have had the money to give Gina for her bond. That maybe he borrowed it from some shady mob people. Then why, in the name of all that's holy, would he stick his neck out for her and then try to railroad her into a plea deal? I mean, in your scenario, Enzo really sacrificed himself to get her out of jail. He's certainly not acting like a man who would do something like that."

"I did say maybe he borrowed it. I also said maybe he got into financial trouble, just out of the blue, and he needs that bond money back. That's a possibility."

I shook my head. "I guess. But that still makes little sense to me. It does make more sense, however, than the first scenario, which was he gave Gina money he didn't have."

"So, what will you ask Tom Garrett to investigate?"

"I'll ask him to investigate Enzo's business. Find out how liquid he is. Maybe you're right. Maybe he used mob money to get Gina out. Or maybe you're right that he suddenly found himself in financial trouble, so he needs money right now. Garrett can find that out."

"Will you stay on Gina's case?"

"I don't know. It's falling apart pretty good right now. Enzo possibly stuck a fork in it. I don't think Gina is telling the truth. I also don't think Enzo's telling the truth. I think the truth is something I haven't even comprehended just yet. If I can just do a bit more investigation, so I can figure out what, exactly, happened, then I might remain on her case. Alternatively, maybe I can get her to plead guilty. I haven't gotten an offer yet from the prosecutor's office. In fact, I haven't even found out who the prosecutor will be for this case."

Harper looked at me and shook her head. "Karma," she said. "I found out for you who's on the other side. BTW, you drew Judge Reiner, Division 33. I personally love that judge, but he's too gruff for most."

I nodded my head. "Reiner. That's good with me. I've always gotten along with him. But who's-" I shook my head. "Ally's on the other side, isn't she?"

Harper smiled. "You know what they say. Karma's a bitch."

Chapter Nine

WELL, that was great. My hand was forced with Ally. I hadn't yet told her about Sarah, and, quite frankly, I was afraid it would blow up in my face when I did. Not that Sarah and I were officially back together. We weren't. We were in marriage counseling and were going out to dinner with the kids, but it would be a long time until my trust was restored. Sarah understood this and had been repeatedly telling me she was willing to wait.

But Ally and I were also still casually hanging out. We got drinks after work sometimes and had been to the movies a time or two. We hadn't yet slept together, and, of course, she hadn't met the kids.

What this meant – that Ally was on the other side of my murder trial – was I would have to step lightly at least until Gina's case was over. I couldn't risk Ally finding out I was seeing my estranged wife. If there would be any break-up between Ally and me, it would have to happen after Gina's case was over. I didn't think Ally would be unprofessional, even if she found out about Sarah. That wasn't the problem. The problem was I knew it would be more than uncomfortable between us if I told her what was going on with Sarah and I didn't want that distraction.

Oh, if only I had listened to Harper when she told me not to shit where I sleep. That was always good advice. Always. Yet, I didn't listen. I was attracted to Ally and wanted to go out with her. That was that. I let my little head rule my big one and now I was paying the price.

Harper was still in my office. She had a sly smile on her face, as if she was amused by it all.

"Be smug all you want," I said. "I know, I know, you told me. I can't think about that, though. I have to only think about Gina's case."

"Yeah, I know. But I'm sure that Ally being the prosecutor complicates matters some."

"It complicates it a lot. Don't get me wrong. But I have to focus on Gina's case and try not to let the noise get in the way."

The problem was, Ally wasn't just noise. She was a human being.

A human being I might have been jerking around.

THE NEXT DAY, I had my first appointment with Bianca Cassavettes, a busty bleached blonde woman with big hair, tight pleather pants and an even tighter blue sweater. I met her at her home, a small house in the Valentine area. It seemed that most of the people involved in this case lived in this area, probably because that was close by where Vittorio and Enzo lived as well.

The Alibi

The Valentine area is a mid-town neighborhood right off Main Street. It's a tree-lined enclave with large homes built in the 19th Century and the early 20th Century. The great artist Thomas Hart Benton once lived in an enormous stone home in the Valentine neighborhood. Because of Valentine's central location, it was a hub for artists and creators. The Uptown Theater, which was an enormous palace that often showed off-beat plays and concerts, was nearby. Also nearby was a run-down strip mall that often accumulated garbage in the parking lot.

Bianca's home was one of the smaller homes in the area – it was only a two-bedroom, tucked away from the street. I walked into her home, and she looked me up and down and smiled. "Hi, you," she said. "Damien, right? We talked on the phone."

"Right. I'm Damien Harrington. Gina Degrazio's attorney."

"Right. Gina Degrazio. Guess she was married to that pervert, Vittorio, huh?"

"Yeah. She was married to him. That's what I need to talk to you about. Vittorio."

She opened her mouth and stuck her finger in. "Vittorio. Yuck."

I looked around the living room. She hadn't yet invited me to sit down, so I stood there, awkwardly waiting in the doorway.

"Well, don't just stand there," she said, motioning to a love seat. "Sit on down."

I sat down on the love seat and Bianca sat right next to me. I thought that was odd, considering there was a reclining chair in that living room, along with a regular-sized sofa. However, I decided to dismiss my gut.

"Okay," she said, putting her arm on the couch and her hand to her cheek. "What did you want to ask me?"

"Vittorio Degrazio," I said. "How did you meet him?"

She looked up at the ceiling. "Oh, God, how did I meet that guy? I'm gonna tell you I really don't remember. I didn't know him all that well, you know. We only got together the one time. After that…" She shook her head. "No way. I wouldn't have gone out with him a second time if you paid me."

"Why is that?"

"You know what happened. Tom Garrett, that investigator guy who came here, he told you what happened. Vittorio put some kind of roofie in my drink and I think he raped me. I went to his house, we started making out, I drank a glass of vodka he gave me, and that was all I remember about that evening."

"That's all you remember?"

"Well, that's the last thing I remember. I mean, I remember stuff about that night, but nothing after drinking that glass of vodka at his house."

"Were you drinking heavily before you got the vodka?"

"No. I mean, I was, but not so heavily I was gonna black out or nothing like that. You know, when I drink, I try to talk to myself. I try to gauge if I'm about to go outer limits and need to pull myself back from the edge. Because I've been in the state where I've blacked out before and I don't like doing that. I don't like losing control."

"When was the last time you drank so much you blacked out?"

"Oh, it's been at least a year ago."

"And when did you meet Vittorio?"

"About a year and a half ago."

The Alibi

I cleared my throat. "So you've been so drunk you blacked out at least once since you met Vittorio, right?"

"Well, yeah, right. But I wasn't that blasted that night. I promise you that."

"And you're sure about that?"

"Of course I'm sure. I had my wits about me. Anyhow, I talked to another girl I knew at the bar. Her name is Coretta Taylor and she told me she also went home with Vittorio one night and she passed out, too."

"Is it possible that both you and Coretta were drunker than you thought and that was why you ended up passing out and not remembering what had happened?"

"I guess it's possible," she said. "But it sounds not right. I mean, what are the chances? I go home with him and I black out. Coretta goes home with him and she blacks out."

"Well, tell me what you remembered from that night."

She took her arm off the back of the couch and her hand grazed my knee as she reached for a bowl of candy on the coffee table in front of us.

"Want some chocolate?" she asked as she tore open the wrapper of a mini Mars bar.

I waved her off and she shrugged.

"Anyhow, let's see," she said. "I went to the bar that night, The Peanut, it's in Midtown, well, 50th and Main, and you know, I go there a lot. I see this guy come in. He's pretty cute, he's dark and Italian, not very tall, just my type. I like guys with black hair, large noses and hairy chests. They usually have a nice package, too, so that's always a bonus. Anyhow, I see him come in, and he sees me, and he sits down next to me." She nodded. "You know, hi, I'm Vittorio, what's your name, yada yada yada. He's buying me drinks. My girlfriend, who I came with, she's splitting with some other guy. She's hooking up too, see?

She wants to get some action with another guy she's met. Anyhow, Vittorio, he's a fun guy, a lively guy, I'm liking him. He's making me laugh. He's buying me drinks. Then he asked me to go home with him." She shrugged. "I'm looking for a good time, so I'm like 'sure, I'll go home with you.'"

"So, you go home with him, and then what happened?"

"Well, he goes all old school on me. You know, he puts on some Dean Martin on the turntable, trying to impress me with his old school moves. And, yes, I said turntable, because he doesn't have a DVD player or a CD player or an MP3 player or any kind of streaming music service. Nothing like that. He's got an old-school turntable, and I have to say, that made me smile a bit. I never knew anybody old-school like that."

"Okay. So, he puts on a record. A Dean Martin record at that. What happened next?"

"Well, as I said, he makes me a drink. A vodka and water. That's what I drink. He gives it to me and he sits down on the couch next to me. He tells me I'm beautiful, I tell him he's hot, he puts his hand on my face and he kisses me. And I'm feeling the kiss, you know, in my ladyparts. So, I'm raring to go, but then I start to feel weird. I tell him I feel weird, he goes and gets a glass of water for me, but I'm feeling more and more weird."

"Weird like how?"

"Like the room is spinning. And, just like that, before I can even figure out what's going on, my eyes are closing and, the next thing I know, I'm in bed with him, naked. He's next to me in the bed. He's also naked. You know, I'm looking at his shoulder – he has this big scar, like this 3" scar, going from the top of his shoulder blade to right under his blade, you know? And I'm just all casual-like, I didn't know what happened, but I ask him about that scar and he gets all freaky and weird on me."

"Freaky and weird? What do you mean?"

"You know, he's all, 'what are you asking me about my scar for? It's none of your business how I got this scar. You wouldn't want me asking you about who did your tits, would you?'" She smiled. "Yeah, I got my tits done. So what? I think my surgeon did a good job, and nobody ever knows the difference, except some men do, I guess. Vittorio figured it out, at any rate."

"So what happened after he got freaky and weird about the scar?"

"He told me to get out. He ordered me right out of the house. Screamed at me to get out. So, I did. I got out. He didn't have to tell me twice."

"Did you ever find out why he was so sensitive about the scar?"

"No. But I'll tell you one thing. I don't ever want to see that bitch wife of his again." She shook her head. "Coretta saw her at the bar. She comes in asking questions about Vittorio and how he had been there talking to us girls. She comes up to me and starts asking me all these questions. I'm all 'bitch, get your ass away from me before I cut you,' because you know I was ready to cut a bitch that night anyhow. I had just gotten fired from my third job this year and I wasn't having any of that bullshit."

"So, you saw Gina Degrazio at the bar and what questions did she ask you?"

"She asked me if I knew Vittorio. I'm like 'get away from me.' But she didn't. She kept on asking me all these questions about what I knew about her husband. I'm telling her I didn't know her husband. Never met him before in my life, you know? She's not believing me, and, well, the two of us ended up stepping outside and, the next thing I know, she's punching me and I'm landing on the street. And I'm like 'it's on, bitch,' and I get up and punch her back. Next thing I know, she's pulling my hair, I'm kicking her shins and the bouncer is coming out of the bar, threatening to call the cops on us both."

"Did the cops come?"

"No. But I tell her not to mess with me no more, because I will cut a bitch. I don't play like that."

"You ever see her again?"

"No. I've never seen her again. I don't go to that bar no more. I go to a different bar. I go to the other Peanut bar downtown. It's a nicer place to go, anyhow."

"Do you have anything against Gina?"

"You mean, aside from her throwing a punch and shoving me to the ground? No, other than that, no. I don't care about her. I could give shit less about her."

I narrowed my eyes. Somehow, Bianca wasn't giving me the vibe that she was capable of killing Vittorio and framing Gina. I had to ask a few more questions, though, to find out if she was capable. I needed to see if she had actual motive to kill Vittorio and frame Gina. So far, I was getting the impression she didn't really care that Vittorio raped her. She certainly didn't seem angry with him.

"Okay. Now, did you tell anybody about Vittorio raping you?"

"No."

"Any reason why?"

She shrugged. "Yeah. I mean, when I talked to Coretta, and I found out the same thing happened to her, I was kinda pissed, you know? I mean, Vittorio's going around doing that to other women, not just me, and that's all kinds of messed up, if you ask me. So, yeah, I was gonna tell the police about what had happened. I mean, I don't really care he did it to me. I thought he was cute, I would have had sex with him if he just asked me to, he didn't have to put a drug in me to do it, but whatever. But Coretta, she seemed upset about what Vittorio did to her, so I was going to tell the cops about what Vittorio did to me."

"And did you end up telling the cops about him?"

She rolled her eyes. "Now, come on, I think you know the answer to that. I mean, you're investigating his death. Did you see anything in his background that would tell you he ended up getting questioned about a rape?"

"No. I didn't see that had happened. But that doesn't mean it didn't happen. If he was just questioned and not charged, I wouldn't necessarily see a record on that."

"Well, it didn't happen. I didn't go to the cops. Vittorio visited me and gave me money to shut my mouth." She looked at me. "Oh, don't look at me like that," she said. "Everybody's got their price. I got my price, too. My price was $100,000."

I sighed. "Okay." I suddenly knew my hunch was right. Bianca didn't kill Vittorio. She wasn't threatened by Vittorio, and she certainly didn't seem to be angry about the situation. I had the feeling I was barking up the wrong tree with her.

"Can you give me Coretta's phone number and address? I want to speak with her."

"She works at The Peanut," Bianca said. "Monday through Friday, she works 10-5. She's a bartender there."

"Well," I said, "thanks for taking the time to speak with me."

"Sure," she said. "You know, you don't got to leave so soon. I was just about to get myself some food. There's some really good places right over on 39th Street to eat. I could really go in for some Cajun food, and Jazz has some of the best. What do you say? Spicy crawdads and etouffee on me?"

I smiled. Going out with Bianca was the last thing I needed to do. "I thank you for the offer," I said. "But I have to get home to my kids."

She looked disappointed but shrugged her shoulders. "Your loss, I guess."

I went out to the street and got into my car. I saw Pearl had called, so I called her back.

"Hey, Pearl," I said. "What's up?"

"Nothing. I just got an order in the mail," she said. "I guess you made a motion to inspect the crime scene. The judge signed it *ex parte*. So, you can go over to Vittorio's house anytime you want."

I nodded my head. "Thanks, Pearl," I said, looking at the clock on my car. It read 3:30 PM. "Maybe I'll go on over there before I head home. The kids never expect me home before 6 in the evening."

I hung up the phone and headed over to Vittorio's home. I didn't know what I would find out when I got there. What knowledge I hoped to gain. But that didn't matter. I knew I had to do my due diligence before I made a decision about Gina's case.

It was increasingly looking like I would withdraw from her case. But I had to make sure I wanted to. I really didn't believe her threat about Nick being in trouble, but that was in the back of my mind, so I wanted to be really sure before I did anything rash.

The Alibi

I GOT to Vittorio's house, which was close to Heather's home in the Hyde Park area. While Heather lived in a small apartment, Vittorio's house was much larger and was an actual free-standing home. It was facing Gillham Park, which was little more than a stretch of greenery in the middle of Mid-Town with tennis courts and a pool. The house was three-story with a large porch that still had Christmas lights up and a rocking chair on the side.

I walked into the living room, stepping around the yellow crime-scene tape, and saw to the right a big-screen television, and, to the left, a large leather couch. Although the outside of the house looked older, the inside was brand-new. Hardwood floors that looked completely new, new appliances in the kitchen, newer furniture and throw-rugs.

On the floor of the living room was the outline of Vittorio's body in yellow tape. I stooped down and saw there was still a puddle of blood on the floor. There wasn't that much blood, however, which told me that Vittorio's heart must have stopped soon after he was hit. Death must have been instantaneous.

I walked through the rest of the house and Bianca's words were stuck in my head. She said she was surprised that Vittorio was so old-school. He played a Dean Martin record on a turntable. She said he didn't have a DVD player, nor did he have streaming capability or a CD player. Yet, I saw very clearly there was a DVD player. I put on the television and saw his television was smart and had Roku. In other words, he had streaming capability. He had a music playlist on his Spotify app on his television and I looked at the playlist. I saw that an eclectic blend of music on his playlist – everyone from Taylor Swift to the Eagles. Some Pearl Jam, some modern rock, some classic rock such as

The Stones. But nothing like Dean Martin or Frank Sinatra or any other crooner.

That's odd. I distinctly remember Bianca going on and on about how old-school Vittorio was, how he had a turntable and no streaming devices or even a CD or DVD player.

I shook my head. I had a sudden flash of insight but I needed to speak with Bianca again.

And then I would have to make a motion to court to inspect Vittorio's body.

I would have to see if he had a large scar on his back.

Chapter Ten

"HIYA, HANDSOME," Bianca said when I reappeared on her porch. "Guess you changed your mind about that dinner, huh? Good. I really got a craving for Cajun food after you left." She went to her coat closet and brought out a leather jacket. "Let's go."

"Oh, I'm sorry," I said. "I didn't come back to take you to dinner. I need to ask you some more questions about Vittorio."

Her face fell when I said that. "Okay," she said. "And then we'll go to dinner?"

"Actually, I still have kids at home who need *their* dinners," I said. "Right now, I'm mom and dad to them."

"Alright," she said. "Maybe another evening?"

I thought about the romantic mess I was already in, between Ally and Sarah, and knew there was no way I would add yet another woman into the mix.

"I'm sorry," I said. "I'm married." That technically wasn't a lie.

She looked at my left hand, which was ringless. "I don't wear my ring," I said. "It bothers me."

"Whatever." She crossed her arms in front of her and glared at me. "Anyhow, what did you need to know about Vittorio? Make it quick, because I'm starving. I guess I'll be dining alone tonight."

Guess so. "Vittorio, would you recognize his house if I showed you a picture?"

"Yeah. I mean, it was dark when I got there, of course, but I left the next day. I would remember what it looks like."

I showed her a picture of Vittorio's house. "Is this the house?"

She shook her head. "No way, man. I mean, that's kind of a cool house, but it's not very big. Vittorio's house, it was one of those big houses in Loose Park. Brick house, white columns, you know, I think they call that style of house Colonial. Big pool in the back." She pointed to the house in the picture. "I mean, that's just a little house like the one I got."

It actually wasn't a "little" house – it was a four-bedroom home with a porch and two stories. But it was made of wood, not stone, it definitely wasn't Colonial and it was nowhere near Loose Park.

"Loose Park, not Gillham Park?" I asked Bianca. "That was where Enzo lived?"

I realized I made a Freudian slip when I asked her where "Enzo" lived, because the whole scenario was becoming more and more clear.

"Enzo, who's Enzo?"

"I'm sorry, Vittorio. That's where Vittorio lived – Loose Park area, not Gillham Park area?"

"Yeah, Loose Park. I know the difference between Loose Park and Gillham Park. It was definitely Loose Park."

The Alibi

"And it was solid brick with white columns in front?"

"Yeah. I told you that. Why do you keep asking the same questions?"

"No reason. Anyhow, thank you very much for being so kind to answer all my questions and taking the time to talk to me."

"Yeah. Listen, I did go out of my way to talk to you. Maybe you should buy me dinner for my inconvenience?"

"Check will be in the mail," I said. "Thanks again."

At that, I walked out of her house, with her shouting after me. "What do you mean, check will be in the mail? You gonna send me some money? Hey, get back here!"

I ignored her, got into my car, and drove off.

―――

THE NEXT DAY, I made a motion to inspect "Vittorio's" body. I would see if Vittorio had a large scar. I had the feeling that Enzo had been using Vittorio's identity all along. That Vittorio was not actually the person raping these women, but Enzo.

The question was whether or not the fact that Enzo was using Vittorio's identity had anything to do with Vittorio's death? The two things might very well be connected – if Enzo was going around telling women he was Vittorio, Vittorio could very well have been popped by somebody Enzo raped.

I didn't want to get too far ahead of myself, though. I had a hunch, but I wanted it proved. And then I would have to get Gina back in here and tell her what I knew. Tell her she was lying, and I had proof. And then see if I could withdraw.

First things first, though. I needed to inspect that body.

TWO DAYS LATER, the order came in from the court, allowing me to go down to the hospital morgue and look at Vittorio. His body was still in a freezer, being held as evidence for trial. The reason why the morgue still had his body was that the results of the toxicology report had not yet come back, plus, I hadn't yet received the autopsy report. I had made a motion to the court, when I got on this case, to preserve the body pending those two results.

I was glad I made a motion to the court to preserve the body. I would find out, once and for all, exactly who I was dealing with. Who the victim in this case was. I mean, I knew it was Vittorio, but I didn't know if Vittorio was the mad rapist.

I called Heather, knowing that going to the morgue to look at Vittorio's body was something she probably would be into. She was that type of girl, I thought – somebody who would actually enjoy going to a morgue and seeing a dead person.

"Cool," she said when I called her. "When are you going?"

"Today," I said. "You get here to the office and we'll go."

"I'm not doing anything today," she said. "I'll be there in a half hour."

A half hour later, Heather appeared in black sweater, tight jeans, thigh-high boots and a grey pashmina. She was wearing designer sunglasses and her long hair was piled high up on her head.

"Let's go," she said. "I've never done this before. I mean, I've seen a dead body. I saw my adoptive mother after I killed her. But I've never seen a stiff before."

The Alibi

I had to smile. Little things, like going on prison visits and going on morgue visits, seemed to get Heather's juices flowing. I remembered, way back when, in the days after I was sprung from prison, feeling the way Heather did. Everything was a revelation to me. Every meal I ate was the best I ever tasted. After all, it wasn't prison food. Every night I slept in my own bed was a miracle - it was an actual bed, not a tiny cot on a metal frame. Trips to the grocery store gave me untold moments of joy. Eating pancakes at IHOP almost brought tears to my eyes. All the little things in life were things I couldn't take for granted. I wondered how anybody could be unhappy when they have freedom, soft beds, all the food that they wanted and could drive to see changing leaves in October.

Unfortunately, that renewed zeal for life didn't last that long. I soon found I, too, was taking things for granted. And life started to wear me down once more.

I hoped Heather's excited attitude might bring that Damien back. The Damien that could get excited about the smallest things.

We got to St. Luke's Hospital, which was the closest hospital to Vittorio's home. It was a beautiful modern hospital, situated right off the Country Club Plaza. It faced Volker Park, the park that was a part of the enormous art museum, the Nelson-Atkins. Vittorio, who lived in Hyde Park, which was just a few miles away from the hospital, was apparently brought here when he was found in the home.

I went to the front desk, showed her the court order that permitted me to inspect Vittorio's body, and she directed me to the basement. She told me I needed an escort to go down there, so Heather and I took a seat to wait for the escort to come.

I also wanted to wait for Ally. Since she was the prosecutor on the case, she wanted to be present for the viewing as well. She still didn't know anything about Sarah, and I still felt guilty whenever I saw her. It couldn't be helped, though.

Ally came to the hospital about ten minutes after Heather and I got there, and ten minutes after that, a person appeared in a white lab coat. She approached us.

"Hello," she said, "My name is Dr. Prorock, and I was the Medical Examiner for Mr. Degrazio. I understand you're the attorney for the defendant in that case, correct?"

I nodded my head. "I am. I have the court order to inspect Mr. Degrazio if you need to see it."

"And I'm Ally Hughes," Ally said, extending her hand. "I'm the prosecutor on the case."

"Please let me see the court order," she said, and I handed it to her. She nodded her head. "Follow me."

We followed her to the service elevator. She inserted her key and the car lurched downward.

"Thank you for accommodating us," I said to her.

"Not a problem." She looked at me. "Is this your first time coming to a hospital morgue?"

"No," I said. "I've been to a few."

The elevator got down to the ground floor and we followed her down a long hallway. She opened up the double doors to a room, and went over to the cooler.

"Okay," she said. "Here is Mr. Degrazio." She opened up the cooler door, and there he was, laying cold on the hard metal slab.

"Could you please lift him up?" I asked. "I need to see both of his shoulder blades."

Dr. Prorock lifted him up on one side and then the other. I carefully looked at both shoulders, didn't see any kind of a scar and nodded. "Thank you."

The Alibi

"Are there any questions you have for me?" she asked.

"Yes. I see that the deceased doesn't have any major scarring on his shoulders. Did you observe the same thing?"

She had Vittorio's file in her hand. She looked through her notes and then shook her head. "No. I didn't observe that Mr. Degrazio had any kind of scarring on his shoulders or any other part of his body. Is there anything else you would like to know?"

"No," I said, looking at Ally. I didn't want to give too much away. "That's all I needed to see."

We all followed Dr. Prorock back to the service elevator and took it to the lobby. "Thank you again for accommodating me," I said to her.

"My pleasure."

We got out into the sun and Ally turned to me. "You're going to be mysterious about why it was so important you view that body, aren't you?"

"Of course," I said. "You're the prosecutor, I'm the defense attorney, I can't give too much of the game away."

She smiled and locked her arm through mine. "Are you going to introduce me to your assistant?" she asked.

"Oh, yes. Heather, this is Ally Hughes, Ally, Heather."

"Hi," Ally said looking over at Heather. "Guess you're working for Damien?"

"I am. And Harper. I'm learning the ropes right now."

"Well, you could do worse than learn the law from Damien. He's a pretty crack attorney."

I smiled. "You're not so bad yourself."

"So," Ally said, getting to her car. "You've been hiding yourself away lately. What do you say we get a drink or something after I get off work? We need to catch up."

I took a deep breath. "About that. I thought maybe we

should lie a bit low until after this trial is over. I don't want anything to distract me from defending my client."

Ally looked disappointed. "Damien, you're a defense attorney. I'm a prosecutor. We're going to have cases together, probably quite a few. If you want to stop dating every time we're on opposite sides of a case, then we might as well not date at all."

Dammit. I felt like she was putting me on the spot, and I didn't know what to say to her.

"I'm sorry," I said. "It's a new thing for me to be dating. I've been with Sarah for so many years. I just have to feel my way around this. I hope you understand."

Heather looked at the two of us. "I'll wait for you in the car, Dami," she said, and then rapidly went over to the car, which was next to a tree, and sat down next to the tree.

"Actually," Ally said, "no, I don't understand. It sounds to me like you're using weasel words to hide what you're really thinking. You're a lawyer. You know how important it is to communicate clearly. So, without using weasel words like 'feel your way around,' tell me what's really going on."

I tried to make a joke. "Hey, weasel words are good enough for a politician," I said. Ally didn't smile. "It's just that-"

"It's just what? What are you thinking right now?"

"I think that maybe I got into dating too soon after Sarah. I mean, I've got my kids at home. My youngest is only 6 years old and she's in recovery from a bone marrow transplant. She was very sick with non-Hodgkin's lymphoma and I almost lost her. Her older brother is trying to deal with his sister being very sick and the breakup of our family, so he's been acting out in school. Add to that this murder case and a class-action lawsuit I'm trying to bring on behalf of people who have been affected by toxic mold.

I'm looking for more plaintiffs so I'll be more than likely get the class certified. That case has been a lot of work, and I already feel guilty for not spending more time with my kids. So…"

She nodded her head. "I get it. I guess that's what I have coming to me. Everybody told me not to get involved with a guy going through a divorce. I didn't listen to them." She pushed the beeper on her keys, and the car unlocked. "You have a nice life, Damien," she said, getting into the car.

I knew by the way she backed up and shot out of the parking lot, her tires squealing, that things were about to get really ugly between us.

Just what I needed.

Chapter Eleven

IN THE CAR, Tom called me. "Good news, buddy. I've been finding plaintiffs for you, left and right. I've just been knocking on doors in the three apartment buildings and I've found most have some kind of mold. I've found lots of other sick people in these places. So far, I've found 15 more people. That makes 22. How many did you say you needed to bring a class-action?"

"About 40. Great work, though. I'll visit all of them in the next few weeks and get them signed up. Keep going. Keep trying to find more people. It looks like we'll have our class in no time."

"I'll email you the info on these new people. By the way, how are things going with that murder case?"

"Well, you won't believe what I found out. Or, maybe you will."

"What?"

"Vittorio wasn't the rapist. Enzo was. He apparently was posing as Vittorio. I have a feeling that might be the reason why Vittorio was popped."

The Alibi

"Oh, really? Sounds like Enzo was a dirty bastard."

"Yeah he was. Good lord. He was going around raping women and telling them his name was Vittorio. Then Vittorio gets murdered. I wonder if it was one of the women Enzo raped. Or maybe there was another reason. I'll have to ask Gina about that."

"Sounds like you got a winner on your hands," Tom said. "I'll send you the names of the people you need to contact for your mold case. And, by the way, I've also been doing a more deep-dive on who is responsible for these apartments. So far, I found out the rich bastard Robert Davis is the main person who owned these apartments but I also found out he had some help. He has a secret partner, and I'm trying to dig out who it is."

"A secret partner? I wonder why he brought somebody else into this mess?"

"Probably because he knew those places were death traps and he wanted somebody to take the blame. Or, at the very least, spread the blame around. Listen, I need to do some more digging and find out who else is involved. I'll get back with you on that."

"Thanks, buddy." We hung up, and I immediately called Gina. "Gina," I said, "I need you to come into my office. Today."

"I can be there at 5," she said.

"It's 2 now. I'll see you then."

In the meantime, I got a flash of insight. "Heather, why don't you and I pay somebody a visit?"

"Who?"

"Her name is Coretta Taylor. She works at The Peanut."

"Let's go."

Chapter Twelve

I WENT TO THE PEANUT, and sat down at the bar. The Peanut was a midtown bar close to the Country Club Plaza, and, as dives go, it had become a bit of an institution. It had a bit of a sports-bar-meets-dive-bar atmosphere, with the Kansas City Chiefs logo on the ceiling, hardwood floors and wood panelings.

An attractive woman with black hair was bartending. She had tattoos on her fore-arms, which were showed off by her sleeveless black t-shirt. Her hair was long, her breasts were large and her face looked like that of a Playboy model. She looked like she didn't take shit yet she also looked like she attracted just that – shit. Men were probably hitting on her constantly.

She saw me sit down and nodded her head. "Just a second," she said, "I need to pour this beer." She poured it and shot it down to the guy at the end of the bar. "What can I get for you?" she asked me.

"Actually, I need to speak with you."

She looked suspicious. "What about?"

The Alibi

"About Vittorio Degrazio."

She took a deep breath. "You a cop?"

"No. I'm not a cop. I'm a defense attorney. I represent Gina Degrazio, who is accused of murdering Vittorio."

"What do you want to know?"

"I need to ask you about an incident with Mr. Degrazio."

She looked over at a guy walking by the bar. "Rick," she said. "Cover for me? I need to go outside for a smoke break."

The guy walked behind the bar and Coretta walked to the end of the bar and came out on the floor.

"Follow me," she said. "We'll talk outside."

I was happy she was so willing to speak with me. I was afraid she wouldn't.

"By the way, this is Heather," I said, motioning to Heather. "She's my assistant."

"Cool."

I followed her out the back door and we were in the alley by the parking lot.

"Okay," she said. "What do you need to know?"

"I got your name from Bianca Cassavettes," I said. "She told me she had been date-raped by Vittorio and she said you were, too."

"I was." She shook her head. "Guy was kinda my type. He used to come in here all the time. You know, I knew the score on him. He would come in, buy women drinks and would go home with them. About twice a week, always the same. But I got a thing for little Italian men and I thought he was cute and pretty funny. I thought it might be fun to give it a whirl, too, you know? So, one night, he stays until close. It's a weekday night, we're kinda dead around closing time, people clear out before 1 on the weekdays. There's some stragglers around and he's one of them. I'm cleaning up the bar, doing my thing before getting out of here, and he comes up and asks me what I'm doing after I get off work."

She got out a pack of cigarettes. "You mind?" she asked, and I shook my head. She lit the cigarette and took a large drag. "So, yeah, I say I'm going home after my shift because I worked a double that day. When I work, I work all day, from open to around five, but I worked a double that day, so I was pretty tired, you know? But he says he wants to buy me breakfast at Town Topic. Well, I gotta say, I love me some greasy spoon late-night food, and, as it happens, I'm not working the next day because I pulled a double that day. That means I can go home and sleep in. So, I ended up saying 'sure, let's go to Town Topic.'"

The Town Topic was a tiny burger joint in the Crossroads Art District that served greasy, yet delicious, burgers, fries and breakfast foods. It was open 24-7, and was the one of the only games in town when it came to after-bar food runs.

"We go to Town Topic, he buys me breakfast, I'm starving, I haven't eaten since noon. Then he asks me to go to his place. I kinda like him, he's kinda fun. I say sure. We end up at his house, this huge house in Loose Park, and I'm thinking 'whoa, this guy is loaded.' Not that that means anything, or nothing like that, but that was what I was thinking."

"And you get to his place, and-"

"Yeah. He puts on a record on a turntable. I think it was Frank Sinatra. I'm thinking it's pretty sweet, you know, you don't see people with vinyl anymore. I always like to pick up vinyl myself. There used to be a cool place on Main called *Recycled Sounds* that was just like in that movie, *High Fidelity*.

God, I miss that place. I used to go there all the time when I was in high school. Anyhow, I digress. But did you know there's a cool second-hand record store in downtown Overland Park that sells vinyl? You can do wine tasting there, too."

She was speaking faster and faster, and I had the feeling she was deliberately stalling. Like she didn't want to tell me what happened next.

"Anyhow, he gets me a drink. It's a whiskey sour, it tastes pretty damned good. I tell him he missed his calling, he should be a bartender, and he laughs. And we're talking on the couch and then boom. I'm down for the count. The room starts spinning and everything gets blurry. It's my first drink of the night. I wake up on his couch the next morning, and, you know, I could tell we had sex. I try to piece together everything that had happened the night before, and I couldn't figure out how I passed out on only one drink."

"How did you figure everything out?"

"Well, Bianca Cassevettes, the gal you talked to, she's a friend of mine. I told her what happened, and she said the same thing happened to her. After only one drink. Well, that pissed me off. It was bad enough he had done that to me, but he also did it to her. So, I went to the police."

I nodded. I was finally getting somewhere.

"You did? When did you go to the police?"

"Well, let's see. This all happened in early February. It was somewhere around the first week of February that I went to the cops."

"Do you know what happened?"

"Not much. I mean, I called the cops about a week later and asked them what the progress was and they just said they had questioned him and released him. They didn't arrest him or nothing like that. I was pissed, but, goddamn if that bastard ended up dead a few days later."

Just then, the guy covering for Coretta poked his head out the door.

"Break's over," he said. "We just got a rush."

She nodded and threw her cigarette on the ground and stepped on it.

"Well, looks like I gotta get back. Anything else you need from me?"

"No. Thanks for taking the time to talk to me."

"No problem. I hope I helped."

"You did. More than you know."

Chapter Thirteen

WHEN GINA GOT to my office at 5, I was ready for her. I knew just how to get the truth out of her, too. Coretta's story sealed it for me. I would speak with her alone, however. That was important, because I needed to break her and the best way I knew to break her was to do it one on one.

"Okay," Gina said when she got into the office. "What's so goddamned important you had to see me right this very minute?"

"Sit down," I said, and she complied. "Okay. I found out some interesting information, and I think I now know what happened to Vittorio."

"Oh yeah? You found out who did it?"

"Yes. I did. Enzo Degrazio killed his brother."

I saw her face go white and I knew I had hit the nail on the head. She sat up straighter in her chair and clutched her purse to her chest.

"Don't be ridiculous. Enzo wouldn't do something like that."

"Oh? Listen, I don't know what game the two of you have cooked up, but I have a feeling Enzo has somehow duped you into the taking the fall for Vittorio's murder while simultaneously undermining you. I'm going to get to the bottom of why that is, but I need to know from you one thing – why are you lying to me?"

"I'm not lying. I told you, I have no idea-"

"Save it. Enzo was drugging women, raping them, and telling these women his name was Vittorio Degrazio. Or perhaps he just said his name was just Vittorio. And that was well and good because he threatened and bribed them to keep quiet. Only there was one woman he didn't get the chance to threaten or bribe. She went to the cops before he had the chance to get to her. And guess who got in trouble for raping this woman? It wasn't Enzo. It was Vittorio."

Gina shook her head, but her eyes didn't meet mine. Her body language was giving her away.

"Well, I would imagine Vittorio wasn't too pleased to be brought in for questioning by the cops about a rape he knew nothing about. And my money's on Vittorio calling his brother Enzo to read him the riot act about raping women and using his name. Something tells me Enzo probably has been a sexual predator going way back, and Vittorio probably knew it. Vittorio knew just what had happened when he was brought in for questioning and it led right back to his pervert brother Enzo."

Gina continued to shake her head, but I just pressed on.

"Yes. So, here's what happened next. Vittorio told Enzo he wouldn't take the fall for Enzo's crimes, he wasn't the rapist of those women and could prove it. Enzo has a large scar on his back. Vittorio doesn't. Enzo knew it was only a matter of time before the dominoes started to fall and the women would be coming out of the woodwork. You've seen

The Alibi

it, time and again – once the first accuser is brave enough to come forward, all the rest come out, too. You saw it with Bill Cosby, Roger Ailes and Harvey Weinstein. It would happen that way. Once somebody was arrested for raping Coretta the dam would break open. Vittorio wouldn't go down for Enzo, and he told him so."

"A fancy story you got there," Gina said, but I cut her off from speaking more.

"Well, Enzo knew there was only one way to prevent Vittorio from going to the cops and telling them who the real rapist was, and that was killing Vittorio. He figured, two birds, one stone. Vittorio couldn't go to the cops and turn him in, and, with Vittorio dead, all those women he raped would think their rapist was dead. That would mean the whole case would die with Vittorio. That was why there was no forced entry. That was why the killer knew right where to get the gun. You told him where to find the gun. Now the only thing vexing me is where you fit into all this. Why did you agree to take the fall for him? What does he have over you? Whatever it is, you're being played for a fool, because he came in here and tried to throw you under the bus."

"Listen, you think you got it all figured out. Well, you don't."

"I think I do. I know I do. It all makes sense. You know, I thought maybe it was one of the women who popped your husband but now I know that it was Enzo. I just can't figure out how you're involved. I will tell you one thing, though – when I first started talking to you about the women Vittorio allegedly raped, you told me not to go there. That means, to me, you and Enzo are in on this together somehow. As I said, you must have told him where to find the gun. But you also let him use the gun registered to you to kill his brother.

That's the only thing vexing me about this whole thing. You agreed to take the fall for Enzo, but why?"

She finally had enough of listening to me. "You think you're so smart. Well, you don't know nothing."

"Oh, but I do. I do. I know just what happened and I know why. I haven't yet put the other pieces of the puzzle together, but I will. In the meantime, you've lied to me a few too many times. I can't trust you and I can't work with you. I'm sorry, but I'll have to withdraw from your case."

"You withdraw from my case and you'll find out what happens to your friend Nick Savante."

"Again with that. Listen, you said something cryptically about that once before, but I think you're full of shit. If you know something, out with it. Don't beat around the bush like that."

"Nick killed a man in prison. And Joey's the only one who knows about it."

Chapter Fourteen

"WHAT THE HELL are you talking about?" I demanded from her.

"You go and ask him about it. Ask Nick about it. He'll tell you. I know he's up for parole in a few months, and, other than this man he killed, he's been an absolute angel behind bars. Joey gives the parole board the word about Nick and Nick will never get out of prison. Ever. He'll just have to rot behind bars until he's 100 years old with his buddy Connor."

I wanted to lunge at Gina. Wanted to smack the smug smile off her face. She had me, at least she had me at that point, and she knew it.

"You're lying. Nick would never keep something like that from me."

"Let me ask you this. When you visit him, are there guards around listening to every word the two of you say?"

"Yes. I don't go in for a professional visit. I go and visit him as a friend. The guards are always around."

"Well, do you think Nick will tell you he shivved a guy in the joint if there are guards around?"

I had to admit, she had a point. "No, I guess he wouldn't. But how do you know all about it?"

"Joey wrote me a letter about it. He wanted to make sure I had insurance you would do all you could to win this case. We couldn't have you going rogue."

"And what's in it for him?"

"I'm not going to tell you about all that. I gotta have some cards up my sleeve."

I took a deep breath. "Get out," I said. "Now."

"Okay. But you're not withdrawing from my case."

"Your arraignment is in a couple of days. I'll decide by then."

"You're not going to withdraw. Not until you talk to your friend and see what he has to say. Once you do that, you won't withdraw at all."

She left and I immediately did two things.

One, I filed an entry of appearance on Nick's case. That way I could have a professional visit with him where everything we said to one another would be confidential.

Two, I called the prison and informed them I would be seeing Nick Savante in the morning.

I would find out what my client was talking about if it was the last thing I did.

THE NEXT MORNING, I headed over to the prison and was led into a private room where I could speak with Nick without anybody being around. Attorneys required privacy because of attorney-client privilege, which is void if there was anybody around except the attorney and the client.

That meant no guards could be within earshot. They were behind a glass but didn't have listening devices.

Nick was brought out in handcuffs and leg-irons. I hated to see him like that, but I knew it was necessary.

"Buddy," he said, when he came out. "I got a notice you're now my attorney and you needed to see me as soon as possible. I have to admit, I don't know what's going on."

I stood up and he sat down across from me. "Sorry about all the confusion," I said. "But I needed to ask you some questions."

"Sure," he said. "Ask away."

"I don't know how to ask you this except coming right out with it. But did you kill a man inside?"

He sighed, and, just from looking at his face, I knew Gina was telling the truth, for once in her life. "Yeah. I was protecting Connor, but yeah. I did."

"Tell me what happened."

"Well, you know I've tried to keep my nose clean in here. So are all the guys. We're not trying to screw up our chance on getting out of here. But there was this guy, and he was psychotic, let me tell you. I don't say that lightly. I'm not the person who says everybody is psycho, crazy or deranged. I pretty much reserve the word psycho for the mentally disturbed. And Ward Johnson was definitely mentally disturbed. He probably belonged in a padded cell, not in here."

"Okay. Now, you said you were trying to protect Connor. What do you mean by that?"

Nick bowed his head and looked at his hands. "Well, Ward came in and started to harass Connor. I don't know, I guess Connor looks just like somebody who was messing with his wife on the outside. He called Connor by the name of Jameson and some of the guys who knew Ward said a guy named Chad Jameson was messing with Ward's wife. Ward beat up Jameson several times because of it."

"Anyhow, Ward beat Connor up several times, and he and Connor both ended up in the hole for two weeks because of a fight they had in the lunchroom. After they got out of the hole, Ward still harassed Connor. He kicked the shit out of him in the yard and Connor ended up in the infirmary with internal injuries because Ward beat him so badly. Ward went to the hole again, and, when he got out, he started telling some of the guys he would take care of Connor once and for all."

"So," he continued, "I couldn't have that. I decided to take matters into my own hands. I knew a guy who could get me a knife and I cornered Ward in the bathroom one day, when there was nobody in there, and I knifed him."

"How did you get a knife in here?"

"I had it smuggled in. I'm not going to tell you anything more than that, because I don't want to implicate the guy who got that knife for me, but yeah. I got it smuggled in."

"What happened after you knifed him?"

"I got the hell out of there but I made a big mistake. I didn't check all the stalls before I went into the bathroom. I didn't check the one closest to the far wall. The handicapped bathroom. Actually, Connor himself was the one who didn't check because I sent him in there to clear it out. He didn't check that stall, but I didn't, either. And Joey Caruso was in that stall. He heard the argument between Ward and me and came out and saw the body on the ground. He has never told anybody about what he saw, and there was an investigation on Ward's death, but Joey was the only one, besides myself and Connor, who knew what happened. He promised he wouldn't tell anybody because he's not a snitch. So, I think we're cool."

The Alibi

I nodded. This was obviously what Gina was talking about when she threatened me – Joey had information that Nick killed that psycho bastard who was beating on Connor. The only question was – why would Joey rat on Nick just on Gina's say-so? I understood Gina and Joey were sleeping together but there had to be something more. There had to be some other connection between the two, otherwise, if Gina tells Joey to rat on Nick, Joey would just tell her to go to hell. I knew the prison code and ratting on another inmate could certainly mean death. Not only that, there was honor among thieves, and most inmates won't rat out another inmate just because it was the wrong thing to do.

"What's going on?" Nick asked. "What are you thinking about?"

"There's a missing puzzle piece," I said. "Joey Caruso knows you killed a man. Here's what's going on – Gina is threatening me. She's telling me that if I withdraw from her case she'll get Joey to rat you out. That, of course, will mean you not only won't get parole, but you might even have to stand trial for the murder of Ward Johnson. That would mean you would never get out of here." I took a deep breath. "But the thing I'm struggling with is why would Joey rat you out just because Gina wants him to? If I can just get around that question, I might not be so worried that Joey could deep-six you."

"Why are you wanting to withdraw from Gina's case?"

"Because I can't trust her. She's lied to me from the start."

"What has she lied to you about?"

"What hasn't she lied to me about?" I shook my head. "I'm between a rock and a hard place right now. I don't see how I can possibly do a good job on her case when I don't trust her to ever tell the truth. Yet, if she has some kind of influence on Joey, then I better step lightly. I need you on the outside, buddy, you and Tommy and Jack. You guys are my brothers. You guys are my family, the only family I've ever had aside from my kids. You've always had my back and I've always had yours. So, I'm going to have to do some thinking and ask some more questions of Gina. I need to find out if she's bluffing."

Nick shook his head. "Buddy, you do what you gotta do. Let me worry about Joey. I don't see him breaking the prison code, but-"

"But I can't chance he will. Again, I have to find out what the connection is between Gina and Joey. Why she can get him to sing if she wants him to. Once I figure that out, I'll know what to do. And, no, I'm not going to let you worry about Joey. If there's even a chance he could turn you in for killing Ward Johnson, I'll dance as much as Gina wants me to."

"Do what you gotta do," Nick said. "I can take care of myself."

"Nick, if something happens, and Joey rats on you and you end up spending the rest of your life in prison, or, God forbid, you get the death penalty, I could never live with myself. No, I won't take a chance when your life is at stake."

Nick nodded his head and smiled. "Womb to tomb," he said.

"Birth to earth."

Nick got up and left because I also needed to speak with Joey Caruso. There was something nagging at me when I found out Enzo was posing as Vittorio. I needed to clear it up with him.

Joey came in about fifteen minutes later. He was around fifty years old, with a full head of salt and pepper hair that looked like it desperately needed to be combed. He was

The Alibi

olive-skinned with large lips and an even larger head. He had about 20 extra pounds.

He looked at me with suspicion in his eyes. "Who's this?" he asked the guard who had entered the room after Nick left.

"My name is Damien Harrington," I said, getting on my feet and extending my hand.

"Ah, yeah, yeah. I remember now. The guard said a Damien Harrington was here to see me, and I was like 'Damien who?' But I remember now. You're Gina's lawyer."

"Yeah, I am. Listen, I need to ask you a few questions. Questions nagging at me."

"Go ahead."

"Okay. Now, I know you were considered the fixer for Vittorio Degrazio, right?"

"Yeah, right."

"And, from what I understand, you fixed things for Vittorio after he raped women, right?"

"Right." He looked at me suspiciously. "I know what you're thinking about, and, yes, I know it wasn't actually Vittorio who was raping women. I knew that it was his identical twin, Enzo."

"You did? Why didn't you say anything to Vittorio? Why didn't you tell Vittorio that Enzo was doing that and using his name?"

"Because I didn't really care. Enzo's money spent just as well as Vittorio's money did. Besides, it wasn't my place to tell Vittorio what his twin was up to."

"But you told guys you know inside that it was Vittorio who was doing the raping, and it was Vittorio you were fixing things for, right?"

"Yeah. Listen, Enzo was paying me well to pretend he was Vittorio, and I wouldn't go against that. Enzo paid me better than Vittorio ever did, because Enzo has more money than Vittorio ever has. So, yeah, I told the guys in here it was Vittorio doing all that."

"But what you said to the guys inside went against Vittorio's reputation on the outside, not Enzo's."

"Yeah. So what? As I said, Enzo was paying me very well to pretend Vittorio who was raping women. I'm not going against that."

I sighed. "Okay. Well, that was all I wanted to know."

WHEN I WAS DRIVING HOME that evening, I got an even worse surprise.

Garrett called me, and I clicked on and talked to him. "Yeah, Garrett," I said, "what's up?"

"I found out who the secret partner is of that bastard Robert Davis," he said. "It took a lot of digging, but I found it out."

"Who is it?"

"It's your client, Gina Degrazio."

Chapter Fifteen

"WHAT? What do you mean, Gina Degrazio is Robert Davis' secret partner?"

"Just what I'm telling you. I found out she was brought on as a secret partner, not a silent partner, but a secret partner, because of her mob ties. She couldn't be a regular partner because she was associated with criminal elements and apparently Robert Davis didn't want the feds banging down his door for having a mob-related partner on board. He wanted her as a partner, but he didn't want her name on any of the titles or nothing like that. But she's a partner, all right. That means there's one more person that we can sue for damages."

I felt my blood pressure start to rise as I considered what Tom Garrett was saying to me. Obviously, I couldn't defend Gina on a criminal charge while simultaneously suing her. That would be an open and shut conflict of interest case. The Missouri Bar would burn me at the stake for that one.

That meant one of two things – either I got off her criminal case, or I got off the personal injury mold case. It was bad enough I had been working the two cases simultaneously anyhow, but I had a good excuse – I didn't know she was involved in the mold case, and it wasn't something that could have just been discovered in a routine conflict check.

That raised the stakes on whether or not I could get off Gina's case 1000%. I had gained the trust of the people I met with. They were in a desperate situation, deathly ill with no place to go. I came in and befriended them and reassured them that everything would turn out okay. I made them believe I was on their side and I would be right with them every step of the way. Yet I was faced with the reality that I might have to betray them. I might have to tell them "never mind." I could find another attorney to take their case, somebody I could trust to do a good job, but I still felt guilty. I felt incredibly guilty for possibly abandoning them.

I didn't want to see their faces when I told them I had to get off their case and send it to another attorney. Yet, that would be the reality *if* I decided to stay on Gina's case.

Goddammit. Everything seemed to be against Gina's case. Everything. I wanted off it anyhow – she didn't listen to me, she hid things from me and she lied to me. I didn't know how I was supposed to win her case under those circumstances.

"Damien?" Garrett said. "You still there?"

"Yeah. I'm still here."

"Can you work both her criminal case and stay on the mold case?"

"No. I can't." I shook my head. "I can't. I have to choose one or the other. And goddammit, I want off her criminal case anyhow. I wanted off it even before you told me the news about her being a secret partner with this Robert Davis guy. Now, I really want off it."

The Alibi

"I was actually excited about the class action mold suit," I continued. "I was energized by the idea that I could actually help people for once. I mean, I know I'm helping people in my criminal defense work too, but in cases like Gina, it just makes me want to take a shower. Helping her beat the murder charge against her husband won't give me nearly the satisfaction I would feel if I won a huge judgment against Robert Davis and those people he hurt were made whole."

I felt so frustrated right at that moment, I felt like screaming and beating my fists on the steering wheel.

"Goddammit, goddammit, goddammit," I yelled at nobody in particular. "I'm sorry, Garret, thank you for calling me about this, but I have to go."

"Don't apologize. I know how you feel. You were really excited about these cases, and now-"

"And now I have to let all of them down. These people who have been let down, time and again, and they're going to be let down one more time. By me." I shook my head. "Goddammit," I said in a low voice. "Goddammit."

I hung up and pulled my car into my underground parking lot and rode the elevator to my office. I would have to talk to Gina once more. I would have to get the whole story from her, and she would have to tell me straight. I knew that, after I spoke with Nick, I wouldn't chance withdrawing from Gina's case.

That meant I had to let all those poor people down.

GINA CAME to my office the next morning. After I got off the phone with Garrett, I knew I didn't have the energy to talk to her. I was just completely drained. So, I went home. I kept Gretchen on the clock that evening because I needed her to work with the kids while I went into my man cave and watched HBO Max and just vegged out. I needed time and space to think about my options.

Several times, I went to my home office, booted up the computer, and started to prepare disengagement letters to each of the mold clients I signed up. But I could only start these letters, not finish them, because I didn't want them to go out. I couldn't face, just yet, the fact that I would have to let these people slip through my fingers. But when I closed my eyes, I saw their disappointed faces. I saw myself telling each one of them, in person, I had to drop them, and I saw each of their faces look devastated.

Would they trust another attorney? Could I find somebody I trusted? I didn't even know. The people I knew practicing law were all criminal defense attorneys. I didn't go to law school locally, so I didn't necessarily know everyone practicing in the area on a first-name basis. I knew all the folks at the Public Defender's Office, and there were a few of those chums who went on to personal injury firms, but these were large firms they joined. Large firms that wouldn't give my clients the personal service I was planning on giving them.

I would have to ask around and see if I could come up with some names to give these people. I would have to personally find somebody willing to be patient and hold these people's hands and really make them feel like they mattered.

That was the bottom line. I needed somebody to let each of these people know that they mattered. That their lives were at stake and they weren't just a number. In other words, I would have to go above and beyond to find the right person to take them on. Then, and only then, would I go through the devastating process of telling each of them, face to face, I could no longer represent them.

I went to bed that night after drinking several shots of whiskey, feeling defeated.

THE NEXT DAY, Gina came into the office. "Well," she said, as she sat down. "What did you decide?"

"I've decided it's time for you to tell me the truth. Your arraignment is tomorrow. After the arraignment happens, we'll be on a tight schedule. Judge Reiner doesn't mess around. He wants his cases docketed quickly and wants them gone just as quickly. He's nothing if not efficient. That means you and I will have to be on the same page, and we have to get on the same page quickly. So, you have to answer every question I have for you, and you have to answer these questions truthfully."

"I *have* been truthful," Gina said.

"Save it. Now. Here's the first question I have for you. I understand you are a secret partner with Robert Davis, and the two of you own some real estate around the city. I need to know exactly what compelled you to invest with him and why you had to be a secret partner. I also need to know where you got the money to become a secret partner with him."

"I don't know what-"

I put my hand up. "Gina, stop. Just stop. I know for a fact you are involved with these apartments and I know for a fact your name does not come up on any title searches. Now, answer these questions straight."

She sighed. "Okay. You got me. Listen, Robert and Enzo are friends. They go way back. Enzo has his restaurant license and his spot downtown because of Robert. Robert's loaded, he knows lots of people in City Hall, he pulled some strings, and Enzo got his downtown restaurant."

"Oh? Robert did that out of the goodness of his heart?"

"No. Of course not. Listen, Robert said he needed an investor to go in with him on buying the apartments. He needed somebody else to partner with him. He told Enzo that if he found somebody willing to invest with him, he would get Enzo that restaurant license and that place downtown."

I raised my eyebrows. "Okay. So, he buys these dilapidated places he ignored and let mold grow and he roped you into partnering with him. I guess because he needed somebody else to take the fall for when the inevitable lawsuits came down against him. I guess you were that patsy. Now, riddle me this. Enzo profited from this arrangement, not you. So why did you agree to be the secret partner for Robert and not Enzo?"

She shifted uncomfortably in her seat. "I owed Enzo a lot of money from way back. Gambling debts he cleared up for me at some Vegas casinos. You ever see *The Godfather*? You ever see that scene where Vito is helping that guy and saying he wants something in return when the time comes? Well, that's the arrangement Enzo and me had when he pulled some strings to erase my gambling debts. I owed him, so I did this for him. Enzo got his restaurant downtown and Robert got his partner."

"Okay. Now, let's roll it back even further. I can only assume Robert got you involved because he knew the properties he was buying were death traps. He probably knew they were mold infested and he probably knew they were lawsuits just waiting to happen. He wanted a partner to

The Alibi

cushion the inevitable fall, so he chose you. First off, did you know that was why he wanted you as a partner? Did you know about the toxic mold growing in those apartments? Toxic mold that's making people extremely sick and even killing some people?"

"No. I didn't know it at the time. I knew there was some reason he wanted me as a partner, but I didn't know exactly what the reason was."

"But why did he buy those properties? What purpose do those properties serve for him?"

She sighed. "He got a tip that an international developer was interested in that land. He knows people who have insider information and he found out the land those apartments are on soon be would be worth 20x the current value. That land developer would tear down those slums and use the land to develop some condos. So, Robert bought those apartments. He bought them before it ever became public that Adium Incorporated, which is the firm that wanted the land, was interested. He knew that Adium Incorporated would file their letters of intent to buy the property and he wanted in before that was publicly known."

"My investigator did an extensive search on these properties and there were no letters of intent filed from anybody. I didn't see that anybody bid with Robert for possession of those properties."

"No, they didn't. They didn't end up bidding. They decided at the last minute they didn't want those properties anyhow, so they ended up bidding on some other properties close by. Robert ended up stuck with the places. It turned out, though, he brought me on as security just in case ended up holding the bag."

"Listen, I didn't find out about the mold issues until he told me about them," Gina continued. "He told me he found out a little boy died in one of the apartments and so did a middle-aged woman. He told me he found out people were getting sick. He told me we needed to be prepared for a multi-million dollar lawsuit. He said he tried to unload the property so that they became somebody else's problem, but apparently that lady, Arnetta Williams, died before he could sell."

I sighed. "Okay. Listen, I was going to be the attorney on these mold cases, but I obviously cannot sue you since you are my criminal client. And, don't worry, anything you told me about these mold cases would be strictly confidential and covered under privilege, so I can't disclose anything you said about the mold to the next attorney handling this case. I probably shouldn't say anything more to you about this, however. In fact, I might have already said too much."

She looked perplexed. "You were going to sue about the mold?"

"I was. I didn't know you were a partner until this afternoon. Now, I obviously will not be the attorney filing suit."

"Does that mean I'll still be your criminal client?"

I took a deep breath. "Unfortunately, yes. I'm feeling slightly more comfortable about that, however, than I was. You seemed to be forthcoming about your association with Robert Davis, so that's a positive sign."

Gina appeared to relax. "So, there will be a lawsuit about the mold?"

"I don't know. I won't be filing it, so I can't tell you if there will be a lawsuit or not. Now, I need to ask you some more questions. I need to find out how you know Joey Caruso and what kind of hold you have over him. You tell me Joey will turn in my friend Nick if things don't go right in your criminal case, or if I withdraw from your case. But why would Joey care? Are you telling you'll

The Alibi

just tell Joey to rat on Nick and he'll just do it because you asked him to?"

"No." She shifted even more uncomfortably in her seat. "Okay. I've been thinking about this a lot, and I've even talked about this with Enzo. He tells me I'm your boss, and what I say goes. That if I tell you not to go to certain things in the trial, you won't go there. That's what he tells me. So, he told me I can tell you everything."

Finally. "Go ahead."

"Well, it started when I got into this apartment deal. I didn't know what I was getting into, and, all of a sudden, I get phone calls from Robert Davis telling me to be prepared for a multi-million dollar lawsuit. I don't have that kind of money. Robert's telling me that if we get judgments against us, we'll owe that money, and even if I went bankrupt, I couldn't get out from under it. So, yeah, I suddenly find myself having to maybe pay people millions of dollars I don't have."

I suddenly realized I probably knew where this was going. "Go on."

"Well, Enzo killed Vittorio, as you've already figured out. We made a deal – Enzo would give me my $3 million bond and I could keep that money after I beat the case, in exchange for me taking the fall for him. We signed a contract, legally binding, I got a lawyer to review it, but we signed a contract that said I could keep the $3 million after I beat the case."

"That contract couldn't possibly be legally binding. You have to have consideration for a contract to be binding, which means that both parties need to give something to one another. The only consideration for this contract was you would take the fall for Enzo's crime. That can't be considered to be legal consideration." I stared at her. "Yet you got a lawyer to tell you that contract was legally binding?"

"Yeah."

"And you told that attorney what the terms of the contract was?"

"No. The contract didn't say I was taking the fall for Enzo. It just said I would keep the money he paid for the bond if I beat the case."

"You got that contract with you?"

"Yeah." She had an accordion file with her, and she brought it out. "Here."

I took about a half-hour to review the contract, and I was satisfied it was binding on both parties. I figured out exactly why the contract was binding on both parties, too – the contract stated that Enzo owed Gina $3 million for prior debts. I didn't know for sure, but I imagined that the attorney who reviewed the contract told Gina and Enzo their current arrangement would never fly, so they needed to put something else into the contract that would be considered legal consideration. Whatever, this was a contract they both signed, the consideration was proper, so it was enforceable in court.

"This contract states you forfeit the money if you're convicted."

"Yeah. I figured it was worth the roll of the dice."

I shook my head. "Worth the roll of the dice? In what world is your freedom worth the roll of the dice?"

"In my world. Listen, those apartments aren't the only thing I'm in hock to. I'm also in hock to Joey. Big time hock to him. A million dollars is what I owe him. He knows guys that will take me out, and I don't mean to dinner. Joey's threatened to ice me more than once. So, I got this promissory note from Enzo that says I'm going to get $3 million

The Alibi

if I beat this case down, so Joey's not so antsy to see me wiped off the face of the earth no more. Suddenly, Joey's hanging back and seeing if I'm going to beat this case because he wants his money."

"Why do you owe Joey so much money?"

"Because he gave me a bunch of money to open up some massage parlors for him. He wanted to launder his money through these massage parlors."

"Okay. And what happened to the massage parlors?"

"Well, they were shut down, all of them, by the city."

"And why were they shut down?"

"The girls were giving happy endings."

I nodded. "That will do it. But Joey had to know that if he gave you money for a less-than-legitimate business that something like that was bound to happen."

She sighed. "Well, it was my fault they were shut down. I told the girls to give happy endings. I wanted the guys to be really satisfied, repeat customers."

"And?"

"And, Joey told me, when he gave me the money for the massage parlors, I was to operate them as completely legitimate operations. No funny business, he said. No prostitution, he said. No happy endings, he said. So, when the city closed down the massage parlors, and he lost his investment, he blamed me. He almost killed me right then and there."

"I have to say, that makes sense. It's kind of pointless to use a dirty business to try to clean dirty money."

"That's what he said."

"Okay. So Joey lost a million-dollar investment because of you. But what does it matter if Joey gets his money now? He's a lifer."

"It matters, because Joey owes a lot of money to some mobsters on the outside. These mobsters, they're threatening to kill his family. Nothing means more to Joey than his two sons. So, yeah, it's basically musical money at this point."

"I don't understand. If Joey owes money to people on the outside, so much so his family is in danger, what is he doing lending money to you?"

"Well, here's the thing. Joey owes the money, but he didn't actually borrow it. It was his son, Antonio. Antonio borrowed the money. He wanted to open up his own restaurant, and he did, but he wasn't a very good businessman, and he lost it all. I think he gambled away a lot of it too, if you want to know the truth. The mobsters are making Joey pay it, though, because Antonio is a deadbeat."

"And Joey is in prison, so how do the mobsters think Joey will pay it back?"

"See, that's where this whole round robin with the money comes in. Joey tells the mobsters he'll get the money from me when I beat down the case. The mobsters know it's a 50-50 shot I actually will beat down the case, but I showed them the promissory note from Enzo that showed I would be $3 million richer when I'm acquitted for Vittorio's murder, so they'll hold off on killing Antonio for the time being. See, everything is up in the air. All I have to do is get acquitted. Then I can pay Joey, Joey can pay Antonio's mobsters, and everyone is happy."

"And if you don't get acquitted..."

"I don't get the money, Joey don't get the money, and Antonio is dead man walking. I'm probably dead woman walking, too, because Joey will have me killed in prison. He knows people inside every prison and my life won't be worth nothing."

"So, I withdraw from the case..."

"And Joey will rat on Nick. Simple as that. He knows his

The Alibi

life depends on me beating down this case, and he don't want to chance my case to anyone but you. Nick told Joey how dynamite you are as an attorney, how many guys you managed to get freed from prison, how smart you are, and Joey wants you. So, that's what I have over Joey. That's why Joey will rat on Nick. He needs Nick as his insurance policy."

"And if I lose the case?"

"If you lose the case, you lose it. But you gotta give it your all. You gotta fight like hell to make sure I'm acquitted. Because if I see you doing a half-ass job defending me, not your very best, then I'll tell Joey you threw me under the bus and didn't fight for me, and that will piss him off enough that he'll rat on Nick then, too. Plus, even if you try your best, Joey's not going to know that. He'll only know you lost, and he'll blame you for losing the case. That means he'll want his revenge on you, which means he'll probably rat out Nick anyhow. So, I guess what I'm saying is you better not lose my case."

I rubbed my forehead. "In other words, in order to make sure Nick is safe, I need to win your case."

"Well, yeah. I guess that's right. You win my case and everybody is happy. Joey is happy, I'm happy, Antonio's happy. Everyone's happy but Enzo, because he's going to be out that money."

"Ay, there's the rub. Enzo will be working against you. His interest is in making sure you get convicted for this. That's why he was in here that one day, throwing you under the bus."

"Right. Enzo wants to see me convicted. He's not going to help."

"So, why did you tell me in the beginning he was your

alibi? You had to have known he wouldn't do a damn thing for your case."

She shrugged. "I don't know why I told you that. It was the only thing I could think of on the spot like that. I didn't think about what I would say to you before I came in here for the first time. I didn't rehearse it in my head or nothing like that. It just came tumbling out of my mouth. Sometimes I just can't stop it. Once I start telling a story, I can't stop myself."

She was finally telling me the truth, but I didn't like it. I didn't like this truth. I had a lot of pressure on me to make sure she was acquitted.

If she wasn't acquitted, Nick's life was in danger.

Chapter Sixteen

"OKAY," I said, "now that we're finally straight, we need to go over strategy. Obviously, I'm going after Enzo. I'll go after him on the stand aggressively. Beat him down. Show the jury Enzo killed his brother. Show the jury why."

Gina shook her head. "No. That won't work."

I closed my eyes and counted to 20. Not to 10, but to 20. I was starting to trust her, and then she throws me for a loop. That was how it had been with us. I still didn't entirely trust her, so I needed her on the same page with me for strategy. That was the least I asked for.

"What do you mean by no?" I asked her, my eyes closed, my teeth clenched.

"I mean, no. You can't throw Enzo under the bus like that."

"Why, pray tell? After all, Enzo did it. Plus, he's a known sex offender. He raped those women. Do you think that he'll stop doing that? He needs to be behind bars for that reason alone."

"Sorry, but I can't let you get Enzo in trouble like that.

He's already told me he'll kill me if I finger him, and if he don't kill me, one of his friends will. Enzo is connected. He says he's not, but he is. He knows plenty of mob guys who will do me in. You have to figure out a different defense."

I took a deep breath. "Here's the thing. I know the truth about what happened. I know you know the truth, too. I can't possibly put you on the stand unless we go with the truthful defense, which is that Enzo killed his brother."

She shrugged. "Come up with something different."

I hung my head. "Okay, I guess I never really explained all this to you. In defending murder, you have several defenses. One is you killed the person, but it was in the heat of passion. You didn't really think about it, you just did it. That doesn't excuse the murder, but it does possibly lower the charge to manslaughter. Two is you killed the person, but it was justified. Self-defense and defense of others comes into that calculation. Three is you killed the person, but you have an excuse. Insanity is a good example of that. Once again, you don't go scot free in that scenario, but you probably would end up in an institution for the rest of your life. Another way I can defend a murder case is that my client didn't do it."

"I know all this-"

"Now, obviously, I'm going to defend you using the fourth method, which is to show the jury you didn't do it. I usually use what is called the SODDI defense – some other dude did it. What that generally means is I have to show the jury who that other dude is. Now, I could use the SODDI defense without giving the jury an alternative suspect. Sometimes that works. But, usually, when you do a SODDI defense, you should have some kind of plausible other person that did it. Otherwise, it's hard to get an acquittal."

"I don't care. I know what you're saying, but you can't

get up there and tell the jury Enzo did it. You'll have to think of some other way of getting me off."

I nodded, regretting I even asked Gina for the truth. If she didn't tell me, then I would feel better about actually using a different defense I knew wasn't the truth. Not that anybody would ever know I knew the truth about what had happened. I would have to go with a defense I knew was a lie.

I would have to sell the jury on a known lie.

"Okay. Well, then, I guess we have our work cut out for us, don't we?"

She nodded. "I guess you do."

"You have me in a box, you know that, don't you? You're telling me that if you're convicted, and Joey doesn't get the money he needs to get his son out of trouble, he might rat out Nick because he'll want revenge on me for losing the case."

"No, I'm saying he probably will rat out Nick if you lose the case. Not that he might, but that he's probably gonna."

"Okay. Yet, goddammit, we have the perfect defense, and I can't use it." I made two fists and raised them to my face. "The perfect defense. We get the women on the stand testifying Vittorio raped them, we get them to testify about the scar on the back, we show the autopsy pictures that show there's no scar, we get Coretta to testify about going to the cops. It all becomes clear as to what happened. Man, we have such a neat and tidy defense."

"And you can't use it. How many times do we have to go over this? I know we got a good defense. I know that. But if you breathe a word to the jury about Enzo being responsible, I'm a dead woman. And, by the way, if that happens, and Enzo kills me, he'll do it before I can collect my bond money. That means Joey won't get his money, either, if Enzo kills me. That means Nick will lose his parole hearing, because Joey's gonna know the reason why I'm dead, and he's gonna blame you. I don't know why you can't understand what I'm trying to tell you. Find a different defense."

I nodded my head. "Okay. Well, I guess that's what I'm going to do." I would have to do something unethical, and that was I would have to present the jury an alternative suspect I *knew* wasn't responsible for the murder. That was the only way I could win Gina's case.

What that meant was that my alternative suspect, whoever I chose to present to the jury, would be under suspicion for Vittorio's death. That was how it worked. One person is acquitted for a murder and the cops keep on looking for the actual murderer. The first place they look is the person I present on the stand as being the likely suspect.

I didn't really see any other choice in the matter. I had to present *somebody* as a likely suspect. Perhaps I could simply get away with telling the jury that Vittorio had many enemies because he was a known sex offender, and leave it at that. That was still unethical, in my opinion, because Vittorio wasn't a known sex offender. He was an innocent party. I knew the truth about that, too. I would have to tell the jury a lie, tell them Vittorio was killed because he was raping women and threatening them, and, apparently, one of the women he raped had had enough. That would have to be the story I would go with. It was a bald-faced lie, and I knew it, but I had no choice. At the moment, that was the only defense I could think of.

Unless…

"Okay. We'll have to figure this out. I have two ways we can play this. One, we try to show Vittorio had a host of enemies, mainly the women he allegedly raped. This could work, because, well, these women had reason to kill him.

The Alibi

There's no doubt about that. However, this is a strategy that probably won't work for two different reasons."

"What are those reasons?"

"One, I need to narrow it down to one likely suspect. That would mean I would be shining suspicion on somebody I know is innocent. Two, there's the issue of the gun being registered to you. If we find some other suspect for this case, I'll have to establish to the jury how she got ahold of your gun. So, that's another roadblock."

Gina nodded and crossed her arms in front of her. "That's one way of defending me. What's another way?"

I took a deep breath. I would throw out something that went against every ethical boundary I knew about. I didn't see any other way out, however, except to ask her to lie. Either way, I would be perpetrating a fraud on the jury. If I chose to throw somebody under the bus, I would be perpetrating a fraud.

If I chose this next avenue, I would not only be perpetrating a fraud, but it would be incredibly risky. I would just throw it out to Gina and see if she bit.

"Another way is justification. He was going to kill you, so you killed him first." I closed my eyes, knowing what I would have to do to make this work. She would have to take the stand and lie, and I would know she was lying. I swallowed hard. I had never suborned perjury before, at least not knowingly.

Then again, I had never been in this position before. I had never been asked not to tell the court the truth before. Usually, in a position like this, it was easy – I tell the truth and that usually worked. But the truth was something I was forbidden to use. This was a first for me, so I would have to get creative. In this case, "getting creative" meant telling a bald-faced lie.

"He was going to kill me, so I killed him first? How's that gonna work?"

I stood up. "Here's how it's going to work. You went to the cops before when he beat you, isn't that right?"

"Yeah," she said. "I called the cops twice. They came out and talked to Vittorio, but they didn't charge him with nothing."

"Did you ever file a restraining order?"

"No. I never filed a restraining order."

"I guess we'll have to live with that. I mean-"

"Listen, the cops questioned me and I didn't say nothing about using self-defense. I didn't say nothing about Vittorio coming after me and me killing him to keep him from killing me first. I don't see how that excuse will work."

"Not excuse, justification. Excuse is something that merely mitigates the sentence. You still have to serve time for murder if you have an excuse, but you might serve less time. Or you might be convicted of a lesser crime. Justification gets you an outright acquittal, which is what we need right now. Now, you're right. You didn't tell the cops you killed Vittorio in self-defense. So, maybe you tell the court you didn't tell the cops that because…" I shook my head. "Let me review your statement to the cops again. Maybe I can figure this out."

I opened up the file and saw Gina's statement to the cops. They took her in for questioning right away and she did the right thing – she asked for a lawyer right up front. They didn't get the chance to question her, really. She just said to the police she wouldn't talk until she got an attorney in there.

Good, good. "I think we're okay on that. You didn't tell the cops you killed Vittorio in self-defense, but you didn't tell them anything else. So, we can still go with that defense if we wanted to."

Gina was looking at me with suspicion. "Okay. So-"

"So, he was coming at you with a belt. He put that belt around your neck and pulled on it. You started to lose consciousness, but you were close to your gun and you shot him." I swallowed hard and took a deep breath. "This could work."

"What happens to me if the jury buys it?"

"If the jury buys it, you'll be found not guilty. Self-defense is an absolute justification, which means you will be not guilty of murdering Vittorio. We can also use the women he allegedly raped as good evidence. It will show he was a violent man."

I felt like crying. I was not only going to suborn perjury, making an entire defense up from whole cloth, but I would keep on perpetrating a fraud by presenting women who thought Vittorio raped them, when it was actually Enzo. Lies piled on top of lies.

I had never in my life done something like this. Yet, I didn't see any other way. I couldn't possibly implicate an innocent person, so SODDI was out. Anyhow, if I did implicate an innocent person, I would still be lying. I couldn't use the truth, because Gina was restricting me, and using the truth could very well end up with her dead and Nick in prison for the rest of his life. It might even result in Nick getting the death penalty for killing Ward Johnson.

One thing was for sure. I wouldn't admit to Harper or anybody else what I was doing. If something happened and this all blew up in my face, and I lost my license to practice law, I certainly didn't want somebody else involved in it. I wasn't sure, but I thought that maybe Harper, if she knew I was going to suborn perjury and perpetrate a fraud, might have a legal obligation to turn me in.

"Alright," Gina said, nodding. "We tell the jury Vittorio had a belt around my neck and was strangling me. I was gonna black out, but I was close to my gun, and I shot him. That probably could work."

I nodded. "It could work. Vittorio was shot at close range, your fingerprints are on the gun, because it's your gun, and there is a record of abuse. There's also a record of rape – don't forget, we can question the cops who questioned Vittorio after Coretta turned him into the cops. Well, didn't turn Vittorio in, but you know what I mean. It could work."

I sighed. What was I getting myself into?

Chapter Seventeen

THE ARRAIGNMENT WAS SCHEDULED for the next day and I went to that with Gina. As Harper had indicated before, the case was assigned to Division 33, Judge Reiner. That meant it would be put on the rocket docket and the case would be tried within a matter of months. I also told Ally of my plan to use the justification of self-defense for Gina.

"Self-defense, huh?" Ally said when I cornered her after the arraignment to tell her of my plans. "Why is this the first I'm hearing about self-defense?"

"I wasn't required to disclose any affirmative defenses before this date," I said. "I'm disclosing it now."

"Why didn't she tell the cops she killed him out of self-defense?"

"She didn't tell the cops anything. She asked for a lawyer right away."

"Okay, then," Ally said. "Self-defense." She looked at me for a few minutes. "Anything else you need to tell me?"

"No, not at the moment." I hesitated. It looked like Ally wanted me to say something more to her. I think I knew what it was. "Listen, Ally..."

"I hear you're getting back with your ex-wife," she said, tears in her eyes. "That's what I hear."

"Who told you that?"

"Somebody in my office. I won't tell you who. But that person saw you and your ex-wife out at dinner one night with your kids."

Was I going to lie again? It worried me that I was finding lying for Gina easier and easier as time went on. I just came right out and told Ally I would plead self-defense for Gina and I didn't even hesitate. I just came right out with it. Could I lie to her about Sarah? I could certainly try to claim we were out with Nate and Amelia just because we were trying to be good co-parents. That might placate her enough that she didn't hate me for the rest of this trial.

No, I decided it was better just to tell her the truth. "Ally, Sarah and I aren't getting back together. Yet. We're in marriage counseling, though, and we're seeing each other once a week. With the kids. I can't trust her after all she has done to me. But I'm not going to say definitively we won't get back together eventually, either. The divorce is on hold at the moment, although the papers are ready to go. I have to do all I can to try to make it work with her. I owe the kids that much. I owe me that much, too." I took a deep breath. "I'm sorry. I should have told you."

"Yeah, you should have," Ally said, shaking her head. "So, all that bullshit about spending more time with your kids, that was all just crap, then?"

"No, I mean, that was the truth, too, I guess. You have to understand that I do need to spend time with my kids and I couldn't bring you around them. I was raised by a

The Alibi

woman with a revolving door of men coming in and out of the house all the time, and that kind of thing is very unstable for a kid. I couldn't bring you around them, so-"

"But you don't mind spending time with Sarah."

"That's different. She's their mother, so I spend time with her and my kids at the same time. I couldn't do that with you. So, yeah, it wasn't a total lie I told you. It just wasn't the whole truth."

"I guess I should have expected to be treated like that by you. After all, you're an ex-con."

The fact that I had served time in prison was well-known in the Public Defender's Office. After all, my attorney in that office, Colleen Sutton, was still working there when I got a job with the PD's Office. I knew, then, that the prosecutors probably also knew my story. I wasn't surprised that Ally knew, but I was somewhat surprised she kept from me that she knew.

"I'm not an ex-con," I said.

"Maybe not. But you were in prison. You learned to lie in prison, I'm sure. That's what you gotta do in prison to survive. Don't think I don't know that. So, yeah, I should've known you would find lying as easy for you as breathing. I just hoped you would be different. I guess you really weren't after all."

Her words stung me. Was she right? Was that why I was finding it so "easy" to lie about Gina? Was I really, in the end, no different from my clients who lie to me? Here I was, so up in arms about Gina lying to me, so angry about it, when, in reality, she wasn't all that different from me. When it suited me, I would lie. When my back was up against the wall, I would lie. I lied to Ally about Sarah and I was going to lie to the court about Gina.

I really was no better than my criminal clients. I always thought I had the moral high ground, but did I really?

"Don't judge me by my record," I said. "Listen, you now know what our affirmative defense will be. You can proceed on that basis."

"Okay. I will proceed on that basis. And I'm going to prove to the court your defense is bullshit. Your client killed her husband in cold blood and I think we all know why she did it. This will be one of my easiest cases to win."

"I wouldn't count on that. Vittorio was a violent man. He beat on my client and she called the cops on him twice. Vittorio also was raping women. One of the women he raped went to the cops and the cops questioned him about it. They didn't arrest him, though, probably because they didn't have the chance. He was killed only days after he was questioned about raping Coretta Taylor. We have plenty of evidence to show his violent propensity. So, yeah, keep thinking this will be a slam-dunk for you. A cake walk. I think it'll be harder than you think to convince the jury that my client killed Vittorio in cold blood for no good reason."

"No good reason? Are you serious? You don't think the fact that your client had a boyfriend in prison, a boyfriend she told witnesses she would marry, had anything to do with it? You don't think the fact that Vittorio was worth more dead than alive had anything to do with it? You're incredibly naïve."

I straightened my back and looked her in the eye. I had no clue Gina was interested in marrying Joey Caruso. Nor did I have a clue about how Vittorio was worth more dead than alive. I didn't even know what Ally was talking about when she said that.

"You think what you want and I'll think what I want. I

have my story, and you have yours. We'll see who the jury believes."

"Yeah, we'll see alright. Look, your client apparently needed money. I know all about Joey Caruso and his son Antonio and Antonio's problems. I know all about how Antonio's life is in danger from some mobsters he stiffed. So, what happens? Vittorio ends up dead. I'm sorry, but if your client is telling you she killed Vittorio in self-defense, she's lying. Plain and simple."

We got to the elevator and I turned to her. "I won't try this case in the hallway. I gave you the notice about my affirmative defense, and that's all I'm going to give you for now. If you need anything more from me, make a formal discovery request, as usual."

"And you do the same. Now, if you will excuse me, I'm going to take the stairs. I need the exercise." At that, she walked down the hall and disappeared through the doorway that went to the stairwell.

Vittorio is worth more dead than alive. I obviously was missing something. I would have to ask Gina about that.

IN THE MEANTIME, I had to continue my search for the perfect attorney to take on my mold clients. And then I would have to tell them, one by one, I wouldn't be their attorney after all. That broke me.

I had assigned Heather the job of finding another attorney, and she had called me a few times to tell me she was looking high and low.

"It's hard," she said. "Most of those big firms are too goddamn big, you know? Your clients will be just a number to them. I've interviewed a few of those attorneys, and I don't think they're quite right."

My luck changed that evening, however, when I was driving home. I called Heather and she informed me she had found just the right attorney for the case.

"Her name is Patricia Pence. She was a partner with one of the mid-sized personal injury firms in town. She's now in a smaller partnership with a couple of other attorneys in the River Market. I told her about the case, she's done her own investigation, and she just called me today to tell me she wants it. I like her, too, Dami. She's a social justice warrior, very smart, and she's outraged about what happened. She's really angry with Robert Davis, especially when she found out why Davis got involved with those properties in the first place. Did you know he just bought those apartment buildings because he thought some large investors wanted that land, and he wanted to buy before those other investors made a bid?"

"Oh? No, I didn't know that." Again, I was lying, but I couldn't betray Gina's confidence. She told me about why Robert Davis wanted the property in confidence. I was already committing so many ethical violations, I would be lucky if I had a license to practice law next year if this all went sideways. "But that makes sense. It makes sense that a greedy bastard like that would buy property he had no interest in, just so he could sell it for an inflated price to a large firm."

"Yeah. So, anyhow, Patricia is angry about all of that. I think she'll be a fighter, but I also think that she'll treat those people like they matter. Just like you say – they have to matter. She'll make them matter."

"Well, good." I sighed. "I'll meet with her and maybe

we'll meet with the mold clients together. They'll know they're in good hands. That's what's most important."

AND THAT'S what Patricia and I did for the next few days. We went to the apartments of the mold clients and spoke with them, reassuring them that Patricia would go to the mat for them. I felt better when it was all said and done, because Patricia won them over. I was also happy that most were in their new apartments and were already feeling better.

"I'm feeling 100%," Mercury said, "and my boyfriend is back with me. I finally got tested for AIDS and HIV, and I'm not positive. When I got those test results back, I got Michael back too."

Juanita informed me that her two boys, Marcus and Jamal, were also feeling much better, although their symptoms were lingering a bit. "The doctors are treating them, though, and they're getting stronger every day. I can't thank you enough."

Candace Kaine told me she was back to work dancing at the club and was hopeful for the first time in a long time. "I was desperate and on my ass," she said. "Now I'm not, thanks to you."

Aurelia could never be made whole – she lost her son, Manuel, and there was no bringing him back. But she was relieved she was out of that apartment, and so was Enrique.

Mariana and Josh also were feeling better and were much happier than when I saw them.

In all, I knew I did good for these people. I got them a doctor, I got them a new apartment and, because of that, they had a new lease on life. Plus, I liked Patricia. As Heather said, she was a fighter and was outraged by what had happened to those people. She was excited to get into this case, and she thanked me profusely for bringing it to her.

While I was happy things were working out on that end, I was sad I couldn't see it through. But it was what it was. I couldn't stay on their cases as long as Gina was my client.

And Gina would be my client until her trial.

Unfortunately.

Chapter Eighteen

May 13 - The Day of the Trial

"HERE WE GO," I said to Gina. She met me in front of the courthouse, looking extremely nervous. "Don't worry. I got this."

I did have it, too. At least, I thought I did. I had witnesses lined up that would testify about what kind of person Vittorio was in life. I had the police reports regarding the incidents where Vittorio beat on Gina. I had the prosecutor's witness list, and I was ready for all of them.

The only problem was I couldn't bring Harper in on this. She had offered to help. She even offered to second-chair. I had to keep a distance from her on this case, though. I didn't tell her why. I just told her I would have to try this case on my own and prepare it on my own. There were no brainstorming sessions with her, no war room strategy meetings. There was only me and my client doing our usual pre-trial prep.

Harper repeatedly asked me why I didn't want her help,

and I didn't know what to tell her. She eventually stopped asking.

We got into the courtroom, and Ally was already there with her second chair, Sheldon Hatch. The judge was also already on the bench. He was early, for once.

"Counselor," he said when I walked in. "Good to see you. I see your client is here, too. I was just asking Ms. Hughes if there was any pre-trial motions I need to listen to. She said she had none, and she thought you probably would have none, either. I hope she's right about that."

"No, your honor," I said. "We're ready to go and there's not anything I need to hash out before trial."

"I understand you're going for self-defense," he said. "I wish you luck on that." He chuckled. "The last few self-defense cases I've tried didn't go so well. One of them was your partner, Harper. Boy, that was heading for a mess, but she pulled it out at the last second. You should ask her about that."

I nodded, thinking that asking Harper about her self-defense case would make her curious about why I was asking about it. I couldn't tell her the truth, so I just didn't go there.

"Yeah, I should," I said to Judge Reiner.

"Well, I guess we're ready to bring in the jury panel," he said. "You guys ready for this?"

"We are, your honor," Ally said.

"Okay, then," Judge Reiner said, and then he nodded to the bailiff. In a matter of minutes, the first batch of potential jurors came through the door. They took a seat in rows of chairs behind the barrier between the lawyers and the audience.

I knew exactly what I was looking for in my jury. I was looking for at least one woman unhappily married to a

The Alibi

violent man. Perhaps this woman had fantasies about killing her own husband. I was a good student of human nature, and I could see beyond the façade. I was also looking for other unhappily married women. Maybe their husband wasn't violent, but perhaps they were simply trapped in a loveless marriage. In short, I wanted women who would see my client and know what she was going through. They could feel the pain she felt in living with a man who would beat on her regularly.

That was what I was looking for in a juror. I knew the power of just one juror who felt passionately about an issue – they could turn everything around. Even if the others wanted to find my client guilty, just one passionate, articulate and persuasive juror could be the person changing everybody's minds.

I just had to get beyond the guilt I was feeling about using this defense and really lean into it. That was the only way this gambit would work.

Ally went through her *voir dire* of the jury. She asked the usual questions – did anybody know the defendant, had anybody read about the defendant's case on-line or in the paper, did anybody know her or me, had anybody been a victim of a crime, etc. After she asked each of her questions, if somebody raised their hand, she followed up and asked them if they could still judge the case on its merits and without prejudice. Everybody answered yes, so she was finished with her questions.

I stood up and walked over to the panel. "You heard all the questions that Ms. Hughes asked you," I said. "And you all answered you could set aside any kinds of emotions and misgivings and judge this case on its merits. I appreciate your responses." I paced around a bit. "I have a few more questions to ask. You're going to hear a story about a marriage that has gone horribly, horribly wrong. I would like to know, with a show of hands, who can relate to this scenario? Perhaps some of you have had physical, violent fights with your significant other. Maybe some of you are in the middle of a divorce. If you don't feel comfortable talking about this issue in front of everyone else, that's fine. I can meet with you during the break, and you can tell me about it in private."

Nobody raised their hands, but I saw a couple of women look like they wanted to speak with me. I figured I probably would be speaking with some of them during the break, just like I asked them to do.

The next question was similar to the first, but, because it dealt with somebody they knew, not themselves, I figured I might get some more open responses. "Does anybody here know of somebody who might be in the middle of an abusive situation?"

A man raised his hand.

"Yes," I said, pointing to him.

"My sister is being abused by her husband," he said. "She's in a battered woman's shelter right now."

"Can you judge the case on its merits and not let your sister's predicament prejudice you?"

"Yes," he said, solemnly. "I can."

Several more women raised their hands, and told their stories. They all said that they could judge the case on the merits, and I made a mental note of each of them. I wanted all of them on the jury. I knew I would get at least some of them, as there wasn't a reason to strike any of them for cause. Ally would probably use her peremptory challenge on some of them, and I was prepared for that. But if I could just get a few of these people, I would be in decent shape.

The Alibi

I asked several more questions, and then it was time to dismiss this batch and call in the next. During the break, I talked to women who confided in me that they were in an abusive relationship, and some women who said they had been in an abusive relationship in the past.

Several more hours later, after Ally and I dickered over this person or that, we had our panel. I was satisfied, because I sat three of the women who had either been in an abusive relationship in the past or were in one right now. I knew they would all be sympathetic to my client, so that was a good thing.

The other good thing was that the trial wouldn't be terribly long. Because I had decided I wanted to try for self-defense, Ally and I agreed, in our first pre-trial conference, to stipulate to certain facts. One was that my client killed Vittorio. That meant there wasn't a need to put on evidence regarding the ballistics and fingerprints and all of that. There wasn't a need to present evidence from the crime scene, either, although I knew the prosecutor would anyhow. Ally would go for the gruesome, because that was one way to stir the emotions of the jury – show the dead body. Blow it up, show the blood, show the victim's face looking lifeless and still. I would not object to Ally showing the crime scene photos, even though they weren't relevant in this case, and they contributed little to the case except inflammation of the jury.

And really, if you think about it, crime scene photos really don't add anything to most juries' understanding to what happened in any given crime and who did it. Unless you have an expert on the stand testifying that the killer was left or right-handed, I never did see exactly why it was so necessary to show every gruesome blood splatter to the jury. I consequently always saw the massive blow-up pictures of people splattered in blood to be prejudicial and not at all probative, but, unfortunately, prosecutors had the right to show these pictures. It didn't mean I had to like it, however.

I also found out exactly what Ally meant when she told me Vittorio was worth more dead than alive, and when I found out what she meant, I almost killed Gina for withholding that piece of information from me. Garrett found it out and told me about it.

Apparently, a mobster by the name of Francesco Veraldi was offering a $1 million bounty on Vittorio's head. Vittorio was working as a spy for the Colombo crime syndicate, which was one of the largest crime syndicates in the area. He apparently had moved up in the ranks of the syndicate, even as he was still posing as a low-level soldier and two-bit gangster. He managed to infiltrate the Veraldi family and was giving information to the Colombo family. Because of this, Francesco Veraldi offered a bounty to anybody who would kill Vittorio or bring Vittorio into Francesco so Francesco could take care of him personally.

This was all top secret, which was why Tom Garrett missed it at first. But he eventually found it. The only reason why Ally knew about this entire arrangement was because she had been working with another mobster who told her about what went down. She learned about the bounty and would use this information against Gina.

What upset me was I thought Gina had to have known about the bounty arrangement herself. After all, Gina was desperate for money. Maybe she killed Vittorio after all. It was only after I did a thorough review of her financial statements that I was satisfied she didn't get the bounty money from Francesco.

Nevertheless, Ally would use this whole scenario against Gina. One of her witnesses was the guy who told her about

The Alibi

the arrangement. From what I understood, this guy was heavily guarded and would go into the witness protection program as soon as the trial was over.

Ally had her theory of the case, and I had mine. Mine wasn't the truth, and hers wasn't either. We both would present a theory to the jury that just wasn't true.

I was also slightly pissed when I found out about the bounty situation because, if I would have known about it, I would have used that information to present Francesco as the alternative suspect in the case. I had a problem presenting one of the women he raped as an alternative suspect, because the last thing I wanted to do was bring suspicion against an innocent woman. Especially since I knew for a fact that all of the women Vittorio raped were innocent.

But it would be much less of an issue to throw a mobster under the bus, even if I knew that the mobster didn't do it. After all, he *wanted* to kill Vittorio. In this case, it would be like that old law school scenario, where a guy comes into a room and stabs a guy who was already dead. Yeah, that guy isn't guilty of murder, because the victim was already dead, but he had sufficient *mens rea* for murder, so maybe there should be some kind of punishment for him.

But I had already explained to Ally that we were trying for self-defense, so I couldn't take that back. The horse had already left the barn, and I didn't get the chance to really investigate whether it would be worthwhile to try to pin the murder on Francesco.

Then again, perhaps it was all for the best. I really didn't want to get involved with pinning a murder on a mobster. That would be dangerous, to say the very least.

The judge dismissed the new jury panel for a short

break. "Be back here at 3 PM," he said to everyone. "And we'll begin the trial with opening statements."

THE JURY CAME BACK, and the trial began.

"Ladies and gentlemen of the jury," Ally said to the men and women who were sitting in the jury box, each of them focused on her with rapt attention. I knew that attention would soon fade when the boring parts of the case came to light, but, for now, she had their full focus. "Thank you very much for your service. I know that each and every one of you have a life outside of this courtroom, and you are making a sacrifice by serving on this panel. I don't ever want you to think I take any one of you for granted."

She took a deep breath and paced back and forth in front of the panel. "You are here today because a man is dead. His name was Vittorio Degrazio and his wife, Gina Degrazio, killed him in cold blood. In cold blood." She nodded and looked each person in the eye. "In cold blood. She didn't have a justification for killing him, no excuse. No, actually, she killed him for one reason – greed, plain and simple. It's a story as old as time, the story of a wife killing her husband for money, but that's exactly what she did. The evidence will prove this, ladies and gentlemen. Here, exactly, is what the evidence will show."

"One, the evidence will show that Vittorio Degrazio was a petty mobster, two-bit, really, until he got a chance to run with the big boys. Specifically, he finally got an assignment from his boss, Vincenzo Colombo, that he could sink his teeth into. Something that would finally catapult him from the low-level shake-down activities he was doing for his organization to a promotion up the food chain of the

The Alibi

Colombo crime family. He was assigned to spy on another crime organization, which was headed up by one Francesco Veraldi. He infiltrated this organization and was caught doing it. That means he was a marked man."

"Francesco Veraldi put a bounty on Vittorio Degrazio's head, ladies and gentlemen, offering a $1 million reward for anybody who could capture Vittorio, dead or alive. That's how much Vittorio was worth to Francesco. And that, ladies and gentlemen, is why Gina Degrazio killed her husband. She killed him because she needed that money. She needed that money because she, herself, was in debt to yet another mobster, Joey Caruso. Joey Caruso needed Gina to pay him back for what she owed him, and he needed that money as soon as possible. I will carefully lay out all the evidence about this complicated arrangement, and you will see that Gina Degrazio killed Vittorio for the money."

"Now, the defense will try to show you that Gina killed Vittorio for another reason. Mr. Harrington, the counselor for the defendant, will try to tell you that Vittorio was trying to kill Gina and that Gina shot him in self-defense. But the evidence will show she didn't tell the officers that when they brought her in for questioning." Ally shook her head. "No, nothing was said to the officers about being in fear for her life or any of that. Instead, she just clammed up and asked for a lawyer. I'll let you draw your own conclusions about that."

I rolled my eyes when Ally started insinuating that Gina must not have had a self-defense claim just because she didn't tell the cops she feared for her life. Gina was simply reacting how I wished all my clients would – she didn't say a word to the arresting officers. Not a word. Thank God for that, because if she would have talked, I would have been sunk. I couldn't have used the self-defense justification.

"And Gina will tell you that Vittorio was strangling her with a belt at the time she shot him. I'll show you her mug shot, ladies and gentlemen, and there wasn't a mark on her neck."

I had that covered, too. After all, Vittorio had been dead for several days by the time he had been found. *Of course* there wouldn't still be marks on her neck when she was brought in for questioning. That was stupid reasoning on Ally's part.

"And here's another thing, ladies and gentlemen. Vittorio had been dead for several days when he was found. Several days. Now, if Gina Degrazio really had killed her husband in self-defense, don't you think she would have gone to the police immediately and told them what had happened? That's what I would have done if I killed my husband in self-defense. I certainly wouldn't have hid out in the house of the identical twin brother of the victim and waited for the police to come and pick me up. No, ladies and gentlemen, the actions of Gina Degrazio after the murder of her husband were not the actions of an innocent woman. They weren't the actions of a woman who killed a man in self-defense. They were the actions of a woman who killed her own husband for the money. For this reason, I would ask you find Gina Degrazio guilty of first degree murder at the close of this trial. Thank you very much."

She sat down, and I stood up and went over to the jury box. "Ladies and gentlemen of the jury, I, too, thank you for your service. Your service is vital to the justice institution, and that cannot be stressed enough. Now, I will admit that Vittorio Degrazio is dead. I will admit that my client, Gina Degrazio killed him. That much is not in dispute. What is in dispute is *why* she killed him."

"You see, under the law, there is a concept known as

The Alibi

justifiable homicide. Justifiable homicide generally is used in cases of self-defense or defense of others. In other words, if somebody is threatening your life or the life of somebody else, you may kill that person. You may kill that person, and, if you do kill that person, you cannot be punished for doing so. It's his life or your life, in other words."

"And that is what happened here. Vittorio Degrazio was a violent man. You heard Ms. Hughes, the prosecutor – Vittorio was a mobster. He was somebody whose job literally was beating people up for a living. He went after people who owed money to the Colombo family and beat them up. That's what he did. Plus, the evidence will show that Vittorio was a serial rapist. You will hear the testimony of two different women who Vittorio raped. Finally, Vittorio and my client, Gina Degrazio, had a violent relationship. Gina called the police on three separate occasions because Vittorio was beating her up. In all three of these situations, no charges were filed, but I can still show you a record of the disturbances."

"Now, with all of this evidence, I ask you if it's really such a stretch to believe that Vittorio was strangling Gina at the time she killed him? No, ladies and gentlemen, it would not be a stretch. It wouldn't be a stretch at all."

"You heard Ms. Hughes. You heard her question why Gina didn't have belt marks around her neck at the time she was arrested. Ladies and gentlemen, Vittorio had been dead for three days at the time he was found. Three days. Of course there wasn't a mark on her neck. Of course. And, in case you might think that Gina would still have marks on her neck three days after almost being strangled, I have an expert to testify that is not the case. My expert will testify that marks made by a belt wrapped around somebody's neck would be gone within 24 hours at the most."

"Then Ms. Hughes questioned why Gina just didn't tell the cops she was defending herself when she shot Vittorio. Well, all I can say is that Gina was doing what she was trained to do, and that was to not speak to the police unless she had a lawyer. Then, she got a lawyer to come to her interrogation, and that lawyer told her not to speak at all. That is always sound advice, ladies and gentlemen – never speak to the police until you've had the chance to have your case thoroughly evaluated by an attorney. Gina was just being smart when she chose not to speak to the police."

"Finally, Ms. Hughes questioned why Gina would have hidden out at Vittorio's brother's house instead of going to the police about what she had done. That, too, is easily explainable – she was scared. Terrified. In shock. She didn't know what to do, where to turn. So, she was paralyzed. Listen, she's only human. Only human. Not everybody will react the way Ms. Hughes would like. Not everybody will do the right thing after a homicide. Many people would react just like Gina, because, after all, a man is dead and she killed him. That's enough to intimidate anyone into running and hiding and hoping that maybe it would all just blow over."

"So, in short, ladies and gentlemen, there is plenty of evidence, plenty of evidence, to show my client killed Mr. Degrazio in self-defense. Because my client was justified, under the law, in killing her husband, I ask for a finding of not guilty. Thank you very much."

I sat down, and Judge Reiner looked at the clock. "Alright, ladies and gentlemen. As you can all plainly see, it is 4:45 PM. That means it's quitting time. You all are excused for the evening, but be back here tomorrow at 9 AM sharp, and I mean sharp. I won't tolerate tardiness in my courtroom." Then he smiled, to show he wasn't that much of a hard-ass. "Thank you very much, and I'll be seeing all of you tomorrow morning."

They filed out, and I went over to Ally. There was one thing I wanted to ask her. She didn't include this person's testimony as a preview in her opening statement, so I didn't know if she would still call him.

"Tomorrow," I said, "are you still planning on calling Enzo Degrazio?"

Chapter Nineteen

I HAD an unpleasant surprise ten days before the trial when I got Ally's witness list. I saw that Enzo would be one of her witnesses. That pissed me off to no end, and it made me almost wish I didn't promise Gina I wouldn't finger him for the murder. I told Gina he would be a problem. He wanted that $3 million he gave to Gina, and he knew that, if she was convicted, he would get that money back. So it was clearly in his interest to make sure Gina was convicted.

That meant he would get on the stand and lie.

Sure enough, when I brought him into my office to talk to him, I found out what he would say. And there wasn't a thing I could do about it, except prepare to cross-examine him and bring him down hard.

Now, I was trying to find out if Ally was, indeed, going to call Enzo as a witness. If she did, that was the one thing that might send Gina to jail. The dominoes would fall from there.

"Of course, I'm going to call him," she said. "He's my star witness."

The Alibi

How ironic the person you call a star witness is actually the killer. I guessed this wasn't the first time the actual killer ended up testifying against the accused, but this might be the first time the defense attorney knew this fact going in.

I shook my head. "Call him," I said. "You'll find out he's unreliable, at best."

"Whatever."

Whatever, indeed. "Okay," I said. "I guess that's the way you want to play it," I said.

"What do you mean? I have a witness who is going to testify against your client and I'm going to use him."

"You'll find out." At that, I just walked away. I knew how I would handle Enzo on the stand. The problem was, I had to not go too far. I couldn't press him too much, because I didn't want him to end up looking like a suspect. Enzo was to be handled with kid gloves, as he was the linchpin for all of the financial shenanigans going on. The last thing I wanted to do was piss off Enzo, so he offs Gina, which would mean Joey Caruso wouldn't get his money, and then Nick would be the ultimate victim.

That, in the end, was my ultimate worry – Nick's future hinged on whether or not I could somehow, someway, help Gina beat down her murder charge without implicating Enzo in the process.

THAT NIGHT, I decided to relax with the kids and Sarah. Sarah was coming over at 6 to fix dinner for us, and I actually was looking forward to it a tiny bit. Sarah and I had become friends over the past few months, nothing more than that. Our marriage counseling was helping to bring us closer together, however. The therapist managed to get beneath the layers and find out what was really driving her abhorrent behavior when Amelia was sick.

At the core was profound fear. I never learned how devastated she was when her brother Noah died all those years ago. She opened up about what had happened to her family after that happened.

"My parents became people I didn't recognize anymore. My mother was angry all the time, when, before Noah died, she was the most patient and sweet woman I had ever met. My father was dead before Noah died, dead from a suicide. I didn't have them to lean on when I needed them the most and I was dying inside. I started to fail in school, started to run with the druggie crowd, started losing a lot of weight. Mom never even noticed. It was like I was invisible. Noah was dead and I was a ghost. It was the worst period of my entire life." She took a deep breath. "Until I found out that Amelia was sick. I thought I put that whole thing behind me – Noah, my parents, my troubled past. But I guess I didn't. I couldn't handle Amelia's sickness. I just couldn't handle it."

Little by little, Sarah and I were becoming fixed.

So, I was looking forward to her coming to the house that evening after the trial.

She showed up with a bag full of groceries and she kissed me on the cheek as the walked through the door. "Hey, Damien," she said. "I'm making sour cream chicken. It's a James Beard recipe. I went to the store and got free-range chicken, sour cream, paprika, onions and chicken stock. I'm going to serve it with new potatoes and asparagus."

"Sounds great," I said. "Nate, Amelia, your mom is here," I called them. They were both in their bedrooms with their doors shut.

Amelia poked her head out. "Hello, Sarah," she said,

The Alibi

and then ducked her head back in. Amelia had not yet forgiven her mother and I didn't really blame her. She was a child. She couldn't understand why her mother abandoned her when she was sick. My only hope was she would someday understand and forgive Sarah, but that seemed a long way off.

Nate, for his part, was still quite close to his mother. He came down the stairs and gave Sarah a hug. "Hi Mom," he said. "Dad said you were coming over and making dinner with us."

"I am," Sarah said, holding Nate close. "And we're going to find a show on HBO or Netflix we can all watch together."

I followed Sarah into the kitchen and put on an apron as I sharpened my knives. I chopped up an onion rapidly and then chopped up some other vegetables we would have in our salad.

"I always admired you for your chopping ability," Sarah said with a laugh. "I never could figure out where you learned to chop like a pro."

"Oh, I watched my share of cooking shows," I said as I put the onions into a hot skillet. "I'm a guy, but I've always wanted to cook for myself, so I learned how. Plus, I knew that chicks really dig guys who cook."

Sarah laughed as she wrapped her arms around my waist. "I don't know about chicks in general, but I know I really dig at least one guy who cooks."

I was starting to respond to her flirtatious moves. When I first started hanging out with her, I wouldn't respond at all. When she would put her hand on my knee, I would remove it. When she would wrap her arms around me, I wouldn't do the same with her. But, lately, I was warming to her.

I turned around, a spoon in my hand, and let her taste the sauce I was making.

"Mmmmm, delicious," she said, "but I was supposed to make dinner, not you. How did you start chopping and cooking and not me?"

"I like to help," I said.

"Well, move over," she said, "I'm going to take over."

She brought the chicken out of the package and put it in the pan with the onions, garlic and oil.

"So," she said, "how did it go today?"

"Okay, I guess. We picked a jury. I got several women on the panel I think might be sympathetic to our defense."

"You're going with self-defense, right?"

"Right," I said. "I mean, it was self-defense." I didn't tell Sarah the truth about Gina's case. I figured I still didn't entirely trust her, and, if something happened, and Sarah and I ended up not getting back together, I didn't want to give her something to hold over my head. I could just imagine telling her the truth, and her going to the Bar and telling them what I did. She would probably do that if I pissed her off enough. "But let's not talk about that tonight. I would like to leave the stress of my trial at the courthouse and not bring it home."

"Point taken." She looked toward Amelia's bedroom. "Is Amelia ever going to stop hating me?"

"I don't know," I said. "I mean, I do know. I think she will. But you have to understand, she's very hurt. She knows you wanted her to die. I mean, I know you didn't want her to die, you wanted her to stop suffering, but she's six. She doesn't know the difference. So, for the time being, she's hurt. She'll come around."

"Maybe we can do some family counseling," Sarah said. "Do you think that would help?"

The Alibi

"I think it would," I said. "It certainly couldn't hurt."

"How is she?" Sarah asked. "I've been talking to her doctors, and they all tell me that she's out of the woods for now. She's in remission. Do you think that's true? Do you think she'll beat this thing?"

"I do. I do. Of course, we can't declare that she's cured until she's cancer free for five years, so we have a long way to go, really. But, for now, it seems like that bone marrow transplant might have done the trick. Her body hasn't rejected it and it seems like this new bone marrow is doing what it's supposed to – help her body fight off the cancer. My fingers are crossed, and, even though I'm not a religious man, I have been praying for her lately."

THAT NIGHT, we ate our dinner and found a movie to watch. Sarah and I sat on the couch together under a blanket, just like we used to, and the kids sat on the floor. It was nice, just like old times, and I almost forgot I was in the middle of a trial. Not just any trial, but a trial with enormous consequences for the best friend I ever had.

I almost forgot about my trial.

Almost.

Chapter Twenty

THE NEXT DAY, it was time to face the music. Ally had her witnesses lined up, and she would be extremely aggressive in showing that Gina killed Vittorio in cold blood. I knew that and was prepared for it. Even so, I knew that breaking down her witnesses wouldn't be easy. Nothing in this job was ever easy, and this trial would be no different.

The first witness she called was Officer Hanley. He was the officer who interrogated Gina at the station, therefore he was the most relevant police officer that Gina would call.

Officer Hanley approached the bench. He was a younger guy, 30-something, with short brown hair and a stiff way of walking. He was tall and imposing and spoke in a baritone voice.

I knew why Officer Hanley was brought in to question Gina – he was the guy that the force brought in for a lot of women, because he had a certain amount of charm with them. He usually played the role of the "good cop," the guy who is polite, sincere and soft-spoken. The guy who would say things like "ma'am, just tell us the truth. Tell us the

The Alibi

truth, and I promise you, I'll go to the prosecutor and ask her to go easy on you." That was the kind of cop he was.

I wondered if Ally would also call Officer Hanley's interrogation partner, Officer Maddox. Officer Maddox played the part of the "bad cop." Where Officer Hanley would be all sweet and polite and accommodating, Officer Maddox would come in and threaten, bully and get belligerent. They were quite the team, those two, and, together, they knew how to break down most witnesses.

But they didn't break down Gina.

Officer Hanley was sworn in and he sat down.

"Could you please state your name for the record," Ally said.

"Officer John Hanley," he said.

"And Officer Hanley, you are currently a police officer on the Kansas City Police Department, is that right?"

"Right." He nodded his head.

"And Officer Hanley, did you get the chance to question a woman by the name of Gina Degrazio?"

"Yes."

"Why did you question her?"

"She was brought into the station after the murder of her husband, Vittorio Degrazio."

"Was she under arrest at the time you spoke with her?"

"Yes."

"Was she informed she was under arrest at the time you spoke with her?"

"Yes. She was read her Miranda Rights and was informed by the officer who picked her up at her house that she was under arrest for Mr. Degrazio's murder."

"I see." Ally nodded her head. "So, she was brought into the station and you and Officer Maddox questioned her. What was her demeanor when she was brought in?"

"Calm. She didn't try to fight with me, didn't try to engage me in conversation. She simply said she wanted an attorney from the second she was brought into the interrogation room."

"So, she didn't try to tell you that Mr. Degrazio was threatening her or she feared for her life or any of that, right?"

"Right. She didn't say any of that. She just said she wanted an attorney and we stopped questioning her right away."

"Now, you've been a police officer for the force for how many years?"

"I'm a 15-year veteran," he said. "I joined the force when I was 21."

"And how many years have you been doing interrogation work?"

"For five years, ma'am."

"And how many interrogations have you done over the years?"

"About 200."

"About 200." Ally nodded and put her hand on her chin, like she was thinking. "And how many times have you questioned a suspect and had them tell you they were protecting themselves when they killed the person you were questioning them about?"

"At least 20 times, ma'am."

"In your experience, have you ever encountered somebody who just wouldn't speak to you, and you later on found out that person had a self-defense claim?"

"No, ma'am. Not to my knowledge, no."

"So, every time you've interrogated somebody who ended up pleading self-defense, that person told you in your initial interrogation?"

The Alibi

"Yes, ma'am. To the best of my knowledge, that statement is true."

"So, is it unusual, to you, that Ms. Degrazio would now be sitting here, pleading self-defense, when she didn't say a word to you about killing Mr. Degrazio to save her life?"

"Yes, ma'am. I do think that is unusual."

"Because people who have killed in self-defense have always told you that was the case, right?"

"Right. To the best of my knowledge, that is correct."

"I have nothing further."

I stood up, knowing I could rip this guy's story to shreds, and I was anxious to do so.

"Officer Hanley," I began, "you just told Ms. Hughes you know of no case where you've questioned somebody on a murder, and that person had a self-defense claim, but didn't tell you about that from the beginning. Is that right?"

"Yes, that is what I testified."

"So, after you've interrogated somebody, you've followed them and their case right to the end, right?"

"Right."

"And you've done that 100% of the time?"

"Well, no, I guess I haven't."

"You mean there have been a few cases where you just lost track of what happened to the person after you interrogated them?"

"There have been a few, yes. I'm a very busy person, and I do many interrogations."

"In fact, the only times you followed a case from interrogation to the conclusion are the cases where you were called to testify, isn't that right?"

He nodded his head. "That's right."

"Which means you only keep track of what happens

with an accused person when the case goes to trial, isn't that right?"

"Generally, yes."

"So, how many cases did you actually track from start to finish, then, over the past five years?"

"I would say about 20 cases."

"So, you've interrogated approximately 200 witnesses over the years, yet you have only tracked about 10% of those cases from start to finish, then?"

"Well, I work with the prosecutors on every case I interrogate and charge. But I don't usually end up working the cases from start to finish, so I'm probably out of the loop with a lot of them."

"So, then, you don't really know if there were some accused individuals who didn't tell you their lives were being threatened at the time that they killed somebody, yet went on to have a self-defense claim anyhow, isn't that right?"

"Yes, I guess that's right."

I was satisfied I got the answer from Officer Hanley I was looking for, so I decided just to rest. "I have nothing further for this witness."

I sat down. "Counselor, do you have any redirect?" Judge Reiner asked Ally.

"Yes, your honor," she said, standing up and approaching Officer Hanley. "Officer Hanley, you indicated you work with the prosecutors on all the cases you interrogate, isn't that right?"

"Yes, that is correct. I work with all of them."

"I have nothing further."

"Mr. Harrington, any re-cross?"

"No, your honor." I figured I got out of him what I needed, and there wasn't a reason to go back in and keep on beating the point.

The Alibi

After Officer Hanley testified, Ally called her ballistics expert and the Medical Examiner, Dr. Prorock. There wasn't anything these witnesses testified to I found remotely relevant. After all, I had stipulated with Ally that Gina killed Vittorio. I didn't see what these people could tell the jury that was helpful. I didn't have any questions for these people for that reason alone.

Ally also showed the crime scene photos, and the Medical Examiner testified on what happened to Vittorio. She said Vittorio was shot once in the chest and this was a kill-shot. The bullet hit his heart and death was instantaneous. I didn't object to the photos, even if they were irrelevant, because they weren't all that gruesome. There really wasn't that much blood, because the bullet hit the heart and that meant there wasn't much bleeding.

It was her next witness I would have to break down mercilessly.

She called Enzo Degrazio to the stand.

Chapter Twenty-One

ENZO CAME IN THE DOOR, dressed in a leather jacket, jeans, and a t-shirt. He was wearing dark sunglasses, as if he thought he was the coolest person in the room. He was also wearing a hat, just like he was wearing when he came to my office to meet me.

He sat down at the witness stand, his stance just as casual as when he was in my office.

"Mr. Degrazio," Judge Reiner said, "could you please respect the court and remove your hat and your sunglasses?"

Enzo shrugged and took off his hat but didn't take off his sunglasses.

"Mr. Degrazio," Judge Reiner said, "please remove your sunglasses."

Enzo sighed and took off the shades. On his right eye was a large black shiner. That eye was also swollen shut. "Yeah, I don't look so pretty right now," he said, looking at the people in the jury. "I've had a rough couple of days."

The Alibi

The jury laughed lightly and Enzo smiled broadly. I could see he was having fun.

Have fun right now. You won't be after I get through with you.

"Can you please state your name for the record," Ally said after Enzo was sworn in.

"Enzo Degrazio, man," he said. "I'm the brother of the late, great Vittorio Degrazio, may he rest in peace." He crossed his chest and took out his cross necklace and kissed it. "Sorry, I just miss my twin brother so much."

I had to suppress laughter at his acting job. I wasn't fooled by him, and I hoped nobody else was, either.

"Enzo Degrazio. As you said, you're the brother of Vittorio Degrazio, isn't that right?"

"Yeah, that's right. That's what I just said, isn't it?"

"That is. Now, are you familiar with Gina Degrazio?"

"Yeah, man, I know her. She stayed with me after she murdered my brother."

"She stayed with you after she murdered Vittorio Degrazio?"

"Yeah. I didn't know she had killed him at the time, man, she just came to my house and told me she wanted to get away from him. She said they were having fights, but my brother had always told me she started all their fights."

"Okay, back up a bit. Now, you just said your brother and Gina got into fights habitually?"

"Yeah, man. They did, like, all the time."

"And that Gina was the one who started all the fights?"

"Yeah. My poor brother, he was abused by Gina. He was a good guy, a really good guy, but Gina ran all over him, man. She attacked him and hit him all the time. Came after him with a baseball bat, gave him a couple of good whacks all the time. Broke his knee more than once."

I suddenly realized the Medical Examiner was more

interesting to me. In fact, I would have to call him back to the stand and I would have to ask him if it was true that Vittorio had broken bones.

"Broke his knee more than once?"

"Yeah, man, broke his knee a few times. He was put into the hospital a few times."

I sighed. Vittorio had never been in the hospital. Tom Garrett did a thorough check and he didn't find that Vittorio had ever been in the hospital for anything. Which was surprising enough in itself, considering the guy was a mobster. The problem was, there wasn't a way to prove he had never been in the hospital. That would be proving a negative, which is always impossible to do.

That was another way of approaching this guy – get him to admit his brother was a mobster, and that would be an alternative explanation for Vittorio's injuries, assuming that Vittorio actually was hurt.

"To your knowledge, did Vittorio Degrazio ever beat on Gina Degrazio?"

"No, man. Not at all. My brother was a peaceable man, may he rest in peace." He crossed himself again and kissed his crucifix again. "I know he is looking down on me right now, man, and I still feel him in my heart. Right here." He made a fist and put it to his heart. "Right here, man. I carry him right here."

"Now, Gina Degrazio's claim is she had to kill Vittorio Degrazio because he was strangling her with a belt and she had to kill him, or else she would be dead. Do you believe that?"

"No, I don't believe that. Not for a second."

"And why don't you believe that?"

"Because Gina told me, man. She told me she was going to kill my brother. She told me she had found out that this

The Alibi

mobster, this Francesco Veraldi guy, was offering money for my brother's head, and she wanted in on that action. She owed this other mobster, this guy she was sleeping with, he's in the joint now, name's Joey Caruso, a million dollars and she had to pay up or else. So, she killed my brother to get the money to pay Joey. And that's what I know."

"I have nothing further."

I sighed loudly, signaling the jury how exasperated I was by having to cross-examine this tool.

"Mr Degrazio," I said, standing up. "Isn't it true you've been in prison yourself? In fact, haven't you been in prison many times before?"

"Yeah, I've been to the joint a time or two. Trumped up charges, man, I had to take the fall for some other guys who were the real criminals, not me."

"Which was it?"

"Which was what?"

"Well, you said two things. One, the charges were trumped up, and then you said you had to take the fall for the real criminals. So, were you in prison because the charges were trumped up or because you had to take the fall? Those are two different scenarios."

"Well, I was in the joint five years ago because I got caught burglarizing a restaurant, but I knew the guy, and I wasn't burglarizing nothing. I was there lawfully, and the guy actually gave me some artwork and lamps from the place, and then he called the cops on me. I didn't even get the chance to sell that stuff. I think I was set up with that one. Anyhow, I only served three months and I was out."

"Three months in jail or in prison?"

"Prison. The big house."

"So you went down for a felony and not a misdemeanor, right?"

"Right."

"And you were also in prison just two years ago, right?"

"Right. Again, I was only in for a few months, though, so it was no biggie."

"No biggie. Why were you in prison two years ago?"

"I was nailed for drug dealing, but I wasn't dealing. I got some drugs from some guy I didn't really know and I sold some to friends. I guess they weren't my friends after all, because I went to prison, even though the cops really wanted the guy who sold me the drugs in the first place. So, that was why I feel I was taking the fall for a bigger fish."

"And now you are-"

"I'm the proud owner of a restaurant downtown, man. Right in the middle of Power and Light – Enzo's." He smiled at the jury. "You all are invited to come on down and dine on some real Italian food, man. I got a little old Italian grandmother from the old country cooking for me." He put his fingers to his mouth and kissed them. "You won't get none better."

The jury laughed and Enzo laughed along with them.

I suddenly knew why this guy could charm those beautiful women and convince them to go home with him. That was one thing I was confused about, but, when he started talking, I stopped wondering. Women ate men like Enzo up.

"So, do you have any background in the restaurant business?"

"What, you mean, before I opened my restaurant?"

"Yeah, before you opened your restaurant."

"No, man. I mean, I've always been a mean cook. I've always made red sauce and meatballs that make women-" He smiled. "Well, you know, they tell me my food is better than sex, and I'll leave it at that."

The jury laughed again.

The Alibi

"So, you got out of prison, most recently in the past two years, and you haven't been in the restaurant business prior, yet you got a sweet spot downtown. Is that what you're telling the court?"

"That's what I'm saying."

"Mr. Degrazio, are you involved with the Italian mafia?"

He stared at me, unsmiling. "No. But your buddy Joey Caruso is, and he has it in for your buddy Nick, so you better watch your back." He raised an eyebrow and crossed his arms in front of him.

I didn't move to strike that as unresponsive. He was brushing me back.

I took the warning.

I turned my back to him and collected myself. I was burning close to the line, and I didn't want to go over it.

"Mr. Degrazio, I notice you have a black eye. Do you mind telling the court how you got that shiner?"

"That's none of your business and I don't have to answer that question." He looked pointedly at Ally, who stood up.

"Objection, relevance," she said.

"Counselor, what is the relevance of asking this witness about why he got that black eye?"

"I'm simply trying to establish his character," I said. "If he's some kind of a street brawler, that goes to his overall character. Since he's the prosecutor's star witness against my client, I feel I have a right to delve into as much of his background and character as possible."

Judge Reiner nodded. "I'll allow it. Mr. Degrazio, please answer the question."

I smiled. I had the feeling the judge was as curious about the black eye as I was.

Enzo's friendly banter and demeanor was gone. In its

place was the *other* Enzo. I could see it in his eyes and his body language. His eyes were narrowed and burning hatred. His body was suddenly closed – his arms were crossed and he was sitting up in his chair. His prior stance in his chair was leaning back, his right arm on the ledge above the table, his right foot crossed over his left knee. His stance now was completely different.

It was as if somebody had flipped a switch and he had turned into somebody else right before my eyes.

"I got it from a chick," he said. "She got pissed at me and hauled off and hit me."

I closed my eyes, suddenly realizing something. It was always at the back of my mind, but this shiner, and his story about a woman doing that to him, brought it to the fore – Enzo was still a sex offender. He was still out in the world, raping women. *That* was the consequences of the course I took in this case, when I decided to take Gina's advice and not pin the murder of Vittorio on the actual perpetrator, Enzo – a sex offender was still loose on the streets, and he would be for the time being. There was little I could do about it right at the moment, though. I had to get through this trial. Maybe after everything was said and done, I could find some way to make sure Enzo ended up where he belonged – behind bars. Hopefully for the rest of his life.

I paced back and forth. "Now, you testified Gina told you she killed your brother, is that correct?"

"Yeah, that's what I said. She told me that."

"And she told you she killed Vittorio because she wanted to collect the bounty that Francesco Veraldi had placed on Vittorio's head, is that right?"

"Yeah, that's right."

"But she never actually collected that money, did she?"

"I don't know, man. I only know she wanted to collect it. That's all I know."

"So, she never actually told you she collected that money, did she?"

"I don't know, man. I don't know."

"You didn't ask Francesco Veraldi if he paid up, did you?"

"No," he said, shrugging, and I suddenly knew that Francesco *did* pay up. He paid Enzo. I could tell it in his eyes.

"Are you and Gina close?"

"No, we're not."

"You're not. Yet, she told you some pretty intimate things, didn't she?"

"What do you mean by that?"

"She told you she killed your brother. That's a pretty private matter, isn't it?"

"Yeah, it is."

"Why would she tell you about it?"

"I don't know, man, you'll have to ask her that question."

"I will. I just want to make it clear what you're asking the court to believe. You're asking this court to believe that a woman who isn't close to you admitted she killed your brother for money. She told you this, yet she didn't disclose to you whether or not she actually collected that money. Is that what you're trying to say?"

"Yes, that's what I'm trying to say."

"And you didn't actually see her kill Vittorio, did you?"

"No, I didn't."

"Mr. Degrazio, were you aware that Vittorio and Gina had physical fights?"

"Yeah, I told that other lawyer that. I told her Gina beat up Vittorio pretty bad."

"Did you visit him in the hospital when Gina beat him up with a baseball bat?"

"Sure, I did."

"Would it surprise you to know that the autopsy of Vittorio did not show he had any previously broken bones?" I knew that to be true, and I would re-call the ME to testify to this.

"Yeah, that would surprise me." The cocky Enzo was back. "Look, man, I don't know for sure that Vittorio had broken bones and knees and shit like that. He just told me that. He might have been exaggerating."

"Exaggerating." I nodded my head. "What a great euphemism. You aren't exaggerating right now, you're lying, aren't you? Vittorio never had any broken bones, because Gina never attacked him with a baseball bat, did she?"

"I said I don't know."

"Oh, now you don't know. You sure seemed to know before, didn't you? You never said on the stand you didn't really know if Vittorio was beat up by Gina, you said he definitely was, didn't you?"

"Yeah, I said that."

"And you testified on direct that Gina told you he would kill your own brother, and she would kill him for money. Isn't that right?"

"Yes, that was what I said on the stand earlier."

"So, Gina is telling you she wanted to kill your brother, and you just said 'oh good?' I mean, you didn't try to stop her or try to talk her out of it or, God forbid, you never thought to go the police about it?"

"No, man, I didn't."

"And why not?"

The Alibi

"Because I didn't believe she would actually do it, man. I didn't think she had the guts to go through with it."

"Did you inquire with Francesco about the bounty on your brother's head?"

"Did I ask Francesco about that?"

"Yes."

"No way, man. I'm not trying to get in the middle of that mess, man. I'm a clean restaurant owner. I don't need no mobster getting up in my business. I figured it was better just to leave it alone."

"Just leave it alone. Your brother's life is in danger, and you just chose to leave it alone. Gina Degrazio was telling you she wanted to kill your brother for money, and you just chose to leave it alone. Is that what you're saying?"

"That's what I'm saying."

I nodded. I had broken him down, and showed how many times he had lied, and I knew my work was done. The man had no credibility. I was able to show that, and I felt satisfied.

"I have nothing further for this witness."

"Counselor," Judge Reiner said, addressing Ally, "any redirect?"

"No, your honor."

"The witness is excused. Ms. Hughes, please call your next witness."

"The state calls Gianni Ricci," Ally said.

Gianni Ricci was apparently the mobster who Ally was calling to establish that Francesco Veraldi had put a price on Vittorio's head. I knew what he would testify to, and that was he would testify that Francesco Veraldi put the bounty on Vittorio's head, Gina knew about the bounty, and apparently Gina was interested in it.

I also knew how I would break him down – little by

little, piece by piece, just like I brought down the lying sack of shit Enzo. I wasn't intimidated by him any more than I was intimidated by Enzo.

Gianni Ricci was short, about 5'4", with jet-black hair slicked on his head. He was slight and muscular and looked like somebody who missed his calling as a light-weight prize fighter. He had the same cocky walk that Enzo had and I had a feeling he would be all attitude, just like Enzo.

The bailiff swore him in, and Ally asked him to state his name for the record. He recited it, and Ally got down to business.

"Mr. Ricci, can you please tell the court why you are here today?"

"Yeah. I'm here to tell the court about the bounty my boss, Francesco Veraldi, put on the head of Vittorio Degrazio."

"Tell the court what you know about that."

"Well, the guy who died, Vittorio, he was working for another family, the Colombo family. And he was caught spying on my boss, Francesco Veraldi. He not only was spying, but he was selling secrets to the Colombos. That's a very bad thing," he said, shaking his head. "It cost Francesco a lot of money, a lot of men and a lot of turf. So, Francesco put a price on Vittorio's head. He wanted him dead, and he didn't really care who did it, as long as it was done."

"And Gina knew about this bounty on Vittorio's head?"

"Yeah, she knew."

"How do you know she knew?"

"She called me up and asked me about it."

"She did? And what did you tell her?"

"I told her she could collect if she killed Vittorio."

"And what did she tell you?"

"She said that it was as good as done."

"I have nothing further." Ally sat down.

"Counselor," Judge Reiner said to me. "Your witness."

I stood up and approached Gianni. "Mr. Ricci," I said, "what kind of arrangement do you have with Ms. Hughes?"

"What do you mean?"

"I mean, what has Ms. Hughes offered you in exchange for your testimony?"

"Nothing."

"Nothing. Really? So, you came in here to testify against a dangerous mobster and asked for nothing in return? No kind of protection or no offer to put you into the witness protection program? Nothing like that?"

"I'm not testifying against a dangerous mobster. I'm testifying against your client, Gina Degrazio."

"Oh, really? You mean, you weren't just telling the court that Francesco Veraldi put a bounty on Vittorio Degrazio's head, a bounty you testified my client accepted?"

"Yes, I was."

"And you don't think your testimony will raise suspicions against Mr. Veraldi and put him behind bars for ordering this hit?"

"No."

I cocked my head. "And why is that?"

"The prosecutor's office gave Francesco immunity on that."

What the hell? "Immunity on what?"

"Immunity on the murder of Vittorio."

I nodded. It all became clear. Ally would get my client and she would do anything in her power to do it. Even if that meant giving a mobster immunity. I had to wonder if she hated me that much, had that much personal animosity towards me that she would go above and beyond the call of duty to get my client. She apparently had Francesco Veraldi dead to rights for this murder and chose to bypass him, a powerful mobster, in favor of sealing Gina's fate.

"Okay. So, she gave Francesco immunity, so you could feel free to testify against my client. Is that what you're telling me?"

"That's what I'm telling you."

"I see." I looked over at Ally and saw she conveniently was looking down at her notes. "So, you testified that Gina told Francesco that it 'was as good as done' when Francesco asked her if she would kill Vittorio for him. Correct?"

"Yes."

"But Gina never actually received that money, did she?"

"I don't know the answer to that."

"Really? What is your role in the Veraldi organization?"

"My role?"

"Yes, your role."

"I'm his right-hand man."

"You are." I nodded. "So, as Francesco's right-hand man, did you ask him, directly, if he ever paid Gina?"

"No, I never asked him."

"But you were the go-between on this gambit, weren't you?"

"What does that mean?"

"I mean, you were the one who was speaking with Gina and relaying her messages to Francesco, right?"

"I guess."

"May I remind you what you were saying on the stand earlier? You said Gina called you and asked about the bounty, and you told her about it, and she said 'consider it done.'"

"Yeah, that's what I said."

"Which makes you the go-between."

The Alibi

"I still don't know what you mean."

I sighed. "Mr. Ricci, did Francesco Veraldi himself call Gina and talk to her about the bounty on Vittorio?"

"No."

"In fact, you talked to Gina, and relayed the message to Mr. Veraldi, right?"

"Right."

"Then you were the go-between." *This is like pulling goddamn teeth.* I had to wonder if this guy was dumb or just playing dumb. "Now, since you were the one dealing with Ms. Degrazio, why didn't you follow up and find out if she actually got that money?"

"I don't know. I guess I just didn't care. Listen, I got a lot to do. Lots of things on my plate. Lots of responsibility to the organization. I don't always get down in weeds. I'm not a details guy. I'm more of a big-picture guy."

"Then would it come as a surprise to you to know that Ms. Degrazio never actually received a dime of that money?"

"I guess."

"You guess. Why would that not be a surprise to you? Weren't you the one who verified she would do it?"

He shrugged. "Listen, I didn't get that involved. I talked to Gina only the one time, and she said 'consider it done,' and that was it. I moved onto the next project after that."

"You didn't get that involved. So why are you testifying in court today? Why would you testify if you didn't really have that much involvement, and you didn't really know exactly what happened? Why would you come to court today if you didn't know what the outcome was on this deal? What are you bringing to the table, here?"

"Objection," Ally said. "Badgering the witness."

"Sustained. Mr. Harrington, please ask one question at a time."

I nodded and took a deep breath. "Mr. Ricci, if you weren't really that involved in this bounty deal, why would you be here testifying in court about it?"

He leaned back in his chair and said nothing.

"Mr. Ricci, did you also get immunity from prosecution on this deal? After all, you were involved in it, no matter what you say, and you would be criminally liable for even helping to set this up. Were you provided with immunity in exchange for your testimony?"

"Yes," he said, and I heard the jury titter and groan. "I was."

"I have nothing further."

I looked over at Ally who knew she would have to try to do clean-up, but I doubted she knew how. Ally didn't have a ton of trial experience, so she didn't yet know how to deal with situations where her witness was made into mincemeat.

"Counselor, any re-direct?"

"Yes, your honor." Ally went right up to Gianni. "Mr. Ricci, you received immunity from prosecution on this bounty deal, as you testified. But you understand the penalty for perjury, don't you?"

"Yes, I do."

"So, you wouldn't come in here and deliberately lie to the court, would you? Immunity deal or no?"

"No. I'm telling the truth."

"I have nothing further."

"Mr. Harrington, do you have any re-cross?"

"No, your honor." I didn't think I could do any better than I already did on my original cross-examination, so I chose to let that stand.

The Alibi

"Ms. Hughes, call your next witness."

"The prosecution rests, your honor."

"Very well. Let's all take a 15 minute break," he said, looking at the clock. "Actually, let's break for lunch. Everybody must be back here at 1:10 PM." At that, the judge got up and walked back to his chambers, and everybody in the jury filed out into the hallway.

"So, how do you think things are going?" Gina asked me.

"Pretty good," I said. "Now, here's how things will go. I'll re-call the Medical Examiner, who will testify he didn't see any healed broken bones on Vittorio. I'll call the officers who came to your house when you called them on Vittorio when he was beating on you. I'll call the two victims who Vittorio drugged and raped. Then I'll call you."

"Do you think it's gonna work?" she asked me in a low voice.

"Yes," I said, also in a low voice. "I do."

I WENT to lunch at the grill across the street and grabbed a quick grilled chicken sandwich and salad. I was always conscious about not eating a heavy lunch when I was trying a case – I had to be mentally sharp and not fatigued, and I knew how a large hamburger and fries affected my energy level for the worse.

After lunch, I went right back to the courthouse. I was there about twenty minutes early, so I closed my eyes and tried to center myself. Everything was at stake at the moment. Well, not maybe everything, but Nick's future was at stake. I didn't know for sure if Joey would throw Nick under the bus if he didn't get the money Gina owed him, but it certainly made sense that he would.

Gina came in and sat down next to me. "Where did you end up going for lunch?" she asked.

"I went to the grill across the street. How about you?"

"I just went to one of the food trucks parked on the street. I sat and ate lunch outside. It was nice. The weather is beautiful."

"That it is." I took a deep breath. "You ready for this?"

"Yeah. I mean, you and me went over my testimony enough times I know just what to expect."

That was true. Gina and I had gone over her testimony again and again. It was important because she was lying. I also went over the possible cross-examination questions. That was even more important. She had to get her story straight which meant she had to remember what she said on direct when it came to the cross.

The jury filed in, and Ally and her second-chair, Sheldon Hatch, came back into the courtroom as well. Before long, the judge also came in and he sat down.

"Okay, ladies and gentlemen," he said, "I hope you all had a good lunch. But I hope you didn't eat too much. I don't want any of you to fall asleep during testimony." He pointed his finger at the jury, and they laughed nervously. "Not a joke," he said. "I know it gets stuffy in this courtroom, and your food is weighing you down, and, before long, you can't keep your eyes open. Just know, I'll be watching all of you like a hawk."

Once again, the jury laughed nervously, but I knew they were taking his words to heart. I personally felt for them, because I knew what it felt like to sit in one place all day, just listening to testimony, and struggling to stay awake. I almost

The Alibi

fell asleep, more than once, in the middle of a day-long deposition, especially if I ate a heavy meal for lunch.

"Okay," Judge Reiner said, addressing the jury. "If you can remember, right before we broke for lunch, the state rested. That means we will start off with the defense." He nodded at me. "Mr. Harrington, whenever you are ready."

I stood up. "The defense calls Dr. Prorock," I said. Dr. Prorock was the Medical Examiner originally called by Ally. I would ask her about broken bones.

Dr. Prorock approached the witness stand and sat down.

"Dr. Prorock, I will remind you you are still under oath," Judge Reiner said to her.

"Thank you."

"Now. Dr. Prorock, the reason why I am re-calling you is because there was another witness who testified the victim in this case, Vittorio Degrazio, had his knee broken several times by my client, Gina Degrazio. I wanted to ask you if there was any indication that Mr. Degrazio's knee had been broken before he died?"

"No, I found no evidence of that."

"And you would have been able to tell, in your examination of Mr. Degrazio, whether or not his knee had been broken and healed, correct?"

"Yes, I would have been able to tell."

"I have nothing further."

I sat down.

"Ms. Hughes, do you have any questions for this witness?"

"No, your honor."

"You may step down," Judge Reiner said. "Counselor, call your next witness."

"The defense calls Officer Dean," I said.

Officer Dean, a tall black man, approached the witness stand, was sworn in and stated his name.

"Officer Dean," I said, "I called you to testify on the stand today to ask you about an incident that occurred January 10 of this year. Do you remember being called to the home of Vittorio and Gina Degrazio that evening?"

"Yes."

"What happened when you went to the Degrazio's home?"

"I was called to that home and I went there with my partner, Officer Jackson, to inquire about a domestic disturbance."

"A domestic disturbance. Who called in the disturbance? Was it Ms. Degrazio, Mr. Degrazio, or somebody else?"

"It was Ms. Degrazio, but there was also a call from a next-door neighbor."

"A next-door neighbor. Do you remember the name of the next-door neighbor?"

"I do. Her name is Laverne Donnelly."

"And she called 911?"

"Yes."

"Why did she call 911?"

"She said she was outside, walking her dog, when she heard loud shouting coming from inside the Degrazio home. She heard Ms. Degrazio screaming and heard the sound of a belt cracking and more screaming."

"More screaming? It was Ms. Degrazio screaming, not Mr. Degrazio, correct?"

"Correct. Ms. Donnelly said she only heard Ms. Degrazio screaming."

"So, did you go to the Degrazio house?"

"I did."

"And did you speak with Mr. and Mrs. Degrazio?"

The Alibi

"Yes."

"What did you ask them?"

"I told them I was there because I got a phone call from Ms. Donnelly and from Ms. Degrazio. I asked Mr. Degrazio his side of the story, while my partner, Officer Jackson, spoke with Ms. Degrazio. Then I spoke with Ms. Degrazio and Officer Jackson spoke with Mr. Degrazio."

"Without testifying to what Mr. Degrazio said to you, could you please tell the court what your impression was of Mr. and Ms. Degrazio at this time?"

"I had the impression that Ms. Degrazio was extremely upset to the point of hysteria, and Mr. Degrazio was extremely angry."

"Did you see a belt?"

"I did. Mr. Degrazio still had it in his hands when we walked through the door."

"What did Ms. Degrazio tell you when you spoke with her?"

"She told me that Mr. Degrazio had been drinking heavily, and was upset because he had recently lost a lot of money betting on horses and at the casinos. She said he was in a violent mood when he came home from the casinos that day and was angry she hadn't cleaned the house while he was gone. She said that one thing led to another and before she knew it, he was punching her and beating her with a belt."

"Did you notice if she had any bruises on her?"

"No. That was why we chose not to arrest Mr. Degrazio."

"Did you believe that Ms. Degrazio had been beaten by Mr. Degrazio?"

"I did."

"I have nothing further."

I knew it would be a problem that they didn't arrest Mr. Degrazio. I didn't necessarily think them not arresting Vittorio to be fatal, though. Unfortunately, over the years I had found out that not arresting the abuser was something that happened all too often.

"Ms. Hughes, your witness," Judge Reiner said.

Ally got on her feet, and I could see she was to ready to go to war. "Officer Dean, you said you got to the Degrazio residence and that Ms. Degrazio told you that Mr. Degrazio had been drinking heavily that day and had lost money in the casinos, and he was very angry and violent, correct?"

"Yes, that is what she told me."

"And he was specifically angry because she hadn't cleaned the house when he was gone, is that right?"

"Right."

"And he had a belt in his hands when you walked in the door, correct?"

"Correct."

"Then why didn't you arrest Mr. Degrazio?"

"We counseled both parties and were there for about an hour, and, by the time we left, the two were calm and sitting on the couch together. Ms. Degrazio told me at that time she didn't want her husband to be arrested, and things were fine, so we used our discretion and chose not to arrest Mr. Degrazio."

"Did you know at the time you chose not to arrest him that the police had been called to their house two other times?"

"I did."

"So, he was a repeat offender and you didn't arrest him."

"Well, I-"

"Isn't it true you didn't really believe Ms. Degrazio's story when you arrived at her house?"

"No, that's not true."

"But is it standard practice to not arrest an repeat abuser?"

"No, that's not standard practice, but we're allowed to use our discretion on whether or not to make an arrest."

"But it is true that if you really thought Ms. Degrazio was in danger, you definitely would have made an arrest, correct?"

"Yes, of course."

"Then it follows you didn't really believe that Ms. Degrazio was in danger, correct?"

"Yes, that's true."

"I have nothing further." Ally looked at me smugly as she took her seat. Her look said *schooled you.*

The next two witnesses were the officers who came to the other disturbances. They didn't arrest Vittorio, either. I felt their testimony could go either way. Either the jury would believe the Degrazios got into violent altercations but had always calmed down enough that the officers didn't want to make an arrest, or they would believe Gina was always crying wolf. Nevertheless, I took the gamble that their testimony would help our cause, not hurt it. After all, trial strategy was never 100%, and most moves you make in trials could go either way with the jury.

My witnesses after that were Coretta Taylor and Bianca Cassavettes. Their testimony was identical to what they told me when I went to see them. Bianca was subjected to vicious cross-examination, however.

Bianca showed up to the courtroom looking like she was trying hard to look legitimate. Her hair was no longer bleached blonde, but was back to its natural brown, and her makeup was toned down. She was dressed in a long pleated skirt and a turtle neck. I thought she was going slightly overboard in her effort to "look the part," but I didn't entirely mind.

She sat down, looking nervous. I kind of felt sorry for her, because she looked like she wanted to be anywhere but where she was right at that moment. She was sworn in, I asked her her name, she stated it, and I got down to business.

"Ms. Cassavettes, do you understand why I called you into court today?" I asked her.

"Yes," she said into the microphone. "I do know."

"And what is your understanding as to why I called you as a witness?"

"You're defending the woman who killed Vittorio Degrazio," she said. "Other than that, I don't really know why I'm supposed to testify."

"Can you tell the court how you came to know Vittorio Degrazio?"

She cleared her throat. "Well, I met him at a bar. The Peanut, 50th and Main."

"The Peanut. Did you end up going home with him?"

"Yes, I ended up going home with him."

"What happened when you went home with him?"

"Well, I don't really know. I mean, I liked him, and I wanted to have sex with him." She looked at the jury. "I mean, I'm not a slut or nothing like that, but I sometimes like to have some fun. But I went home with him, expecting to have sex with him that night."

"And did you have sex with him?"

"Yes, but not in the way I planned."

"What do you mean by that?"

"Well, we were at his place and he made me a drink. I

The Alibi

think it was a vodka and water drink. I took a swig and the room started to spin. It seemed like he was a long way away, and I started to feel dizzy and woozy. The next thing I know, I'm naked in his bed, and he's next to me."

"And he had sex with you while you were unconscious, then?"

"Yeah. It was a Cosby thing."

"And how do you know he had sex with you while you were unconscious?"

"Well, I could tell." She pointed down. "You know, my ladyparts could tell." She looked over to the women in the jury. "I'm sure you ladies know what I'm talking about. Plus, I woke up without clothes on and he was naked, too."

"I have nothing further for this witness."

"Ms. Hughes, your witness," Judge Reiner said.

Ally stood up and walked over to Bianca. "Ms. Cassavettes, you say that Vittorio Degrazio had sex with you while you were unconscious, right?"

"Right. He raped me."

"But you went home with him, intending to have sex with him, isn't that right?"

"Yeah, but, you know, if we were going to have sex, I wanted to have a say in it."

"Of course, of course. But you simply took a sip of your drink and you passed out. Is that what you're telling the court?"

"Yes, that's what I'm saying."

"But you didn't call the police about it, did you?"

"No."

"And why didn't you?"

She shifted in her chair. "He paid me not to," she said. "$100,000."

Ally seemed delighted by that admission. "$100,000. Oh, really? That's a lot of money, isn't it?"

"Yeah. It sure has helped my finances a lot."

"Isn't it true that Vittorio didn't rape you at all, but you blackmailed him by threatening to go to the cops about something that didn't actually happen?"

"No. That makes no sense."

"It makes perfect sense. You go home with a man, you sleep with him, and then you threaten that you're going to cry rape unless he pays you. Oldest trick in the book."

"That isn't what happened."

"Is it a habit of yours to go home with strange men?"

I stood up. "Objection, relevance," I said.

"Sustained," Judge Reiner said. "Move along, Ms. Hughes."

"I have nothing further."

My next witness was Coretta Taylor, and she was much more unimpeachable in my estimation. She *did* go to the police, so there was no making her look like a scam artist who was trying to shake down an innocent man.

She didn't try to dress the part, but that was okay. She was still gorgeous. She was wearing a long-sleeve t-shirt, so her tattoos were at least covered up, tight jeans and black leather boots. Her black hair was in a pony-tail and she wasn't wearing makeup.

She was still one of the most beautiful women on the planet.

She was sworn in, I asked her her name, she stated it, and I started to ask her questions.

"Coretta, you are currently a bartender at The Peanut on 50th and Main, isn't that right?"

"Yeah. That's right."

The Alibi

"And you met Vittorio Degrazio at that bar, isn't that right?"

"That's right."

"And did you end up going home with him one night?"

"I did."

"And what happened when you went home with him?"

"He put something in my drink to make me pass out and he raped me while I was unconscious."

"Did you call the police after that?"

"Yeah, I did."

"And what was your understanding about what happened after you called the police?"

"They questioned him and released him. I have no idea why they didn't arrest him."

"And when was he questioned and released?"

"I think it was on Valentine's Day of this year."

"Valentine's Day - that was when he was questioned and released, according to your understanding?"

"Yeah."

"And did you find out later he was found dead?"

"Yeah. Just a few days later, I guess. I mean, I kept calling the police station to ask them when they would charge the bastard with raping me, and they eventually told me he was found dead. I can't say I shed any tears about that one."

"I have nothing further."

I looked over at Ally. *Checkmate.* Her eyes narrowed and her lips pursed. She knew there was nowhere to go in cross-examining Coretta. I knew she wouldn't even try. Any question she asked Coretta would just dig the hole that much deeper.

"Ms. Hughes, do you have any questions for this witness?"

Ally gave me the stink-eye. "No, your honor."

"Mr. Harrington, call your next witness."

"The defense calls Gina Degrazio."

I looked over at Gina. *Showtime.* I nodded at her, and she nodded back. She was about to commit perjury and I was suborning it. I still wished there was some other way around it, but there just wasn't. At least, there wasn't any way around it that didn't involve implicating innocent people.

She was sworn in.

"Please state your name for the record," I said.

"Gina Marie Degrazio."

"Now, Ms. Degrazio, you are the wife of the deceased, Vittorio Degrazio, correct?"

"Yes. That's right."

"And what kind of a relationship did you have with Mr. Degrazio?"

"It was a bad relationship. Very bad."

"Why was it bad?"

"Vittorio, he wasn't a good husband. He drank too much, played the ponies too much and played too much cards. He was always losin' money, hitting the bottle, and then beating on me."

At least this much was true. "So, he was an avid gambler, a heavy drinker and a violent man."

"Yeah. But, you know, his job involved him being violent, too."

"What was his job?"

"He was a mob enforcer for the Colombo crime family."

"What does that mean? What did he do for the Colombo family?"

"He shook people down. If somebody owed the family something, and they didn't pay, he beat them up to make

The Alibi

them pay. He also went around and got more territory for the family by shaking down store owners to make them pay up too. If there was somebody spying from another family, he beat them up, too. He didn't kill nobody for the mob, though. That was left to other guys."

"So, he beat people up for a living."

"Yeah, he did. Is it any wonder he would beat on his wife, since he beat on perfect strangers all the time?"

"Did you call the police when there was a domestic disturbance?"

"Yeah. Three times I called, and three times a police officer would come out and talk to us."

"But they never arrested Vittorio, though, right?"

"Right. They never arrested him."

"Why didn't they arrest him?"

"Because they know Vitty. They were afraid of him. They knew that if they arrested Vitty for beating on me, Vinny Colombo would be paying them a visit. He didn't like his men getting arrested for nothin'. That was why they never took Vitty downtown."

"Now, let me take you back to February 18 of this year. Do you remember that day?"

"Yeah, I remember that day."

"What happened that day?"

"Well, Vitty had been out all day at the boats."

"By boats, you mean casinos, right?"

"Right. The boats. Anyhow, he had been at the boats all that day, and got home about 6 o'clock. He was hungry like a bear, and he had been drinking all day at the boats, too. Well, I didn't have supper ready. I was sleeping on the couch and didn't feel like cooking."

"And then what happened?"

"Well, Vitty got real mad at me. Started screaming

about how he expected dinner when he got home and I better start acting like a real wife or he was gonna do something to make me act like a real wife."

"By real wife, what did he mean by that?"

"He meant he wanted me to cook and clean. He wanted me to have dinner ready for him whenever he got home. I told him he was being an ass, 'cause I had no idea when he was coming home. It ain't like he called me from the boats to tell me he was on his way or nothin' like that."

"And what happened when you said that to him?"

"He slapped me."

"And what did you do after he slapped you?"

"I slapped him back. And so he hit me with a closed fist. He hit me in the chest."

That was important she said he hit her in the chest and not the face. If he hit her in the face, she probably would have had a bruise in the mug shot.

"He hit you in the chest?"

"Yeah. Then he pulled me by the hair and. When I was down on the ground, he took off his belt and wrapped it around my neck and pulled."

"Were you able to get on your feet?"

"Yeah, I was."

"And what did you do when you got to your feet?"

"Well, I struggled against him for several minutes. I almost passed out. But I remembered I had a gun hidden in the drawer of the lamp stand. I was close to the lamp stand, so I opened up the drawer, got my gun and shot him."

I got out a picture of her living room. "Here is the lamp stand, right?"

"Right."

"And you took this picture of your living room, right?"

"Right."

"And this picture is a fair and accurate representation of your living room?"

"Yeah."

"I would like to mark this picture of Ms. Degrazio's living room as Exhibit A."

"Any objections?" Judge Reiner asked.

"None," Ally said.

"It is so entered. Proceed, counselor," Judge Reiner said to me.

"Okay, so you reached into the lamp stand's drawer and got out your gun and shot him, right?"

"Right."

"And he died instantly, right?"

"Yeah, right."

"And you were arrested several days later, right?"

"Yeah. The cops traced the gun used in Vitty's murder to me and they arrested me."

"Did you tell the cops you shot him in self-defense?"

"No."

"Why didn't you?"

"Because you know, you always see on the movies that people get in trouble when they talk to the cops without a lawyer being around. I knew to ask for a lawyer right away."

"And did you get a lawyer that night to accompany you in the interrogation room?"

"Yeah."

"Was it a Public Defender?"

"Yeah. His name is Vern Reynolds."

"And what did Vern tell you?"

"He told me not to talk to the cops."

"I have nothing further."

I sat down and Ally got to her feet and approached

Gina. "Ms. Degrazio," she began. "That was a likely story you just told the jury. But it was all a lie, wasn't it?"

"Nope. It happened just how I said it did."

"Really? How big was Vittorio Degrazio?"

"He wasn't very big. Only about 5'6" and weighed about a buck fifty."

"So, he was strangling you and you were about to pass out, and you still managed to get into that drawer and get that gun?"

"Yeah."

"And he allowed you to get that gun?"

"What do you mean, he allowed me?"

"I mean, he saw you reaching into that drawer, and he didn't try to stop you?"

"No. He was drunk and out of his mind. Have you ever been around somebody who is so pissed he doesn't know who he is or where he is?"

"I'll ask the questions, if you don't mind."

"Well, he had this look in his eye that told me he wasn't in reality no more. He didn't even notice I was reaching into that drawer until it was too late."

"Did he know what you had in that drawer?"

"No."

"Why is it he didn't know what you had in that drawer?"

"I never showed him."

"And you didn't keep the gun locked up?"

"No."

"Why didn't you keep the gun locked up?"

"There was no reason to. We never had any kids around the house or nothin'. Why would I lock it up? And I kept that gun for protection, if somebody broke into the house. I couldn't get to the gun to use it on an intruder if it was locked up, now would I?"

The Alibi

I smiled at Gina. She was holding up so well. Reciting just what I told her to say.

"Isn't it true you found out that the mobster, Francesco Veraldi, had placed a price on Vittorio's head?"

"No, I didn't know about that."

"But you called Gianni Ricci and said you were interested in that bounty."

"No, I didn't."

"Mr. Ricci testified you did."

"Mr. Ricci was lying, plain and simple."

"He had no motive to lie."

"Yes he did. You offered him immunity from prosecution if he lied about me. That was his motivation right there."

I had to admit, Gina had Ally there.

"Isn't it true you owe another mobster, Joey Caruso, $1 million?"

"Yeah. Joey gave me a million dollars to open up a bunch of massage parlors, and they all went bust."

"And isn't it true that Joey was pressuring you to pay up because he needed that money to get his son out of trouble?"

"Yeah, that's true. Joey went to prison for offing his old lady so he don't have no access to his money. Yeah, he needs me to pay him."

"And how do you propose to pay him?"

She shrugged. "I don't know yet."

"You don't know yet? Listen, I know what happens when a mobster tries to collect and he can't. You'll be dead woman walking if you don't pay him."

"I guess that's right, yeah."

"So, you had motive to kill your husband. You needed a million dollars, Francesco Veraldi was conveniently offering a million dollars, and you saw your way to pay your debt to Joey Caruso. So, you shot him, killed him and collected that million dollars. Admit it."

"I won't admit it, because that's not how it happened."

"Again, how do you plan on paying Joey?"

"I guess I'll have to take a mortgage out on our home."

"Your home is worth about $200,000 and it's already mortgaged to the hilt." Ally did her homework, unfortunately for me.

"Listen," Gina said. "I've been out on the streets this whole time. I didn't spend more than a day in jail. Joey still don't have that million dollars I owe him. If I offed Vittorio for the money, don't you think I would have already paid Joey?"

"How do I know you didn't pay Joey?"

"Because you know. I talked to Joey and he said you saw him and talked to him. You found out I never paid him."

"Move to strike as non-responsive," Ally said.

"Actually, counselor, I think her answer was very responsive to your question," the judge said. "Live by the sword, die by the sword. Motion to strike overruled." Judge Reiner seemed amused that Ally boxed herself in her own corner.

At that point, Ally had Gina's mug-shot photo in her hands. "Ms. Degrazio, please take a look at this picture. I would like to enter Gina Degrazio's mug shot as Exhibit A," Ally said to the judge.

"Any objections?"

"No, your honor." I figured it wouldn't do much good to object to entering the mug shot into evidence, so I didn't even try.

"It is so entered."

"Now," Ally said, "please take a look at this picture of you that was taken at the police station when you were

The Alibi

arrested. This is commonly known as a mug shot. Is this the picture taken of you on the day you were arrested for Vittorio's murder?"

"Yes, that is my mug shot," Gina said, examining the picture. "That's me."

"Take a close look at the picture, please."

Gina studied the picture and then handed it back to Ally. "Alright, I looked at it. So what about it?"

"I see you were wearing a shirt that exposed your neck."

"Yeah I was."

"Do you see any marks on your neck?"

"No."

"But you testified in court that Mr. Degrazio was strangling you with a belt at the time you shot and killed him, right?"

"Yeah, that's what I said."

"Yet you didn't have any marks on your neck in this picture."

"Right. This picture was taken three days after I killed Vittorio. Three days."

"I have nothing further."

Ally sat down, glaring at me. I smiled back. I didn't know how it would go – it did look bad, very bad, that Gina owed Joey so much money and apparently didn't have a way to pay it back. I knew she did have a way to pay it back, but that could never come in, because that would give the whole game away. I knew Ally might have drawn blood with that exchange.

I hoped she didn't.

———

ONE MORE WITNESS came on the stand, and that was the expert I hired who testified that the belt ligature wouldn't have made marks that would have lasted on Gina's skin for two days. That was a formality at this point, and, in the big scheme of things, anti-climactic.

After that witness, I rested. I felt I had put it all out on the table and hoped I did enough.

I prayed I did.

Nick's life and future depended upon it.

JUDGE REINER, after I rested and Ally informed the judge she didn't have any other evidence to present, informed the jury that it was time for closing arguments. It was time to pull everything together for the jury. I had to make it good, because these words would be the last thing the jury would remember when they went into the deliberating room.

Ally started with her closing arguments. "Ladies and gentlemen of the jury, you were just sold a bill of goods. A bill of goods. The defendant claimed she was fearing for her life when she shot the victim, Vittorio Degrazio. She tried to show that was the case by bringing in officers who responded to calls regarding domestic disturbances at the home she shared with Mr. Degrazio. Yet, none of those officers made an arrest. None of them. You heard the defendant desperately needed money, because she owes a powerful mobster, Joey Caruso, one million dollars. You heard that another mobster, Francesco Veraldi, placed a bounty on Vittorio Degrazio's head, a bounty of, you guessed it, one million dollars. Therefore, the defendant, Ms. Degrazio, had a powerful motive to kill Mr. Degrazio. She needed to kill him so she could collect the bounty for

The Alibi

killing Mr. Degrazio, so she could, in turn, pay the money she owed to Joey Caruso."

"And that's exactly what happened. She killed her husband for the money. Granted, she needed that money, because if she didn't get it, she wouldn't live another month. That doesn't excuse what she did, however. That doesn't excuse it at all."

"Now, let's say for the sake of argument that Mr. and Mrs. Degrazio actually had a tumultuous and abusive relationship. Let's just say that Mr. Degrazio actually beat on the defendant. If that were true, the defendant had another motive to kill her husband. So, if you choose to believe that Gina Degrazio was being beaten by Vittorio Degrazio, that doesn't mean that Ms. Degrazio's self-defense story becomes more plausible. On the contrary, it becomes even less plausible. It just gives her one more motive to kill Mr. Degrazio."

"I remind you of the testimony of Gianni Ricci. He testified on the stand he told Ms. Degrazio about the bounty on her husband's head, and she could collect it if she killed her husband, and she told him 'consider it done.' I remind you of the testimony of Enzo Degrazio, Vittorio's identical twin brother. He said Gina told him she would kill Vittorio Degrazio, because she had found out a mobster had put a bounty on Vittorio's head and she quote 'wanted in on that action' unquote."

"There you have it, ladies and gentlemen. Two different witnesses, both with the same story. Gina Degrazio killed her husband for the money. That's what happened, ladies and gentlemen. Don't believe the story about self-defense. That's all smoke and mirrors. Focus on what these witnesses are saying. Focus on what they are saying. Thank you very much."

I stood up when Ally sat down, and I approached the

jury. I went over to the jury box and leaned down on the railing that separated me from them. I looked each person in the eye and then exaggeratedly sighed and shook my head.

"I can't even," I said, motioning to Ally. "Ladies and gentlemen of the jury, I don't know about you, but I can see that everything Ms. Hughes just told you is a bald-faced lie. I mean, look at the witnesses she brought on the stand to testify against my client. You have Enzo Degrazio, Vittorio's brother, who testified Gina wanted in on the action, as he put it, the action being a mobster putting a price on Vittorio Degrazio's head. And you heard him, ladies and gentlemen, he did nothing about that. Nothing!" I slapped my hand on the rail.

"This is the same guy who was kissing his crucifix and talking about how much he misses his brother. How much he carries his brother around in his heart. Yet, I asked him what he did when he found out that his brother had a price on his head and that Gina Degrazio was ready to collect that price, and that Gina Degrazio told him she would collect, and he's all like 'oh, well.'" I shook my head. "If somebody put a price on your loved one's head and somebody else is saying she wants to collect that price and kill your loved one, would *you* just shrug your shoulders and go on with your lives? Would you?"

"No, you wouldn't. Any normal person wouldn't. Yet, Enzo, if his testimony is to be believed, did just that. He said he thought Gina wasn't serious, but he certainly didn't try to find out if she was serious, did he?"

"So, that was one of Ms. Hughes' star witnesses. The other one was Gianni Ricci, and he was a real piece of work, too. You heard him. He was involved in carrying out the bounty on Vittorio's head and he received immunity in

The Alibi

exchange for his testimony against Gina. He just got his get out of jail free card, and all he had to do was come in here and throw my client under the bus. That's all he had to do, ladies and gentlemen. That's a sweet, sweet deal, so of course he's going to come in here and lie about Ms. Degrazio. Of course he is. I'm quite sure that Ms. Hughes offered him that deal and he jumped all over it, and I don't blame him. I don't blame him."

"What other evidence did the state provide to show that my client killed her husband for the money? None. She only provided those two witnesses, Gianni and Enzo, and they both came off looking like the lying weasels they both are. Now, she tried to break down my client, asking her how she would pay back Joey Caruso, a mobster she admittedly owes a lot of money to, and my client truthfully admitted she didn't know. I fear for my client's life, because she really doesn't know how to pay back Joey Caruso. I fear for her, because, as she said on the stand, Joey hasn't received that money she owes him. He hasn't received that money, and, as my client established, Ms. Hughes knows Joey hasn't received that money yet."

"And why hasn't Joey received that money? After all, if my client actually carried out a hit on her own husband in exchange for $1 million, she would have already received that money from Francesco Veraldi, and she already would have paid Joey Caruso that money. She's been out of jail this whole time. Don't you think, ladies and gentlemen, that if she had the money for Joey, and she just hadn't paid him yet, Joey would get wind of that and would have already had her killed? I mean, think logically about this scenario, ladies and gentlemen. Think logically about it."

"So, I think I've established you can just discount the witnesses for the prosecution. They were clearly lying.

Gianni Ricci came in to lie in exchange for immunity for his role in the bounty deal. Enzo Degrazio was lying for some other reason. I don't know what the reason is, but it's very clear he was lying. So, let's just stipulate that both of the prosecution's star witnesses were lying. That out of the way, it's time to look at the evidence the defense provided, and these witnesses were damning."

"First, you saw the testimony of Coretta Taylor and Bianca Cassavettes. They both told their stories about how Vittorio raped them. He drugged them and had sex with them while they were unconscious. That's really disgusting behavior and it showed how low Vittorio's character was. These women had no motivation to lie. None whatsoever. Oh, Ms. Hughes tried to make it look like they were lying, but she didn't get very far, did she? And then you saw the testimony of the officers who came to the Degrazio's house several times in response to calls regarding domestic disturbances. Officers came to the house three different times. Three different times. That shows, right there, that the Degrazios had a violent relationship."

"Finally, you saw the testimony of my client. Ms. Hughes desperately tried to trip her up but my client was unshakeable. Absolutely unshakeable. Ms. Hughes didn't break her down. Her story was that solid. And her story was powerful. She testified she didn't cook dinner and Vittorio came home that night, totally drunk and angry after having lost money yet again at the casinos. She said a fight broke out, and that Vittorio, completely drunk out of his mind, threw a belt around her neck and strangled her. She had no choice but to try to save her life. No choice. She reached into her lamp stand drawer, brought out a gun, and shot Vittorio. It was her life or his, ladies and gentlemen, and she chose to live. She chose to live. Any one of you would do the same."

"Ladies and gentlemen, the facts of this case dictate a finding of not guilty. Not guilty. And I also wanted to remind you that the prosecutor has the burden of proof in this case. The state has the burden of proof. The state, who provided completely inadequate and lying witnesses, has the burden of proof. And no way did the state meet that burden. No way." I shook my head. "No way. I also wanted to remind you that the state must prove its case beyond a reasonable doubt. That means that if you have any doubt in your mind about my client's guilt, then you must acquit. If you think that it's even a faint possibility that my client actually did kill her husband in self-defense, you must acquit. My client gets the benefit of the doubt in this situation. I ask for a finding of not guilty. That's the only verdict that would be just in this situation."

"Thank you again for your service. I know you will go and deliberate and do the right thing. I know it, because I know that all of you are not the kinds of people who will make a woman pay for saving her own life."

At that, I went and sat down.

AFTER WE GAVE the jury our closing arguments, Judge Reiner dismissed the jury. He gave instructions on the elements of murder, and instructions on the elements of self-defense, and then he thanked them for their service and sent them on their way.

On the elements of murder, he told the jury that "if you believe that the defendant knowingly killed the victim, Vittorio Degrazio, and killed him after deliberation, then you must find the defendant guilty of murder in the first degree. However, if you believe that the defendant killed Mr. Degrazio because she felt that lethal force was necessary to defend herself, and that her belief that this force was necessary to defend herself was reasonable, then you must find the defendant not guilty. That said, if you believe that Ms. Degrazio was the initial aggressor, then you must not find that the defendant was justified in killing Mr. Degrazio, unless Ms. Degrazio withdrew from the encounter, and Mr. Degrazio pursued it further after her withdrawal."

After Judge Reiner gave the instructions and thanked them, the jury filed out to deliberate.

And it was time for me to wait.

AT 6 PM, Judge Reiner informed everybody the jury was still deliberating. They had gone out at 3 PM, so they had been at it for three hours. "You might as well go on home," he said to Ally, her second-chair Sheldon Hatch, Gina, and me. "We'll be in touch when the jury has a verdict."

I sighed. I wanted there to be a verdict that day, but I couldn't possibly force the jury to come back with their decision just because I wanted them to.

"What does that mean?" Gina asked me. "Why can't they make up their minds?"

"I don't know. I do know that we picked a decent jury and we left it all out on the table. I will have to admit I'm a bit worried just because Ally really dug into the fact that you owe Joey Caruso so much money. It does look like you had a reason to take that million dollar bounty from Francesco Veraldi. Especially since you didn't have a good answer for how you are prepared to pay Joey back."

The Alibi

Gina looked worried. "Do you think they'll find me guilty?"

"I don't know. I don't know."

We left the courtroom, got the elevator and took it down. I left the courthouse, found my car, and sat in the front seat.

I left it all out on the field, but what if it wasn't enough? What if Gina got convicted, and ended up stiffing Joey, which, in turn, makes him so angry he turns on Nick to spite me? What if Nick ended up spending the rest of his life in prison because of all this mess? What if he got the death penalty because of it?

I couldn't think about that. That thought couldn't possibly enter my mind. It wouldn't happen like that. Gina would be found not guilty, and that $3 million that Enzo gave her as bond money would revert to her. She would use that money to pay off Joey. Joey's son would be spared, and Nick would be, too. It had to happen that way.

It just had to.

Chapter Twenty-Two

THE NEXT DAY, I went to the prison. I needed to see Nick and let him know how things went with the trial. I still hadn't heard back about a jury verdict, and I was on pins and needles, so I needed something to take my mind off it.

I got to the prison and he came out. I chose to visit him as a regular visit, with guards around, because I hated seeing him in leg irons and handcuffs before.

He smiled. "Damien," he said, "I didn't know you were coming today. If I would have known, I would have baked you a cake."

"I wanted to see you and tell you how things went with the trial."

He sighed. "Listen, Damien," he said. "If things don't go your way, they don't go your way. Really, I'm okay either way."

I wanted to tell him I wasn't okay either way. I wanted to tell him he was my brother and I needed him to get out of this hellhole. I wanted to tell him that seeing him spend

The Alibi

the rest of his life in prison would devastate me beyond measure.

I didn't say any of that, though, because the guard was around and listening to every word we said.

"Well," I said, "how are things going right now?"

"Good. You gonna come back and see Jack, Connor and Tommy sometime soon?"

"Sure. As soon as the trial is completely over and the verdict is read. I just wanted to see you because-"

"I know. I'm the one who has the most at stake in the trial." He nodded his head. "You know, it's funny. The first year in this place, every second seemed to drag on like a lifetime. I never thought I could get used to this place. The food, the pissing in front of everyone, the hard beds, the fights, the guards watching your every move. But it's been 17 years, and I can't even imagine what life is like on the outside. Would I even recognize it?"

"Well, you might not. We didn't even have smart phones when you went inside."

"I know. Those smart phones sound pretty cool, though, and I hope I can get one."

"You will. That will be the first thing I get for you when you get out. That and an electric car. That's another thing I don't think you even know about."

"I'm sure I don't." He shook his head. "The world went on without me, man."

"You're going to get out," I said. "If it's the last thing I do, I'm going to make sure you get out."

He nodded but looked sad. "We'll see." Then he looked around. "Well, I think I gotta get back. You come and see the other guys next time, okay?"

"I will, buddy. I will."

I watched him being led away and I felt a pang. What if things went sideways? Could Joey ever be trusted, even if he got the money he needed? I just didn't know.

I went back to my car, turned on my phone and saw a text message.

The jury was back with a verdict.

Chapter Twenty-Three

MY HEART WAS POUNDING as I sped back to Kansas City. I knew they would wait for me to arrive, but that didn't make it any easier. I felt like I couldn't breathe. Like I was swimming underwater and couldn't surface.

I realized at that moment just how terrified I was that everything would go down the tubes. That Gina would be convicted and couldn't pay Joey, and Joey would rat on Nick as revenge on me. If that happened, I'd be devastated. Absolutely devastated.

I got to the courthouse and didn't even wait for the elevator. I took the stairs, two at a time, and arrived in the courtroom to find that everybody was already there.

"I'm sorry," I said, "I was visiting a client in Cameron."

"Well, you're here now, counselor," Judge Reiner said. "Get on in here and get your verdict."

I took my place next to Gina, who looked absolutely terrified. "Here we go," I whispered. "Are you ready for this?"

"No," she said. "But it is what it is."

Judge Reiner addressed the jury. "In the case of State of Missouri v. Gina Degrazio, has the jury reached a verdict?"

"We have your honor," the foreman said.

"Will the defendant please rise?"

I drew a breath and stood up. Gina followed, getting unsteadily onto her feet.

"In the case of State of Missouri v. Gina Degrazio, on Count One, Murder in the First Degree, how does the jury find the Defendant?"

"The jury finds the Defendant Not Guilty, your honor."

Gina started to crumple and shook her head.

"And this is the unanimous verdict of the panel?" Judge Reiner said.

"It is, your honor."

"Very well. The Defendant is free to go."

I realized I had been holding my breath, and I let it out slowly. I closed my eyes.

Thank God. Thank God. Thank God.

Ally came up to me. "Well, looks like you got another sleaze back on the street," she said. "Congratulations."

Gina looked like she wanted to kill Ally. "What's her problem?" she asked me.

"Nothing. She hates me, that's all."

"Whatever. Anyhow, Damien, great job. I'll-"

"You'll get your bond money back and then you're going to see Joey ASAP."

"Goes without saying."

"I know, but I'm saying it anyhow."

Gina and I left the courthouse and got into the street. "I'm going to be paying Joey a visit in a week," I said. "I know it might take a day or two for you to get that bond money back. You need to make sure you get it to him."

The Alibi

"I will, I will." She took a breath. "Anyhow, Damien, thanks. I couldn't have done it without you."

I nodded. I broke every ethical rule to get this verdict, but hopefully the ends would justify the means.

A WEEK LATER, Tom Garrett, who I assigned to monitor the Joey-Gina-Nick situation reported back. "The mobsters who were after Antonio Caruso, Joey's son, were paid yesterday, so Antonio is out of the woods. I heard Joey is pretty happy with the outcome. So, it looks like your guy Nick will be fine."

"I hope you're right," I said. "I just hope Joey is as good as his word."

"He will be. Prison code. He has no reason to break it anymore. Relax. It'll be okay."

"I hope you're right."

I also found out the mold clients settled their case with the slum-lord, Robert Davis, for $30 million. He really wanted to keep the entire situation out of the papers, which was why he settled it so quickly. As for Gina's liability for the buildings, her lawyer successfully managed to convince the court overseeing the case she had been coerced into the arrangement, therefore she should be held harmless in the suit. Gina was able to show just how she was duped, so the court agreed, and Gina didn't have to pay any of the damages.

I was happy about this. Extremely happy. Those people deserved that money after what they went through. I looked at their happy faces in the paper and my heart soared. It was a great ending for them. All of them. They could get their lives together, and that was all that mattered to me.

In the meantime, I picked up a new murder case. A prominent New York City artist, Marcus Jackson, was in town for a showing of his work. He was found murdered in the back of his gallery.

Dill Halloway, a diminutive gay man, came into see me. "I heard you're one of the best lawyers in the city," he said. "My husband was arrested for the murder of Marcus Jackson. Needless to say, the media has been crawling all over our loft. I need you to represent him. He's innocent, and you need to prove it."

Next in the Kansas City
Legal Thrillers series

vinci-books.com/reasonable

When a renowned artist is murdered, a suspect with memory loss becomes the key to unlocking the truth.

In the heart of the city, a celebrated artist from New York is found savagely murdered in the back of an art gallery. The prime suspect? A well-known art dealer, tormented by the possibility that he might have committed the heinous crime but unable to recall the events of that fateful night.

Turn the page for a free preview…

Reasonable Doubt: Chapter One

I MET WITH DILL DEWITT, the husband of Leland Dewitt IV, a prominent gay socialite who lived in an enormous mansion located just off the Country Club Plaza. I had no idea how this particular case fell into my lap, especially since Dewitt had been on the cover of the *Kansas City Star* just about every day since the internationally famous artist, Jackson Michaelson, was found murdered in the back of a downtown art gallery.

Jackson was considered to be the hottest artist in New York City at the time of his murder. He had had showings in Prague, Paris and London which were sold out, as wealthy patrons from around the world paid top dollar for his paintings, sculptures, installations and sketchings. He was also extremely active in the gay community, giving millions to charities that focused on bullying, HIV awareness and teen suicide.

I pulled up to the house and immediately saw the throngs of reporters waiting just outside Leland's gate. I drove through the gate, with the reporters banging on my

The Alibi

window, asking me to speak with them. I just shook my head. There was no way I would make a statement. I didn't know what to say, for one. Also, I made it a point never to speak to the media about a case.

I drove up a long driveway and hit a circle drive with a large fountain in the middle. Leland's home was one of those turn-of-the-century mansions with 20 rooms. I understood his home had a temperature-regulated wine cellar, a movie theater, a recreation room, an outdoor pool complete with old-world statues and a hot tub that seats 10, an entire room dedicated to clothes and shoes, and a kitchen as large as that in a restaurant.

This was a murder made for the media. Leland Dewitt IV was only 32 years old but was one of the richest men in the city. He was from old money. His great grandfather, Leland Dewitt, was a robber baron. He made his fortune around the turn of the century during the height of the industrial revolution. He supplied lumber for railroads and shipyards and died in 1960 at the age of 81. He was a billionaire at the time of his death.

Leland Dewitt IV and his brother Roger were the sole heirs after Leland Dewitt III and his wife, Loretta, were killed in a TWA plane crash in the 1970s. Which meant that both Leland and his brother were billionaires in their own right after the crash.

Since Leland Dewitt was the suspect in this murder, and the victim was an internationally known artist, I knew the media would be all over this case like flies on shit. I didn't particularly want this case for that reason alone. I never wanted the spotlight. I turned away from it whenever it tried to shine on me. Since I had such a chaotic and impoverished upbringing, I didn't feel secure having the spotlight on my face.

I went to the front door, an enormous wood structure, and rang the doorbell. I heard the sonorous chimes and waited for somebody to open up the door and let me in. Which happened a few minutes later.

A tall and thin man with a mustache, dressed in a suit, answered. "You are here for Mr. Dewitt, correct? You are Damien Harrington?"

"I am."

"Dave, let him in," a high-pitched male voice admonished from behind the door. "Honestly, David, do you always have to act so butlery?"

The man, who I assumed was David, stepped aside and I walked in. Leland was standing in the enormous foyer, with the 30 foot ceilings, Greek columns and marble floor. To the right was a large marble staircase that led to the second floor, which overlooked the foyer and an atrium around 20 feet away from the foyer.

"Come in, come in, handsome," Leland said as he approached me.

Leland was a slight man, only around 5'5" and probably weighed 120 lbs. His hair was light blonde and shaggy, his face was tanned and slightly worn, and he had big blue eyes. He was dressed in plaid shorts and a pink golf shirt, with a sweater wrapped around his neck. He had bare feet.

He walked right up to me and extended his hand. I shook it and he beamed. "Me and Dill were just sitting out by the pool, waiting for you. Follow me. It's such a hot day, I knew it was pool time."

I followed him through the house and through two enormous French doors which led to the pool area. The pool was enormous and kidney-shaped, and the terrace that surrounded the pool was, just like the rest of the house, made of marble. There were statues surrounding

The Alibi

the pool and an island in the middle of it that featured a wet bar.

In the pool was, apparently, Dill. He had dark hair and sunglasses and was floating in the middle of the pool while he sipped a red drink from a straw. He saw me, smiled and waved. "You must be Damien," he said, still waving. "Thanks for coming out here to see Leland."

"Well, come on in," Leland said to Dill. "You need to talk to Damien too."

At that, Dill rolled off his float and swam to the side of the pool. He went around to the pool steps, stepped onto the terrace and toweled off. "Thanks for coming," he said again. "Sit down."

I sat down at one of the tables surrounding the pool, across from Leland and Dill. Leland was sitting very casually – his right leg crossed over his left knee. He had put on a pair of sunglasses. Dill, for his part, hadn't bothered to put on a shirt. He was sitting to the right of me, dressed only in his swim trunks. On the table was a pitcher filled with tomato juice.

"A Bloody Mary?" Leland asked me. "David might be a stiff, but he makes one helluva good drink."

I nodded. Why not? It wasn't usually my habit to drink on the job, but when in Rome...

Leland poured me a glass and I took a sip. I had to admit that David really did make a mean Bloody Mary. I considered myself to be a bit of a Bloody Mary connoisseur and this was one of the better ones I had tried. It was spicy without being unbearable, and it tasted unbelievably fresh.

"This really is an excellent Bloody Mary," I said.

"Well, David squeezes actual tomatoes. Me and Dill buy them at the Farmer's Market on Saturday afternoon, and David uses them to make the drink. That's really the secret to truly delicious things, by the way – use fresh ingredients and you get a fresh taste. That's pretty basic, but sometimes the most basic ideas are still the best ones."

I took another sip. "Does David squeeze and ferment the potatoes to make this vodka, too?" I asked as a joke.

"No," Leland said. "But I admit, I like the high-dollar stuff. I get this stuff called Magnum Grey Goose. $800 a bottle."

"Well, that would do it," I said. "If you're going to spend that much for vodka, it better taste damn good."

"Right?" Leland said. "Well, drink up. You're going to need it after you get through with my story." He shook his head. "Poor Jackson. He was so young. So full of life. He really had the tiger by the tail, that one. The tiger by the tail. He certainly didn't deserve…" At that, he choked up. He bowed his head, shaking it, while Dill scooted over and put his arm around Leland's shoulders. "He didn't deserve what happened to him. The world will be deprived of a great, great man. Imagine if Beethoven was cut down at the age of 27. We wouldn't have ever gotten the Fifth Symphony, the greatest masterpiece the world had ever known. Now, Jackson is dead at 27, and who knows what masterpieces he had yet to create?"

"Oh, that's right," Dill said. "That's so true. In a parallel universe, Jackson is still alive and creating, and the people of that other universe will be enjoying many more years of his work. But in this universe, he's cut down in his prime. In his prime." He sighed. "I wish I could teleport to that other universe so I could see just what Jackson would create when he got to be old and grey."

Leland smiled. "Dill really believes that stuff, by the way. He really believes in other worlds, parallel universes and worm holes. I think he's been watching too much *Dr. Who*, but to each his own. Anyhow, in this world," he said, shooting Dill a look, "Jackson has joined the 27 Club."

I nodded. I was familiar with the 27 Club. The term referred to the fact that so many of our geniuses, both musical and artistic, died at the age of 27. That club included Amy Winehouse, Kurt Cobain, Jimi Hendrix, Janis Joplin and Jim Morrison. It also included the great New York artist, Jean-Michel Basquiat, whose 1982 painting, which was Untitled, set a record high for any US artist at an auction, selling for $110 million.

As if he read my mind, Dill said "You know Basquiat died at Jackson's age. His art is selling for hundreds of millions of dollars. Jackson might have that kind of legacy, too, you know."

"Yeah," Leland said. "I wouldn't be surprised if Jackson's art commands that kind of price tag in about 20 to 25 years." He shook his head. "And you know a movie was made about Basquiat. I fully expect a Hollywood producer will want to make a movie about Jackson's life and death. That's how beloved he had become in such a short, short time."

I nodded and took another sip of the Bloody Mary. I thought about how nice it would be to not have to worry about money. Not having to worry about working for a living, just living for traveling the world and playing tennis in personal courts, and sitting on the veranda sipping Bloody Mary drinks made with freshly-squeezed tomatoes. I was comfortable enough - I was still living off the millions I got from that wrongful death case a year or so ago - but nothing like *this*.

"And how did you know Jackson?"

"I was one of his earliest and largest patrons," Leland said. "I found out about him 10 years ago, when he was 17 years old and living on the streets of Hell's Kitchen. He was literally a starving artist back then, but I saw some of his graffiti he created around the city, and I was just blown away. I had an eye for guys like him and I set him up in a loft in the Village and paid his living expenses so he could just create art without having to worry about where his next meal was coming from or whether or not he could sleep in an actual bed."

"Don't worry," Dill chimed in. "Leland's interest in the boy wasn't sexual. At least, that's what Leland tells me."

"Well, I wasn't exactly a dirty old man at the time I met him," he said. "I was only 22 when I met Jackson, but he really wasn't my type. Too blonde, too skinny." Leland shook his head. "No, I wasn't sexually attracted to him. I just saw his graffiti work around the city and I knew talent when I saw it. He was definitely talented."

"Of course he was talented," Dill said. "After all, he became the toast of Europe when he went over there. The *bon vivant*."

Leland rolled his eyes. "He's always using foreign words wrong. Dear, *bon vivant* means a social and luxurious person. Jackson certainly wasn't that. I mean, he was. He was a social guy. He had to be. But luxurious, no. He wasn't. He always told me he was more comfortable sleeping on a hard floor than on a luxury bed. That was why I used to go to his loft, and this was after I lined up wealthy patrons for him, mind you, and saw he slept on the floor. A blanket on the floor, with a pillow. That was all." He shook his head. "I guess that came from the fact that he lived on the streets, from the time he was only 16 years old. Could you imagine that? Living on the streets at 16? I'm surprised he didn't end up joining a gang."

"Oh, no gang would have wanted him," Dill chided.

The Alibi

"He was too gay, too sensitive, too skinny, too everything. He did get along by being a rent boy, though, to several different men over the years. Funny, that. He never let anybody actually get him an apartment, though, until Leland. I guess because Leland was interested in him professionally and not sexually."

"I guess," Leland said, obviously not convinced. "I don't know why the boy let me take care of him. But Dill is right. Jackson let me set him up in an apartment. He let me give him a monthly allowance. He let me introduce him around to my friends. I was very connected in the New York art scene and he totally allowed me to hook him up with all my wealthy friends. I mean, not hook up in the sexual sense, but hook up in the professional sense."

"Anyhoo," Dill said. "So, yeah. That's the story in a nutshell about how Leland and Jackson know one another."

"Now, let's see," I said, looking through my file. "In your statement to the police, you told them you didn't remember going into the living quarters of the gallery. The night that Jackson was killed. Is that right?" In Leland's gallery, he explained to me that he had an entire studio apartment attached to the back of the gallery – complete with a kitchenette, dining room, and a couch that pulled out into a bed. That was where Leland was apparently arrested the night of the murder.

"Oh, yes, that's right." Leland nodded his head. "I was blotto that night. It's not often that I drink to excess like that, but I did that night. The crazy thing was, I seemed to be semi-coherent to everyone around me, including Dill. Nobody knew I was three sheets to the wind. I think that it's also because I have been prescribed Ambien for sleep. I took one right before midnight that night."

Dill gave Leland a look and then shook his finger at him

like he was being particularly naughty. "I know. I always tell Leland about that. I always tell him not to mix Ambien with alcohol, but does he listen?"

"I know, Daddy, I know," Leland said with a roll of the eyes. "Anyhow, I try to take Ambien an hour before I go to bed. And I planned on sleeping in the back of the gallery that night." He shot a look over to Dill. "Dill was being a pill and I didn't feel like going home. I set up an entire bedroom in the back of that gallery for just those occasions when I don't want to go home. And that happened to be one of those nights."

"And, let's see, it looked like Jackson's time of death was-"

"2 AM, the morning of April 9. I know. That's what the police told me when they brought me in for questioning."

"Right. 2 AM. So, what happened on the evening of April 8, then?"

"Well, it was Jackson's Kansas City debut. It was a First Friday, you know, when all the art galleries are open late and have little parties for the people. And there was a lot of excitement about Jackson being in town. A ton of excitement about him. Our gallery was filled with people that day, from the time the First Friday got going to the time we closed. First Fridays are always packed, you know. There's always thousands and thousands of people that come to Crossroads and go through the galleries and appreciate all the wonderful art that each gallery has to offer."

I nodded. I had never actually been to a First Friday, but it was one of Sarah's favorite things to do. She was the art aficionado, not me. In fact, I had never even heard about Jackson Michaelson, but Sarah knew all about him. She had been a fan of his from years back and was devastated to find out he had been murdered. But she was extremely impressed to know I would be defending Jackson's alleged murderer. That is, as long as I was convinced that his alleged murderer, Leland, didn't do it. If I thought he did it, Sarah wouldn't be speaking with me for awhile.

"This will make your career, Damien," Sarah had said.

"That's all I need," I had said. "To be known as a celebrity attorney." I rolled my eyes. "I'll see what he has to say before I agree to represent him."

"Okay," I said. "So, it was a First Friday, and Jackson was the star attraction."

"Yes. The star attraction. Our gallery got so much foot traffic that day, I tell you what. I usually buy at least a case of wine for the guests, but I knew I would need more wine, so I bought four cases. Four cases, and they were all gone by the end of the evening. Not to mention about twenty wheels of Brie cheese and tubs and tubs of fig spread. Thank God for Costco." He smiled. "I mean, I got money to burn, but I don't always like to spend it so much. I like a bargain as much as the next guy."

"Nothing wrong with that." I drew a breath. "So, there were thousands of people in your gallery that evening."

"Tens of thousands, probably."

Dill snorted.

"What? Listen, each First Friday attracts at least 10,000 people, and I swear to God, every last one of those people ended up in my gallery at some point."

"And what was Jackson doing?"

"He was holding court. You know, he was dressed in ripped jeans and a t-shirt, five o'clock shadow, his hair hadn't been combed in God-knows-how-long, but he didn't care how he looked. Nobody else did, either. They were fascinated by him. He was going around the gallery, talking about the inspirations for his paintings and just selling himself and his art. I don't usually sell a ton of work on those First Fridays, but I did that night. Even at $50,000 and up, his art was selling like crazy."

"Selling like crazy? How many paintings did you sell that night?"

"I sold 20. I had displayed 25 and sold 20. We're talking the most expensive painting was $100,000, and most of them were between $50,000 and $75,000. I considered that to be a very successful night."

"And how much did Jackson get of that?"

Leland shrugged. "I just give him all the money. I don't take a commission from him. Why would I? I have more money than God. No, I just give him all the money."

"And how much did the gallery collect from people that night?"

"Well, we ended up doing $1.4 million in sales."

"Wow. $1.4 million. And Jackson got to keep all that money for himself?"

"Every dime. But you know, money meant nothing to him. Zero. He gave most of his money away. AIDS charities, anti-bullying programs, all sorts of animal rights organizations. He gave most everything away. Oh, I mean, he kept some money for himself. After all, he has to eat and he does still have that loft in New York. The same loft I got for him back in the day – he still lives there. He insisted on buying it from me and I let him. So, he has the upkeep of that loft. But, other than that, he never spent much money. The kid was a saint when it came to charitable giving."

Dill nodded. "A saint," he said, echoing Leland. "What kind of a kid would just make millions of dollars a year and still sleep on the floor of an old loft and give most of the money away?"

The Alibi

I nodded, thinking hard. Was his charitable giving tied to his murder? Or was it something else?

"So, he was very generous with his money."

"Too generous. But that was Jackson. See, he had a hard upbringing. He was living on the streets at the age of 16, you know."

Dill put his arm around Leland. "Dear, he knows that. You already told him that."

"Oh, right, I guess I did. But he was." Leland's voice got low. "You see, I think, although I never did find out for sure, but I think his stepfather used to do stuff to him. Molest him. I didn't know about all of this, but I found out soon enough, that his family had more money than my family does."

"Oh? What do you mean?"

"Just what I say. Jackson's family was extremely wealthy."

"But they let him live on the streets?"

"Well, they didn't *let* him do anything. He lived on the streets and evaded detection for many years. He told me he got good at it. His family reported him missing, and you know, his face was always in those newspapers. You know the ads, where it shows the kid when he went missing and then shows an age progression. I'm sure you're familiar with these ads. Everyone has seen them."

"Yes, I am," I said. "So, his family put his face on these ads?"

"Yeah. They even hired a private detective to find him. But Jackson was always too smart for all of them. So he lived on the streets for years, hiding in plain sight, while his family looked for him, high and low."

"That's where his career as a rent boy came in," Dill said. "He never let them give him money or any of that, but he allowed them to take him in from time to time. He would stay with this john or that john whenever he thought the police were getting wise to where he was. And these johns, they never turned him in, because they all knew why he was running. They all understood it so they never turned him in as a runaway."

"And his parents lived in New York City, too?"

"Oh, no. I mean, his father was an international financier in Lower Manhattan. His mother was from old money. He lived with his mother and stepfather out in Connecticut, and his stepfather was, shall we say, a-"

"*Bon vivant*," Dill said with a smile.

"Yes, a *bon vivant*. He used that term right that time. A *bon vivant*. He loved to party and loved all the luxuries that life can bring. And he apparently loved Jackson a little too much." Leland shook his head. "I didn't mean that. Of course he didn't actually love Jackson at all. If he loved him, he wouldn't have done what he did. Anyhow, the stepfather was just an all-around awful person. He was a sexual predator and went through his wife's money like water. He had mistresses and also had boys on the side. I always say there are no bisexuals in the world, but I think I might be wrong. The stepfather seemed to be somebody who loved men and women about the same."

I carefully made notes while I listened to them speak.

"The stepfather, what else can you tell me about him? Is he still married to Jackson's mother? Is he still living in Connecticut? Is there any way possible he might have killed Jackson?"

Leland sighed. "Yes, he still lives in Connecticut. No, he's not still married to Jackson's mother. He and Jackson's mother, Marie, were divorced five years ago. As to whether

The Alibi

or not he killed Jackson, I don't know. I don't know what kind of motive he might have had to do that."

Dill piped in. "I do. I know what kind of motive he would have."

"Enlighten me, dear," Leland said.

"Pretty simple, really. Jackson was getting more and more famous. That means newspapers are talking to him. Reporters are interviewing him." He turned to me. "Did you know Netflix was going to produce a special about him? About his life?" He nodded his head. "That's how famous Jackson was getting."

"A special? Like a documentary?"

"Yes, a documentary. One of those things where they visit the hometown and talk to the people who knew him growing up and then talk to the people who know him now. Show his art work, you know the drill. I'm sure you've seen a Netflix documentary before. It's always the same standard format."

I nodded. "Yes. I have seen Netflix documentaries. Well, that would definitely give the stepfather reason to kill Jackson, wouldn't it? If that documentary gets produced, there's a good chance the stepfather's secrets will be revealed. So, I'm going to have to find out the stepfather's name, where he works and all that. I'll either send my investigator to speak with him, or I'll do it myself."

"Yes," Leland said. "That's a good place to start. His name is George Mason. He lives in Greenwich, Connecticut. He works at Goldman Sachs as an investment banker."

"Are you sure he still works there, honey?" Dill asked.

"Yes. I'm sure." Leland turned to me. "That's actually the first person I thought about when I was arrested for this. I thought maybe George was behind it all."

"Good," I said. "I'll be sure and speak with him. Now, can you think of anybody else who could have done this?"

Leland bit his lower lip and then took a sip of his drink. "Dill, honey, could you do me a favor?"

Dill looked at Leland suspiciously. "What?"

"I need to speak with Damien alone. Could you check on David and see if there's anything he needs?"

Dill rolled his eyes. "You promised me you wouldn't keep secrets." He crossed his arms in front of him. "Or don't you remember promising that?"

"Stop being such a drama queen, Mary," Leland said, using the gay slang term for somebody annoying or effeminate. "And see if you can give David a hand."

Dill didn't move a muscle. "You're going to tell him about Mystic Anna, aren't you?" Dill looked at Leland accusingly. "You're completely wrong about her. She wouldn't do something like this."

Leland rolled his eyes. "Will you just please give us a bit of privacy?"

"Okay," Dill said. "But you better not tell him what I think you're going to tell him."

"I'll tell him whatever I want," Leland said. "It's my life on the line, you know."

"Now who's being a drama queen?" Dill still didn't look like he was going to move.

"With all due respect," I said to Dill, "Leland isn't being a drama queen when he's telling you his life is on the line. It absolutely is."

"You mean," Dill said, "they're going to try to give him the chair?"

"Actually, in Missouri, it's lethal injection. But no, they aren't seeking the death penalty for Leland. At least, they haven't certified him yet for that. But they might upgrade the charges and seek the death penalty in the future. Even if they don't, he'll probably be sentenced to life in prison without parole if he gets convicted for this. So he's facing very serious time. If he knows something about somebody who might have done this, I need to know about it."

Dill suddenly looked very worried. "Well, he won't go to prison because he didn't do this. Right?"

I looked over at Leland who was trying hard not to also look worried.

"Leland hasn't yet told me he didn't do it. That said, even if he blacked out from the Ambien and the alcohol, I doubt very seriously he killed Jackson. I've done research on the topic of Ambien blackouts and I've found that a person won't do something on Ambien that he wouldn't do while he's conscious. In other words, if Leland didn't have cause to murder Jackson and Leland doesn't have violent tendencies, it's unlikely he murdered Jackson."

"Well, then, if he didn't murder Jackson, he won't be convicted." Dill seemed pretty satisfied with that answer, even if that was an answer he made up himself. "So, I'm not worried."

I looked over at Leland. "Go ahead and tell me what you were going to tell me. It looks like Dill is pretty set on not leaving us alone to speak, but I need to know everything you might know about somebody else who might have done this."

"Okay, then," Leland said. "I'll go right ahead and tell you."

Dill gave Leland a look, but Leland studiously ignored him.

"And?" I said to Leland.

"Her name is Mystic Anna. She's Dill's psychic. I personally think she's the most likely one to have killed poor Jackson."

Reasonable Doubt: Chapter Two

"OKAY," I said. "Tell me about Mystic Anna."

Dill piped up. "There's nothing to tell about her," he said. "She's a fine person. She never would do something like this."

"Oh, shut up," Leland said. "You never want to think she does anything wrong." He turned to me. "Dill relies on her for everything. He's just afraid that if she gets sent up the river that he'll curl into a ball of goo and die. He literally can't make a single move without her say-so."

"Well, you're just trying to get her out of the way because you don't like my relationship with her."

"You have no relationship with her. She's a charlatan who takes all your money. Or should I say she takes all of my money." He addressed me. "Dill doesn't actually work for a living. I take care of him and all his needs. He's my husband, so it's only right. But he's absolutely on the nose when he says I don't like the way he relies on her for everything. He can't even eat a bowl of cereal in the morning without calling and consulting her." He lowered his voice. "He pays her a half-million a year."

I cleared my throat. "A half-million a year?"

"A half-million a year."

Dill rolled his eyes. "As if you'd miss that money. That's pocket change to you."

"Can I ask what you did before you met Leland?" I asked Dill.

"What do you mean?"

"Did you work? Did you have your own money?" I didn't quite know what to think of the two men. I got the impression Dill was the *bon vivant* and latched onto Leland for his money. Not that that meant anything, but perhaps that would give me another lead on who might have done it. I had to clear Dill, in my mind, of murder.

Maybe Dill was jealous of Leland's relationship with Jackson? Threatened? Maybe he believed Leland would one day leave him for Jackson? That would be motive for murder, especially if there was a tight prenup and Jackson might be left with little to nothing in the event of a divorce.

"Why are you asking all these questions?" Dill whined. "You're making me feel like I'm under suspicion."

"I just wanted to know."

Leland sighed. "Dill was somebody I met up in New York. He was working at Lips New York as a drag queen. His drag name was Helen Heels."

"And that's how you met? At the bar?"

"Yes, that's how we met." Leland nodded his head. "He was serving cocktails and lip-syncing to Christina Aguilera tunes. Now, can we please move on to Mystic Anna?"

"Certainly. Tell me about her."

Leland glanced at Dill, who was still staring daggers at him, his arms crossed in front of him. "Mystic Anna is Dill's personal psychic. She works out of her New York City home. I've been there with Dill." Leland shook his head and made a face. "Her home looks just like you might think. Crystal ball, incense, beaded curtains in the doorway, the whole nine. I was surprised she wasn't wearing a scarf around her head."

"There's a reason for all of those things, if you must know," Dill said indignantly. "The crystal ball actually helps her see the future. The incense helps her clients relax." He rolled his eyes. "And she happens to really like crystal beads."

"Whatever. Anyhooo...Dill relies on Mystic Anna for all his big decisions."

"She told me to marry you, didn't she?" Dill asked.

"A broken clock is right twice a day," Leland said dismissively. "As I was saying. Mystic Anna fancies herself to be some kind of latter-day Jeane Dixon or Edgar Cayce. You remember who those people are, don't you?"

"I do remember something about Jeane Dixon. Didn't she make a bunch of predictions in the *National Enquirer?*"

"Yes," Leland said, with another roll of his eyes. "She would make predictions like 'Charles and Diana will have marital problems,' long after everyone knew they were having marital problems. Her predictions, the ones that came true, were ones that didn't take a rocket scientist to figure out. Most of the things she said didn't come true, though. She was a real charlatan, if you ask me."

"Yet she was a wealthy charlatan. Didn't Nancy Reagan rely on her advice?" I asked.

"She did," Leland said, with a nod of his head. "And yes, she managed to make her charlatanism into a cottage industry for herself. A sucker's born every minute and Jeane Dixon reached those suckers."

I looked over at Dill, who looked like he was getting more and more pissed by the second. He was glaring at Leland and shaking his head. But he didn't say a word.

"And Edgar Cayce, he was famous for being a seer too, right?"

"Right," Leland said. "Anyhow, this Mystic Anna wanted to be taken seriously. She has this blog where she makes predictions for the coming year. Most of them were bullshit, but she predicted the death of poor Jackson."

"Yes she did," Dill said triumphantly. "She did. She predicted it just last month."

This piece of news got me interested. "Really? Let me see that blog post."

Grab your copy...
vinci-books.com/reasonable

About the Author

Rachel Sinclair was a criminal defense attorney for eleven years, so she doesn't scare easily. She graduated from the University of Missouri-Kansas City School of Law in 1998, and worked for the Public Defender's Office for several years before striking out on her own. She currently lives in San Diego, California, with her boyfriend, Joey, and her two fur babies, Annie and Toby. In her spare time, she likes to read, bicycle all over town, Boogie Board at the beach, and watch trashy television.

www.ingramcontent.com/pod-product-compliance
Lightning Source LLC
LaVergne TN
LVHW030241250326
834688LV00047B/1749